Gary L. Ivey

BACKLASH 2:
Justice Denied

Backlash 2: Justice Denied

BACKLASH 2:
Justice
Denied

Gary L. Ivey

2018

Published by

Studio IV Productions, Kailua Kona, HI 96740

ISBN: 0-9993968-1-1

ISBN-13: 978-0-9993968-1-0

www.backlashbook.com

Cover photography iStockPhoto and DreamsTime.

Design by Gary L. Ivey

Acknowledgements

Many thanks to those who read the first "Backlash" and encouraged me to write a sequel, which I had not initially planned to do. My appreciation also to Ruth Arthurs and the members of the Living Stones Church Writers Group for their constructive criticisms, which sharpened my focus and forced me to question my first efforts. Thanks also to Bill Barley for his insights on the legal profession, which helped steer me away from at least one foolish error. Finally, thanks to my wife, Toni, for suffering through my reading of the entire book aloud and helping me recognize continuity lapses and inauthentic character behavior.

Backlash 2: Justice Denied

PROLOGUE

The black Lincoln Town Car sped along Market Street on the route it followed every day to the Thomas F. Eagleton Federal Building in St. Louis, Missouri. The driver glanced in the rearview mirror at the back seat, where Judge Everett Walker of the United States District for the Eastern District of Missouri munched on a croissant and read a brief from the defense in his first case of the morning.

His tailored suit was becoming as wrinkled as his face, but it wouldn't matter because his day would be spent cloaked in the traditional black robe of a Federal Judge. With the first spring blossoms on the trees and the frost gone from the air, Walker probably wished he could spend the day at the country club. *Perhaps he could get away early for nine holes, as he often did*, the driver thought.

The judge's driver turned right on 10th, where he always did, give or take five minutes, every day of the week. Traffic was no heavier or lighter than usual. The routine of the route allowed his mind to wander to his weekend plans to watch the Cardinals with his current girlfriend at their favorite sports bar.

Then, in his peripheral vision, he became aware that a gasoline tanker truck was changing lanes and getting closer to his car as it pulled past him in the rush-hour traffic. Suddenly the large tanker truck swerved in front of the limo and he had to slam on the brakes, tires screeching on the pavement.

"What the…!" he exclaimed, struggling to control the car. His anger turned to consternation when he realized the tanker had slammed on its brakes and come to a stop across two lanes in front of him. He instinctively stomped on his own brake pedal repeatedly to avoid a collision.

The judge was pitched forward against his shoulder strap and his open briefcase and its loose papers flew off the back seat and fell to the floor in a heap. The driver took in what had happened and had only a moment to be thankful that they hadn't hit the tanker, when there was a thunderous BOOM!

When the tanker exploded, a cloud of fiery gasoline went in all directions and the judge's limousine was covered in flaming fuel. The occupants strained at their seatbelts to get free, but the fiery vapor reached the fuel lines of the car and a secondary explosion blew off the hood and shattered the windshield, exposing the driver to the flames from the tanker. It only took another split second for the fire to find the limousine's gas tank and the third explosion caused the vehicle's rear end to fly up into the air and then fall hard to the asphalt.

The judge was already dead when it landed.

CHAPTER ONE

FOUR MONTHS EARLIER

Large, silent snowflakes fell softly, gradually turning the dormant grass into a moist, white blanket. A thin sheen was forming on the motionless surface of the slowly freezing reflecting pool. In the darkness, the flakes danced like fireflies in the beams of car headlights as vehicles moved along the rapidly slickening pavement.

Stately Roman-revival buildings and monuments were lit from below by massive floodlights which appeared to ignite the snowflakes, looking like so many floating Christmas lights. The real Christmas lights still hung from the street lamps, though Christmas was ten days past.

Patrick Garrity glanced out of the car window at the moonlight on the Potomac River, taking a rare opportunity to belatedly enjoy the season as he drove home from work. It had been a long day. As he glanced in the rear-view mirror he thought he might have seen some gray among his trademark red hair, something he wasn't ready for in his early 40s.

For him, as Political Editor of the *Washington Herald*, Christmas with his preteen daughters had been via FaceTime® to his ex-wife's house. He ached with the thought of not seeing his daughters for Christmas, but even without his brutal work schedule, he would have had difficulty affording the trip, since a large share of his salary was still earmarked for child support.

Even Christmas Eve mass had almost been crowded out by preparations to cover the incoming freshman class of Congress who had been swept into office by a historic upset, precipitated by the backlash against the punishing gasoline tax of the "Petroleum Independence Act." Veteran Senators and Congressmen from both parties had been turned out because they supported the tax, meaning there was a multitude of new legislators for him and his staff writers to get to know. New Year's Day had just been another day at work for him.

The freshman class in Congress understood why they had been sent to Washington as did those veterans who remained, so they had already stitched together a bill to repeal the gas tax. There was little doubt that it would pass, and the new president who would be sworn in less than three weeks hence would certainly sign it.

For most people in the country, the repeal of the extra dollar the tax had forced onto already high prices could not come too soon. In some parts of the U.S., premium fuel was at $6.00 per gallon, the new cap put in place by Federal statute when the tax was added. But diesel fuel was included in the tax, so the prices for all consumer goods had risen suddenly when the impact of the gas tax was felt, since all consumer goods were delivered by diesel-powered trucks. Pretty much everybody felt the effects of the tax and had voted their pocketbooks last November, causing the fruit-basket upset in Congress.

Patrick shifted his lanky frame inside his compact sedan to stretch his muscles after sitting all day, chained to his computer or sitting in meetings.

The odd thing was that most of the former congressmen and senators who had supported the gas tax were Democrats, but the former president, who had signed the gas tax bill was a Republican and, since virtually everyone who supported the tax was now out in the cold, the incoming president was a Democrat who would have to work with Republican majorities in both houses of Congress; *a very interesting prospect for a political reporter,* Patrick mused.

Of course, the new president, William Lowndes Toland, might have been more comfortable ideologically with moderate Republicans in Congress than with the far-left wing of the

Democrat party. But after the gas tax debacle, there would be few of the latter in either chamber.

Toland was a "blue-dog" Democrat from South Carolina who had served that state's legislature and two terms in the governor's mansion in Columbia. South Carolina had a reputation for being volatile and unpredictable going back to the Civil War, which, Patrick assumed, some in the state were still proud to have started. Toland's family tree was well documented back to that state's legislature which was the first to secede from the Union. In fact, Toland's middle name, "Lowndes", was testament to his pedigree, going back to the second president of the state, when it was briefly a republic, prior to the American Revolution.

All this went through Patrick's mind as stream of consciousness, as he smiled at the beauty of the falling snow. For a political reporter, Toland was tailor-made for great copy.

Then he smiled a little broader and his blue eyes danced as his thoughts left Washington, D.C., and wandered to Texas.

* * *

There weren't many New Year's decorations to be taken down, Jacqueline Marie James, the relatively new CEO, noticed as she rode the elevator from the lobby to her top-floor office in the 20-story black-and-gold tower that stood beside an Interstate highway in Houston, Texas. Axiom Oil Incorporated's policy manual only allowed minimal holiday decorations in its headquarters. *However,* Jackie thought, *perhaps we should allow some serious party decorations when Congress repeals the punishing gasoline tax.*

The law had been crafted specifically to punish the oil companies, boxing them in between the artificial price cap and the $2.00-per-gallon tax on motor fuel. This effectively prevented any possibility of companies like Jackie's to make a profit and her company was feeling the strain.

It was only a matter of time, Patrick had assured her on one of their frequent late-night phone calls, until the new Congress would do just that and the price of gasoline would be allowed to fall to market levels again.

Concerning Patrick, she wasn't sure where their relationship was going, or even if it was a "relationship." They had been together only a few times and they both had incredibly busy schedules and heavy responsibilities. With him in D.C. and her in Houston, phone calls and texts were their mainstay.

She was surprised when the notoriety brought on by the gasoline tax also brought her an admirer. After being abandoned by a fiancée years ago, Jackie James had thrown herself into her work and had not given much attention to her own needs, preferring to put her energies into building the company that began as a family business. Now she feared her work might prevent a real relationship.

She was certain that they looked like an odd couple to other people. He was a cynical reporter from the seat of national power; she was a native Texan with oil in her veins. He was tall, she was petite. He had bright red hair, hers was a deep brunette, He was Catholic, she was Protestant. In fact, she was Southern Baptist, which was pretty much its own domain within Protestantism.

But the biggest difference between them from some people's perspective was the fact that, even though he was relatively well paid, Jackie was one of the wealthiest women in the country, although she wasn't focused on that. In fact, when she was Vice President of Operations for the company she got familiar with all the jobs her employees did, often working alongside them, earning their respect, because she respected them.

As she exited the elevator, her mind returned to the thing always on her mind these days: the end of the gas tax. Even after the repeal, there would still be gas taxes, but the punishing $2.00-per-gallon tax imposed by the Petroleum Independence Act, only a dollar of which the statute allowed the company to pass on, would be a thing of the past.

What most people don't realize, Jackie thought again for the thousandth time, *is that oil companies like Axiom had only about a five-percent profit margin on gasoline sales, whereas the government – Federal, state and local – imposed taxes that were many times that.* So, when the media crowed about the profits the oil companies were making during good years, they failed to mention that the various levels of government were receiving as much as five times the oil companies' profit in

9

taxes, without having to incur any of the risk or do any of the work required to find oil, refine it, transport gasoline and oil and retail the products in a volatile worldwide market. And the government's share didn't go down during the bad years. Add Federal and state regulations to the mix and, even for large, established companies like Axiom, just surviving could be a challenge. And Jackie was acutely aware that her employees and stockholders, not to mention their customers, were heavily dependent on the success of the company.

Once in her spacious, top-floor office, Jackie drew one set of floor-to-ceiling curtains apart to let in the pink morning light. The wall of glass in the high-ceilinged office dwarfed her, making her look lonely in the large room, silhouetted as she was against the window. While she was powerful within her company, there were many forces beyond her control.

Turning to the large desk which had been her father's, her eyes were drawn to the framed picture of him and her mother just to the right of her computer screen. She could hardly believe it would soon be eight months since her father died suddenly and she had replaced him as CEO of the multinational gasoline retailer her grandfather founded.

Thirty-eight-year-old "Jackie", as she was known to pretty much the whole country, had become a household name during the company's boycott, which had been her idea, after all. With her petite frame, dark, shoulder-length hair and flashing eyes, she had become something of a folk-heroine. The boycott had been precipitated after an environmental terrorist attack on one of Axiom's oil platforms in the Gulf of Mexico, which some in Congress took as their opportunity to pass the gas tax to punish the company for what they portrayed as an "accident." That caused Jackie to hatch the idea for "Operation Backlash."

For three months, the company had instituted a moratorium on gasoline and diesel-fuel sales, even though selling motor fuel was its main business. The company's reasoning was that, since with the tax they would lose money on every gallon they sold, they shouldn't sell any.

Admittedly it was a bit of a stunt, but "Operation Backlash" had for three months attracted attention, both positive and negative. Because of the higher fuel prices, the economy had slowed to the point that the tax revenue increase expected by those who enacted the gas tax plan failed to materialize. In fact, overall revenues to the Federal treasury had fallen, due in part to Axiom's temporary boycott but more due to the drag on the economy caused by the government-mandated, overnight dollar-a-gallon increase in the price of gasoline.

Axiom's boycott had only been for three months and that had ended September 30. During October, November, and December the company had sold gasoline as before, so was paying the tax and the bottom line was showing the strain. While she had pledged not to lay anybody off during the boycott, the company could not continue that policy for long.

She had prayed for wisdom and for a speedy end to this ordeal for the sake of her employees, stockholders and customers. However, she sometimes wondered if God involved himself in business affairs. She hoped so, because it directly affected so many people that He did care about and cared for.

Though she didn't make a big deal about it publicly, her faith was very important to her, and the church she and her mother attended had a wing with her father's name on it.

Congress could not act too soon to suit Jackie.

CHAPTER TWO

"Jonesy! Gimme that ball peen!"

Tobias "Jonesy" Jones looked up and handed the hammer to his supervisor, Carlo Minetti, who took it and carefully tapped the stubborn nut that didn't want to break free. He had spent five minutes trying to free it with an inch-and-a-quarter open-end wrench and a dousing of WD-40, but it hadn't budged. They needed to replace a valve on an FCC, or "Fluid Catalytic Cracker" unit, but one of the nuts was corroded and wasn't cooperating. Minetti's brow was furrowed under his short, stiff black hair.

At 55, Jonesy, who was also called "Toby" at times, was stocky, about 30-pounds overweight and had perpetually dirty fingernails. His jumpsuit was tight around his belly and his boots showed the wear of hundreds of days of hard work on his job at the Axiom Oil Incorporated Refinery in Gary, Indiana. He stood watching as Carlo tapped the nut then put the wrench on it and tapped that counterclockwise to get it loose.

The "Cracker" they were working on was just one of many complex chemical processing units in the huge refinery which broke down crude oil into useable hydrocarbons for making a dizzying array of products people used every day.

The refinery was a sprawling industrial installation where crude oil came in and gasoline and diesel fuel, plus a variety of other petroleum products from solvents to polymers for plastics, went out. Many of those secondary products would be sent to other manufacturing plants where they would be further refined and combined with other raw materials to become products as varied as asphalt paving, pharmaceutical capsules, guitar strings, food additives, house paint and clothing, to name just a few products.

The installation, like most refineries, included acres and acres of huge storage tanks where crude oil was stored initially, and then refined product was stored in a separate area, awaiting transport to market in large, gleaming, semi-trailer tanker trucks. Large buildings with 30-foot ceilings and high windows and skylights housed the chemical processors.

Crude oil flowed through a spaghetti-like mass of pipes, many of which rose several stories above the buildings and travelled through them, as product was pumped through the refining process. Hundreds of people worked their shifts around the clock to keep everything running continuously to meet the demand for the multitude of materials that had once been oil – as much as three-and-a-half gallons of crude oil was required per person per day in the United States to meet the demand for the wide variety of products which at least partially started life as crude oil!

Jonesy looked at his watch. The shift whistle would sound soon and he would be able to gather his lunchbox and windbreaker and leave the plant like he did every day in his green 1998 Chevy S-10 pickup.

Just then the nut broke free.

"Whew!" Minetti exclaimed. "You take it from here Jonesy."

"Right, boss." He could just get the unit replaced and the tools put away before the whistle.

* * *

Jason Wood sat looking out the window of his luxurious office, dressed in a tailored $3,000 suit and spun-silk tie. The headquarters offices of Champions of Mother Earth occupied the top three floors of an office building in downtown Seattle, Washington. As president of Champions, the non-profit game had been good to him. He turned around and walked the several feet from the window to his large, glass-topped, custom designer desk and sat down in his one-of-a-kind red leather office chair. He crossed his long legs, then turned and absentmindedly looked at the huge abstract original oil painting on the wall to the right of his desk. However, under his trimmed blonde hair, his mind was on other things.

The nonprofit organization had chapters all over the country and its monthly magazine, EARTH VIEW, had a subscription base of more than one million. "Champions" raised tremendous amounts of money in donations from environmentally concerned people all over the world. Thanks to that money, the organization had been able to make tremendous strides in defending the Earth against those who carelessly abused her. The funds pouring into the organization's coffers also made possible the Class A office space the headquarters occupied.

The past few months had brought little besides bad news. If it wasn't enough that the Petroleum Independence Act was likely to be repealed, Marvin Borelli was in jail awaiting trial on charges that he had funded the bombing of an offshore oil platform that had given Congress the impetus to pass the Act.

The flamboyant Borelli wasn't a Champions employee but a contract lobbyist who worked for other organizations as well, although Champions of Mother Earth had been Borelli's biggest client. The organization was now quietly distancing itself from Borelli. Even before his arrest, Wood had worried about Borelli's extravagant lifestyle and the attention it could draw.

The 52-year-old Wood knew they had to cut ties with Borelli because the money used to finance the bombing had come indirectly from the coffers of Champions of Mother Earth.

Much more of the organization's money had gone to the re-election campaigns of politicians who helped push the Act through. He had no idea if someone in the government was connecting the dots. Right now, he was trying to figure out when the other shoe would drop and how he could prevent it from dropping on him.

Wood hadn't become president of the huge NPO without being able to think politically. Whatever happened he was totally committed to the Cause. After all, if the Earth's environment was ruined, no one would survive. So, he must protect himself and his organization no matter what it took.

The idea that was taking shape in his bright mind could very well solve two problems at once. That was just the way he liked to do things.

* * *

Jackie James sat at the end of the huge, lacquered conference table with her executive assistant at her side, the matronly but supremely efficient Doris Maxwell, taking minutes. Jackie's right hand, the slender Wayne Simpson, was seated in a wingback chair against the polished, paneled wall, taking his own notes. Jackie had brought him with her from Operations when she became CEO because the Type-A Simpson always anticipated what she needed and had it ready.

This was a meeting of the Finance Committee, so Dennis Trask, the burly, mustached Chief Financial Officer of Axiom was there, his large frame looming over those seated at the table as he gave his report. Around the table were a half dozen accountants, analysts and internal auditors.

Also present was Benny Tyson, Axiom's solid-as-a-rock president. He had been in that job a long time, though he was still relatively young. Jackie had leap-frogged over him to become CEO, and with all that had happened Tyson didn't seem to mind that he hadn't been tapped for the top spot.

"How bad is it this time?" Jackie asked sardonically, wishing these meetings could be avoided.

"You know how much I prefer to give good news," Dennis replied. "But until the gas tax . . ."

"Yes, I know," Jackie interrupted. Dennis smiled, not at all ruffled. These meetings had become a bitter joke, with no possibility of positive news as long as the gas tax was in place.

"Is there any change at all?" Jackie asked.

"Not really. You see the bottom line in the report," Dennis adjusted his reading glasses on his nose to better see the figures on the stapled report of the company's financial performance for October, November and December, the company's fiscal first quarter. "Revenues are down substantially as people conserve and the tax is stealing the cash flow we can usually count on. I guess the good news is that the gas tax has only been in place for six months. We probably have at least one month to go before we can expect it to be reversed.

"Otherwise," Trask continued cautiously. "We'll have to look at layoffs and perhaps shutting down some operations."

"I don't want to do that yet," Jackie shook her head vigorously. "In this bad economy, I don't want to lay people off until we have no choice. Everyone working for Axiom from vice presidents to the clerks at our convenience stores deserves the best we can give."

"I guess we can hold on for another month."

* * *

After the meeting, Wayne followed Jackie to her office instead of going to his own office across the hall.

"Was there something else?" Jackie asked.

"I was just wondering how you're doing," Wayne said.

"Fine, I guess," Jackie answered, unsure what Wayne meant.

"It's just that, everything that's happened; you've hardly had a chance to catch your breath."

Jackie sat down at her desk and motioned for Wayne to sit in one of the leather wing-back chairs facing her. He was certainly right about that. Her father had died unexpectedly on a Monday, she had been elected CEO the following Monday and the very next Monday the Gulf Pride oil platform had been attacked by eco-terrorists. Ever since, there had been nothing but pressure.

"It hasn't been any better for you," Jackie said reassuringly. "You've had to run to keep up with all that's happened."

"Yes, but the brunt of everything has been on you. I'm concerned about you," Wayne said.

Jackie was almost uncomfortable as he said this. Wayne was unquestionably devoted to her, which was a real advantage to her when she needed reports and presentations assembled and organized, but the way he said "concerned" and the wide-eyed look on his pale face made her wonder if there was more to his devotion than duty to the job.

"You know I appreciate all you do," Jackie said. "I couldn't do this job without you, but you don't need to worry about me. Maybe I should be concerned about you. Do you have an outlet outside work? Hobbies? Friends? Church?"

"I'm okay," Wayne said, looking down at his feet.

"Okay, just be sure you have a life outside this building."

* * *

Although former Senator Nathan Taylor still had a home in Vermont of course, the majority of his time for the past thirty-plus years had been spent in his Georgetown townhouse. Now it looked like he would need to sell it and go back to Vermont; starting over in his 70s.

He still couldn't believe what had happened. Vermont had re-elected him to the Senate for decades without a real contest. Sometimes the Republicans didn't even field a challenger to oppose him. This time, an unknown Libertarian had won "his" seat. *It's an outrage!* he again fumed from his main-floor study, as the rising sun coming through the nine-foot-tall, crimson-draped windows turned the room's wood panels from dim gray to golden brown.

Everyone was saying he lost because he had spearheaded the passage of the Petroleum Independence Act. *Do the people of Vermont care so little for the Environment that they would turn me out over that?* It appeared so.

He didn't know where to begin to get the townhouse sold, although there would certainly be plenty of new faces in Congress who would need homes in the Washington, D.C., area. A place like this would likely be out of reach of many of those new faces, however. Here, property values would frighten those just coming in from the rest of the country. Better to sell to someone who had been in Washington for a while.

He tried to think of the name of the real estate agent who facilitated his buying of the townhouse more than three decades ago, but couldn't remember it. No matter, she was likely retired now anyway. Or dead. In the past, as late as last week, he would have just turned something like this over to a staffer, but he had no choice but to let them loose to return to Vermont or find employment elsewhere in the massive D.C. machine. He would have to find his way himself.

Or perhaps he should just stay here, in familiar surroundings; perhaps get a lucrative position at some think tank. Yes, that might be possible. After all, though he was up in years, he was still vigorous and his mind was sharp. He was slender as a 20-year-old and his bushy white hair gave him a distinctive look that automatically conferred power to his very aura. He knew many influential people and he could use that influence to help a worthy organization.

He was beginning to run down a mental list of possible organizations to contact when he noticed a light blinking on the desk phone, meaning he had a message. He pushed the button.

"Senator Taylor, this is Special Agent Samuel Jorgensen of the D.C. field office of the FBI. At your convenience, sir, I need to ask you a few questions about the genesis of the Petroleum Independence Act. Please call me at . . ."

Taylor heard the number but didn't write it down. He was unable to move and just continued staring at the phone as the message clicked to a stop.

* * *

"It's good to SEE you," Jackie emphasized the word "see" because she was using her new iPhone® to "FaceTime®" Patrick for the first time. She was sipping a cup of hot chocolate, bundled in a soft velour robe as defense against the winter night, sitting in the king-sized bed in the master bedroom of her stone-sided home in her gated community.

"Yeah, pretty cool, huh?" Patrick answered. He was seated on the couch in the living room of his two-bedroom apartment. "Like it better than your Blackberry?"

"Yes, I do. It's real 'Dick Tracy'."

"Whoa! That's reaching back into ancient history. Aren't you too young to remember Dick Tracy?" Patrick teased.

"Hey, my daddy used to read the funny papers to me every Sunday," Jackie said, giggling. "Every Sunday he was in town, anyway. But isn't "Dick Tracy" still running?"

"I don't know," Patrick answered.

"You don't know? Don't you work for a newspaper?" Jackie asked, laughing.

Patrick laughed too. "I guess I don't pay much attention to the funny papers. Anyway, it's good to SEE you too. I just wish it wasn't long distance."

"Me too," Jackie replied. "I'm trying to find a hole in my schedule to come to D.C."

"A likely story!" Patrick teased.

"I am!" Jackie insisted, laughing.

They continued to flirt like teenagers for another five minutes until Jackie said she would have to get to bed so she could stay awake at work tomorrow.

"Yes, I know that feeling. I'm looking for a way to get to Texas, too."

"Can't be too soon for me. SEE you later."

"Bye."

After she ended the call, Jackie realized neither of them had said anything like "I love you" as they hung up. In fact, neither of them had ever said "I love you" or much of anything that would categorize their relationship. So, what do you say when it's too early to say that? *It's been too long since I've been in a relationship*, Jackie thought.

CHAPTER THREE

"Congrats, you ol' dog!"

"Couldn't happen to a nicer guy!"

"Now you gotta pay for a wedding!"

Jonesy smiled and raised his bottle, returning the heartfelt wishes and laughter of his friends upon hearing that his oldest daughter, Amber, was engaged. He had managed to keep it secret from the guys he worked with for several months because he knew they would razz him, but now, as the big day drew near, he realized he was proud and didn't mind the good-natured ribbing.

He and his buddies were at McHenry's, their regular watering hole. Most of the guys worked at the Axiom refinery with him and had been Axiom employees for varying lengths of time. McHenry's was an old-school Gary, Indiana, pub with a fiercely loyal clientele and Jonesy was definitely one of them.

Bottles and glasses clinked together as Jonesy's friends celebrated with him, but the remark about paying for a wedding started Jonesy thinking. He had two daughters and he had admittedly spoiled them, right through high school until now that they were both in private college. It stretched his budget pretty thin. Margaret, Jonesy's wife, had gone back to work as a clerk in a discount department store after the girls left for college, but it was tough. Not even Margaret, and certainly not his precious daughters, knew how tight things were.

He made good, middle-class money as a union pipefitter at the refinery and he and Margaret had put money in a college fund, but he had been unprepared for the private college tuition at the College of the Holy Cross: $25,000 per year each for tuition was only the beginning. There seemed to be no end to the living expenses and fees that were added. Jonesy had thought he had saved for the girls' college, but the reality was so much worse than what he imagined.

Amber was a junior and now Leslie was also in college as a freshman and the reality was truly hitting the family.

College was made possible, just barely, by cutting living expenses to the bone, dipping into savings, selling a little Axiom stock from his 401k, taking whatever overtime he could get, and getting a Stafford loan for each of the girls. Luckily, the girls could pay on the loans once they graduated and were working.

Jonesy took care of the checkbook, even though Margaret might have done it better, but in Jonesy's world, that was the husband's job. So, he knew what no one else did, that things looked OK, but there were a lot of things he would have ordinarily done that he had just let slide.

For instance, the bungalow that had been home for the family for 25 years seriously needed to be reroofed, but that was a several-thousand-dollar expense, so Jonesy had liberally applied black roof patch to try to forestall the inevitable.

The same was true of his Chevy S-10 pickup. He had missed two oil changes now and had actually used a welder at the refinery to patch a hole in the radiator. Then there were the tires. When one needed replacing, he opted for used tires, which were cheaper but also wore out sooner.

But he kept things looking as normal as possible at home by making sure the obvious things were taken care of: he kept the grass mowed and the hedges trimmed in the summer, the leaves raked in the fall, and the snow shoveled and the oil furnace operating in winter.

After college he could replenish his meager savings.

* * *

"It'd be better for you if you'd just tell us what you know."

Marvin Borelli said nothing as Special Agent Samuel Jorgensen looked at him and sighed. They had done this dance almost every day for a month in the Washington, D.C., FBI field office, but Borelli had stubbornly kept his mouth shut.

He just sat sullenly, looking intently at the scratches on the gray, metal table top; his hands secured to it by handcuffs through a steel ring. His black hair was uncharacteristically unkempt, unlike the slicked-back style he preferred.

They had let him suffer the indignity of jail in Virginia for several weeks after his arrest. When that failed to get him to talk, they had moved him back to holding in D.C., which was many times better, but he was growing more and more desperate as the days dragged by.

Inside, his blood was boiling as he barely listened to Jorgensen's questions. *Why on earth can't my smarmy, five-hundred-dollar-an-hour lawyer get me out of here?*

His attorney was sitting beside him, logging billable hours but contributing nothing to the conversation. Joseph Panckowicz' impeccably coiffed gray hair and custom-tailored suit spoke volumes about his Washington, D.C., law practice, however. He had said something about the government using the Patriot Act to keep him locked up. *So, I'm a terrorist now?*

Borelli's life in Washington, D.C., had been the opposite of what one thinks of when one pictures a terrorist. He wondered what had happened to his Maserati. He figured it was just one of many things that had fallen victim to the government's asset forfeiture laws. He was pained as he remembered the high-dollar transactions he had brokered as a lobbyist, the evenings of fine dining with powerful people. And the women – political groupies basically – had all been his life before his arrest.

Now that was all gone and he didn't really know how they had fingered him. He figured his well-healed clients had run away as they would from someone with leprosy when he had been arrested. The Feds had probably cleaned out his small, but luxurious office as well.

Most of the time, Borelli was the only prisoner in the holding area of the Washington field office of the FBI, which was not the same as the J. Edgar Hoover Building, the FBI headquarters across town. Other prisoners had come and gone but they had been either released or moved to Federal prison. Meanwhile Borelli just continued to be held. His lawyer hadn't even been to see him for a few days. He was here now just to make sure Borelli didn't say anything.

"See, we know your role in the whole thing," Jorgensen continued, since no one else was talking. "We know you gave them the money for the oil platform bombing. We just need to know who gave you the money and was pulling the strings."

Borelli had heard it all before. He was sick of this boy scout of a Special Agent in a crew-cut and a cheap suit. He knew that telling him what he knew would not get him released; it would only get him tried and convicted, so why should he cooperate? Even an immunity deal would still mean prison time.

"Your buddies in the 'Knights of Mother Earth' are singing like canaries," Jorgensen chided, referring to the local environmental radical group that had carried out the bombing and were in custody in Texas.

"They aren't my buddies," Borelli snapped. Panckowicz touched his arm and shook his head. *The flunkies in the "Knights" can sing all they want*, Borelli thought. *There's a firewall between them and the author of the plan.* Unfortunately, Borelli WAS the firewall.

"Yeah, they aren't quite in your league, are they? Yet you used them, more than once apparently." Jorgensen glanced down at the file in front of him. "The bombing of the oil platform was just the warm up. Then there was Atlanta. An innocent man died there too, you know?"

Nobody's innocent! Borelli fumed. The greedy oil companies were stripping the Earth of its resources and they needed to be stopped. There was no doubt about the rightness of his Cause. Violence against the Earth demanded violence in return.

Then Borelli realized that Paul Stoddard, the leader of the Knights, was the only member of the group who knew him and the only one who knew enough to cause trouble for him. *So, Stoddard must not have talked too much, or the FBI wouldn't be continuing to question me.* That was just one more reason for Borelli to keep quiet.

"Do you know former Senator Nathan Taylor from Vermont?" Jorgensen asked. This was the first time this question had been asked.

Borelli wanted to ask why the Senator was "former", but he was determined to say nothing. His arrest had come before the November election and he hadn't had access to much news. *I need to ask Panckowicz.*

Taylor had been a key figure in the origination and passage of the Petroleum Independence Act. Borelli had clandestinely passed him information and had even supplied wording for the bill, while keeping him in the dark as much as possible about other aspects of the plan to allow him plausible deniability. He had also funneled a lot of cash to his reelection campaign, but if the FBI was asking about him, it meant they were suspicious that the Act itself was due to a conspiracy.

Conspiracy? Borelli had never applied that word to what he had been involved in, but of course that's what it was.

"Got nothing to say again today, huh?" Jorgensen sighed. "Well, see you again tomorrow. Or the next day."

Borelli just stared at the tabletop. Panckowicz stood up as Jorgensen left the interrogation room and another agent came in to un-cuff Borelli and take him back to holding.

"Thanks for nothing!" Borelli snarled to his lawyer.

CHAPTER FOUR

"Aye!"

"The member from Colorado votes 'Aye'", said the Speaker of the House to the recording clerk.

A voice vote was being taken in the chamber of the House of Representatives on H.R. 4592, the bill to repeal the Petroleum Independence Act.

After registering his vote, Colorado Representative Carl Kellerman listened to the votes as they were cast and made a few notes. The vast majority of the members were voting in favor of the bill. A few abstentions marked those who had survived the recent election and had voted for the original bill. They did not have the courage to vote "Nay" on this popular bill, but they wouldn't vote for it either.

Kellerman had been among those who tried to stop the passage of the Petroleum Independence Act in the first place, but it had been a losing battle. He suspected that cash had been spread around to grease the skids, because the bill had passed so easily. The election changed the political landscape, however, and the unpopularity of the gas tax meant that no amount of campaign cash could save many of those who voted for the bill.

So, Kellerman and others who voted against the original bill survived in the election and most of those who voted for the Act had now been replaced with freshmen whose mandate was clear: repeal the gas tax.

Soon Kellerman stopped taking notes. There was no need. The vote would not be close at all. The bill to repeal the Petroleum Independence Act would sail through the House virtually unopposed.

* * *

Patrick Garrity noticed Congressman Kellerman from across the House Floor. Kellerman had occasionally served as a good, if cagey, source for him.

Suddenly Patrick realized he was almost bored. The only newsworthy thing coming out of this was the overwhelming affirmative vote and the total lack of real opposition. He had expected the bill to pass, but this result seemed to be almost as automatic as the passage of the original bill had been. Just as there had been no stopping the Petroleum Independence Act and its tax, there would be no stopping its repeal.

Garrity was an old hand at following politics, but the juxtaposition of the two bills, barely eight months apart, was surprising even to him.

He decided he could afford to take his attention away long enough to send a text message. He took his iPhone® out of his pocket and began pecking away with both thumbs.

* * *

Jackie's iPhone® chimed indicating a text had arrived. As she reached for it on the corner of her massive desk, she saw the source and smiled, eagerly swiping it to read the contents.

"So far vote is all pos. Will def pass House."

She shouted a cowgirl's "Yahoo" and jumped up from her high-backed leather office chair, dancing an impromptu gig on the plush carpet. She then sat back down and answered Patrick's text.

"Yay! Keep me posted!"

* * *

"It's over 90% for repeal so far."

President William Lowndes Toland was being kept apprised of the vote by his chief of staff while he sat at his desk in the Oval Office reviewing intelligence reports.

"Thank you," Toland answered, only briefly looking up before lowering his graying head again.

It was obvious that Congress would pass the bill to repeal the Petroleum Independence Act by a wide margin; the Senate probably less decisively than the House, but it would certainly pass both houses and then make its way to his desk.

There was no doubt that he would sign it, too, though he dreaded facing the leftmost members of his party, for whom the gasoline tax had been a tremendous moral victory. Many of them still refused to admit that it had been an economic disaster, however, and still maintained their allegiance to the idea that fossil fuels must be stamped out.

Personally, Toland appreciated that tremendous progress had been made in terms of emissions standards since the bad old days of 1970s gas-guzzling, smoke-belching mega-cars. His Democrat party could take most of the credit for the implementation of those C.A.F.E. standards and other regulations on manufacturing that had cleaned up the air and water to a degree that surprised him.

And tremendous progress had been made in "green" technology such as hybrid cars and even fully electric vehicles. Of course, Toland knew that most people who ostentatiously bought and drove the gasoline-free vehicles wouldn't want to be reminded that petroleum was still essential in the manufacture, transport, and lubrication of the electric vehicles, not to mention all the plastic and synthetic-rubber parts and hydraulic fluids without which they couldn't exist or function. Also ignored by their enthusiasts was the fact that the electricity which powered the cars was likely produced in coal-fired plants. But at least they weren't powered by petroleum!

But he was also surprised by the lack of appreciation of those advancements on the part of his colleagues in the party, especially those close to the "green" agenda. Some of them seemed to have the attitude that no ground had been gained. The term "sore winners" occurred to him.

From the new president's perspective, the FBI's investigation into the bombing of the oil platform and potential ties to Washington lobbyists and politicians was especially concerning. As the titular head of the party, preventing fallout from that investigation while not appearing to impede it would have to be a priority in his administration.

But he would definitely sign the bill to repeal. The people had spoken loud and clear last November and he had become the "leader of the free world" because of his promise.

* * *

"Hi, Paula," Patrick greeted the receptionist for Congressman Kellerman's office as he often did. Usually she had some smart remark, but today she just glanced up and then back down at her desk, which was covered in multiple, foot-high stacks of files, books and papers.

At one time, Patrick had thought he might ask Paula out, as she was a fetching, willowy blonde, but she was not interested in the least; that she had made abundantly clear. She was no happier to see him now than any other time.

"Is he here?"

"If you're referring to the 'esteemed Congressman from the Great State of Colorado,' no he's not. I don't really know where he is. Probably huddling with a fellow committee member in the halls."

"I saw him leave the chamber after voting."

"Well, he didn't come back here."

"What is all this stuff anyway?" Patrick asked, gesturing to the piles of files and loose papers on her desk.

"I guess the congressman decided since everyone else is moving in or out of Congressional offices that we needed to clean house too, so I'm having to go through all these files – and other junk, whatever it is – and decide what to throw away or keep or whatever."

"Oh. Poor you."

"Yeah, I can tell you're all broken up."

Then Patrick noticed something on top of one of the stacks. It was a brochure for the lobbying firm of Marvin Borelli.

"Hey, what's this?"

"How should I know?"

"This is a brochure for the lobbyist the FBI arrested last year. Borelli. He was involved in the Axiom bomb plot."

"If you say so."

"Can I take this?"

"Please do. In fact, can you take a couple of stacks, please?"

"Thanks, I'll come back later when he's more likely to be in."

On the way out, Patrick looked through the brochure. Pretty standard stuff: general information, a client list, case studies. *Well this is now a collector's item,* Patrick thought, *since Borelli isn't servicing any clients where he is.* Then Patrick realized he wasn't actually sure where Borelli was right now. He hadn't heard anything about a trial.

* * *

His lawyer had insisted, so, against his better judgement, Nathan Taylor had agreed to be "interviewed" by the FBI. He and his attorney were ushered into a window-less room by a young, respectful FBI agent. *Pitiful newbie,* Taylor thought.

Taylor's lawyer was 20 years his junior, but had still been his attorney for 20 years. They sat quietly. They had discussed their strategy before coming to the Washington field office.

Soon, an older agent came in and introduced himself as Special-Agent-in-Charge Samuel Jorgensen. He was accompanied by another agent with a notepad.

"Thank you for coming in, Senator," Jorgensen began. "We have a few questions and, hopefully, this can all be cleared up."

Taylor watched the agent, trying to size him up and anticipate where the questioning would go. He knew he needed to react as little as possible, regardless of how close the FBI was to the truth.

"Can you tell me about how the Petroleum Independence Act came to be?" Jorgensen asked.

"I don't understand," Taylor answered, feigning confusion. "Why is the FBI interested in how legislation is created?"

"That's part of our investigation that I can't share. I'm sure you understand," Jorgensen smiled.

Taylor inwardly seethed, but he returned the smile as the agent continued.

"So, we just need to know how the Act came about. Whose idea was it?"

"Mine, of course. I have been a crusader for the Environment for a long time." Taylor instantly regretted using the word "crusader." Jorgensen looked up and their eyes locked.

"Did you write it?"

"Are you asking how the sausage is made?" Taylor willed his facial muscles into a joking, relaxed mask.

"Just answer the question." The agent wasn't smiling.

"Well, I certainly roughed out the broad outlines, but there were staffers and consultants who contributed."

"So, you didn't write it?"

"Not every word, no. In any legislation, the details have to be hammered out by people who are experienced in the field. It's important that laws like this one have real-world practicality."

Jorgensen appeared skeptical. "So, who were some of the contributors? Anybody I would know?"

"Probably not. Do you know the chairman of the Climatology Department at Stanford?"

"Can't say I do. What's his name and what was his contribution?" Jorgensen looked over at the agent who was silently taking notes.

"Dr. Bertrand Lewis. He's an expert on global climatology."

"What did he write?"

"Well, I don't know that he actually wrote anything in the legislation, but he was given a copy for his comments and he replied with valuable input."

"Uh-huh," Jorgensen said. "Who else?"

Taylor gave him a couple of additional names, but admitted that they had mainly consulted with comments on the finished legislation.

"What about this guy?" Jorgensen reached into his thick file folder and pulled out an eight-by-ten photo that looked like a mugshot. It was Marvin Borelli. "Do you know him?"

"I believe he's a lobbyist," Taylor said slowly after a pause.

"That's right. In fact, you know him very well, don't you?"

Taylor said nothing.

"Here's another picture I want you to look at." Jorgensen took another eight-by-ten from the file. It was a grainy printout of a video frame. Taylor instantly recognized that it was taken in the Senate Commerce and Energy Committee room when they had interrogated the upper management of Axiom Oil about their moratorium.

"That's Marvin Borelli sitting right behind you in the Committee hearing. Isn't that spot usually reserved for close aides? Is that what Borelli was to you, a close aide?"

For the first time since they had sat down, Taylor looked at his lawyer, who discreetly shook his head and closed his eyes with pursed lips.

"Did Marvin Borelli write the Petroleum Independence Act?"

Nathan Taylor looked down at the institutional table and said nothing.

"Got nothing smooth to say now?" Jorgensen put the pictures back in the file. "Did Marvin Borelli give money to your reelection campaign?"

"No," Taylor answered finally. He felt safe answering that question, since the money that Borelli had funneled his way had actually come from others, not Borelli himself.

"Is that so? Why then am I able to go down the list of your contributors and find the same people and organizations on Marvin Borelli's client list?"

Taylor scowled.

"You see, here's what I think happened. Borelli had this plot to destroy the oil companies, so he hatched the attack on the oil platform in the Gulf and you just HAPPENED to have this legislation ready to go. And next thing we know, Borelli is sitting behind you in hearings and getting contributors to line up to contribute to your reelection effort for a 'safe' seat."

Jorgensen paused, but Taylor remained silent.

"So, got nothing to say to that? If I decide I'm right and you took money to pass this legislation, I'll arrest you and compel your testimony!"

"Do you know who you're talking to?" Taylor exclaimed, ignoring his panicking attorney. "I was a member of the House of Representatives when you were in grade school and I've been a sitting United States Senator for more than 30 years!"

Jorgensen almost appeared bored. "So, that just means you should have known better."

* * *

Every television in Axiom Oil Incorporated's Houston headquarters was tuned to a cable news channel and many were watching the live stream online as the new president signed the bill to repeal the gas tax. The Oval Office ceremony lasted all of ten minutes, long enough for the president to make a forgettable speech, to go through several pens that would become instant collector's items and for photographers to get pictures and video of him with a bevy of beaming politicians in the background.

Although the margin of victory had been less than in the House, the Senate had passed the bill without a problem, so now the president could make it the law of the land.

Jackie watched in her office, along with Doris and Wayne. As the president completed the signing ceremony, they cheered and "high-fived", then headed downstairs for a "staff meeting" that had been called to celebrate the event.

There would be catered food and drink and even a DJ to help them have a serious celebration. It was only two o'clock but Jackie had decreed that work was over in the black and gold tower for the day.

Tomorrow new projections could be made with a fresh look to the future of the company, its employees and their families.

* * *

Judge Everett Walker regarded the television on one wall of his chambers with disdain, as if the blow-dried talking head had included a personal insult in her news report of the passage of the bill to repeal the Petroleum Independence Act. *These politicians are little better than trained monkeys the way they spin around with the changing winds of public opinion,* he groused. Even in an age when all public figures' every word seemed to be recorded and played back on the interminable 24-hour cable news networks, they thought nothing of reversing opinions they had convincingly proclaimed only weeks before.

Disgusted, he snapped off the TV with the remote in his wrinkled right hand and turned back to his work in his wood-paneled chambers in the Federal Building in St. Louis. Walker's chambers were a throwback to the days when juries were all male and courthouses were all dark wood paneling and deep red carpet: masculine to a fault.

As a Federal Judge with three decades of judicial experience under his belt, Walker knew, of course, that many of the Congressmen and Senators who voted this repeal were new to politics, but there were plenty of veterans still left in both houses who had voted for the Petroleum Independence Act just a few months before and now they had voted to repeal it.

Cowards.

And what of the new president? His pledge to repeal the Act during the campaign was a direct betrayal of everything the Democrat party stood for.

Judges, at least Federal Judges, Walker huffed, *don't have to bother with the fickle winds of public opinion to get reelected. We can stay true to our principles.*

CHAPTER FIVE

An old Def Leppard tune blared from an equally old turntable connected to a "component" audio system that was must-have for audiophiles in the 1970s. A 60-something man in wrinkled jeans and a faded 'Earth Day' T-shirt absent-mindedly nodded to the beat as he dipped a teabag in a chipped mug. His salt-and-pepper hair was tied into a ponytail with a leather thong.

Only when the song ended did he realize someone was knocking on the front door. He didn't bother to hurry.

"Hello, Mr. Donaldson? My name is Robert Thorne," the bespectacled, impeccably dressed, 30-something young man at the door said. "I'm with the firm of Fischer-Williams in Bellingham, Washington."

"You a lawyer?" the man with the gray ponytail asked, sounding like it galled him to pronounce the word.

"Yes," Thorne said, with a brief look that said, *Obviously, Einstein!*

"What're you doing way over here in O'Fallon, Missouri?"

"I'm here to make a contribution to your organization, the Aquarian Community."

"Why would you wanna do that?"

"Oh, not me personally," Thorne said, thinking *Missouri really is the "Show Me" state.* "I represent a party that wishes to remain anonymous."

This earned the lawyer a more skeptical, guarded look.

"My client wishes to donate $100,000."

The aging hippy gasped audibly. "What? Why? We haven't done squat in years."

"I'm sorry," the young lawyer continued. "I don't remember your first name."

"George. George Donaldson. People call me 'Slats'."

"OK, George, Mr. Donaldson. You are still committed to saving the Planet – er, Mother Earth, right?"

"'Thout a doubt."

"Then my client has something for you to do with half the money. The Aquarian Community can keep $50,000. The other $50,000 is for a court case important to the Environment."

"You know, I completely forgot my manners," said Donaldson, his tone now considerably friendlier. "Please come in and have a seat so we can talk this out like normal people."

The odd pair was able to sit down on the threadbare furniture only after Donaldson cleared away a month's worth of newspapers and a plate and fork from last night's supper.

"So, what's the court case that's so important?"

"You are aware, are you not, of the Petroleum Independence Act?" Thorne asked.

"Of course, I'm reminded every time I fill up!"

"You're not driving a hybrid?"

"I would if the durn things weren't so expensive! Anyway, what's the deal?"

"You know Congress passed a law repealing the gas tax?"

"Yeah."

"Which will cause more gasoline to be sold and more pollution to be put into the air?"

"Yeah, I suppose."

Thorne's look said, *what kind of environmentalist are you?* but he said, "So my client wants to get a Federal judge to issue an injunction to stop the repeal of the tax."

Donaldson squinted at the youngster, but said nothing.

"That way the tax will continue and less gasoline will be sold, so less pollution," Thorne said, finishing as if it was all obvious.

"But if you're with a law firm, why are you hiring another lawyer here in Missouri? Why not just file for the injunction yourself back in Washington state?"

"Because there's a judge in St. Louis who is sympathetic and we are a lot more likely to be successful if a Missouri lawyer files in the District Court here."

"Judge shoppin' are ya?"

"We don't like that term."

"No, I don't suppose you do. Why do you need me? I mean I appreciate the fifty grand and all, but why don't you just retain the lawyer yourself?"

"Because, as I said, my client wishes to remain anonymous."

"And I don't?" Donaldson laughed loudly. "Young fella, I'm about as anonymous as it gets! My ex-wife can't even remember my name."

"Well, for the $50,000, you would need to appear publicly."

"To do what?"

"Why to appear in court, as the plaintiff, of course, or 'petitioner' I should say."

"Me?"

"You and your organization, the Aquarian Community."

"So, you want me to pretend that this was my idea?"

"You and your group, yes. In fact, you might be able to raise more money this way."

"What're you talkin' about?"

"There will be press coverage. It will be a big deal. You'll be David fighting the Goliath of the Government-Industrial Complex. People might come forward to help with the effort."

Donaldson leaned back in his worn, favorite chair and rubbed the soft, white stubble on his chin. He had been a crusader once. Perhaps he could get the old gang together and be one again.

"Well, Mr. Thorne, I might have one battle left in me."

"Excellent, Mr. Donaldson," Thorne said, opening his fine leather briefcase. "There are just a couple of documents I need your signature on, including the information you need for the lawyer, and then I can give you your check."

"Right on!"

* * *

Jackie James had not had time to follow it closely, but the trial of the Knights of Mother Earth group was going forward, including the leader who had broken into her house and threatened her life. Some of the proceedings had been on TV, and she sat down one night to see the late news and suddenly realized they were describing the verdict.

She sat on the edge of her bed in her spacious master bedroom, transfixed as she watched the jury file in and the judge in the New Orleans courtroom ask for a verdict, as a reporter narrated the moving images.

The charges were severe, with the entire group charged with conspiracy to commit murder and terrorism, as Jackie knew from earlier news reports. Now, however, at the handing down of the verdict, the reporter telling the story related that the group had cooperated with law enforcement. Some in the group had only participated in bombing the oil platform, so they would serve time in prison, but their charges were now reduced to manslaughter instead of murder.

That was not true of the leader, however.

"Paul Lucas Stoddard, the Knights' director, unlike the rest of the group, will stand for murder – three counts, plus kidnapping and making terroristic threats," the Houston TV station reporter said, "because of the deaths during the oil platform bombing and the firebombing of an Axiom service station in Atlanta, and he murdered a policeman after he broke into the home of the Axiom CEO and held her at gunpoint."

Jackie shuddered at hearing the reference to her and the memory of that night. She did not relish the media attention at this time, either.

The reporting of what had transpired earlier in the day continued as Jackie watched closely. The judge asked the jury for their verdict. "Guilty" said the foreman, when asked to judge each of the participants. "Guilty," was the judgement of the jury concerning each of Paul Stoddard's murder charges.

He will surely be in prison for the rest of his life, Jackie thought. Though she knew others were involved, it gave her comfort to know that this man would be behind bars and unable to threaten her.

She was glad she didn't have to testify. There had been plenty of evidence against the Knights of Mother Earth without her testimony.

* * *

Amber Jones, at age 20, was beautiful in her way, not model-tall or model-thin, but, with wholesome good looks, a better-than-average smile and an outgoing personality, she attracted plenty of attention from the opposite sex at The College of the Holy Cross in Notre Dame.

Now that she was engaged, Tobias Jones wanted more than anything for his daughter to have the wedding she had always wanted, but he knew that it would be very expensive. Even for his blue-collar, middle-class status, expectations would be high.

The reality turned out to be even worse than he feared, as he learned how picky his beloved daughter could be about everything from just the right embossed, double-enveloped invitations to the hors d'oeuvres for the reception.

Amber's sister, Leslie, was thrilled that Amber was getting married and would naturally be the maid of honor, but she was also envious and was in the middle of all the plans. Being less than two years apart, the girls were very close and, as Jonesy watched them together, it dawned on him that Leslie could get engaged as suddenly as Amber had and there could be another wedding in his future. The thought barely had time to warm his father's heart before it caused him to break out in a cold sweat, thinking about bills.

Jonesy had only met the fiancé, Ryan Peterson, once. He seemed nice enough, a senior majoring in marketing, which people said could pay well, but Jonesy had no idea what someone with a marketing degree did for a living. Anyway, the fiancé and he were totally irrelevant to the wedding plans. Jonesy's daughters and his wife were in total control of that project, except when it came time to pay for things.

And that's when Jonesy resorted to plastic. He had been proud of the fact that he never allowed the family to rack up a pile of credit card debt, but that had to change now. His primary Visa card was filling up at an alarming rate. Reluctantly he responded to an offer for a card at another bank with an introductory zero-percent rate and a high credit limit. He didn't want to think about what the rate would be after the zero-percent offer expired.

One day, Jonesy's stress got the better of him when, on his way to the refrigerator, he walked by what had been the dining room table, but was now wedding-planning headquarters. Margaret and Amber were looking at a shopping website on Amber's laptop when Amber looked up and said, "Daddy, see the absolutely divine wrist bag I'm buying for my honeymoon."

"Wrist bag? What's that?"

"It's a clutch with a strap so you can hang it from your wrist and put your money and phone and driver's license in it."

Jonesy looked at the picture on the screen briefly and said, "Hmm."

"We got a good deal on it. It was on sale for only $199.00."

"What?!" Jonesy shouted. "What the heck kind of bag costs two hundred bucks?!"

"It's Louis Vuitton, Daddy!"

"It'd better be gold plated at that price!"

"Now Toby," said Margaret. "She needs nice things for her trousseau."

Jonesy said something unintelligible that was more of a growl than anything and went out to the garage, slamming the back door behind him.

CHAPTER SIX

For his initial visit to the lawyer's office, George Donaldson's main concessions to convention were to wash his salt-and-pepper hair and put on an old corduroy sport coat. He sat waiting in the large law firm's plush waiting room, tapping his toes against the soles of his sandals, looking like a rotary phone in an Apple store. He didn't have to wait long.

Blake Reardon the Third breezed into the room with the air of a man always in a hurry. Every graying blonde hair was perfectly in place and his manner was as starched as his gleaming, white shirt. His eyes flickered only briefly when he saw Donaldson for the first time.

"Mr. Donaldson, pleased to meet you. I'm Blake Reardon. Come right this way."

Reardon led the way down a long hallway and around a corner, then through a tall door opening into a luxurious corner office and motioned for Donaldson to sit in a leather chair.

"You called about your desire to get an injunction against implementation of the bill to repeal the gasoline tax, right?"

"Yes, I think the gas tax should continue, for the Environment," Donaldson said, just like he'd practiced.

"You think if less gasoline is sold, there will be less pollution, is that right?"

Donaldson saw Reardon's eyebrows go up and suddenly he felt like a fourth grader whose teacher was asking leading questions trying to get him to multiply three times six.

"Yeah, that's pretty much it."

"Well, let's see, you said you represent a concerned citizens group called the Aquarians?"

"The Aquarian Community."

"Right. Does your group have funds for a retainer?"

"Yes, we have $50,000 set aside for this," Donaldson said beginning to feel like he was in a play in which the script was already written but had yet to be shared with all the actors.

"That will be fine. I will require $20,000 as a retainer and the other payment when we have presented the case."

Donaldson nodded, not knowing what else he should say. He wondered if he was supposed to negotiate the price, but it seemed Reardon already knew the amount Donaldson had.

"What I will do, Mr. Donaldson, is draft a petition that will outline the concerns of your organization and submit it to you for approval, and then we will file it with the court."

"How long will that take?"

"Shouldn't take long at all."

Especially since it's probably already written, Donaldson thought.

* * *

The petition on the desk in front of Melissa seemed to vibrate and pulsate as she read the words. *This is so exciting! The judge will be so pleased by this petition!*

Melissa Bertram, Judge Everett Walker's lead clerk, knew his preferences from the Amaretto creamer he liked in his coffee to the position he would likely take on any given case. She stood, gathering the brief that had only just arrived via courier and started down the hall to the judge's chambers in the Federal courthouse in St. Louis.

"Sir, I think you're going to like this," Melissa said after knocking and being bidden to enter.

"What's that?" Judge Walker asked, taking the brief and peering through his brass-rimmed reading glasses, pinched at the very tip of his nose and brushing back an errant silver hair.

"Ah, good!" the judge exclaimed as soon as he saw the first page of the document. Melissa smiled as she watched his reaction, but she wondered why he didn't seem as surprised as she expected him to be.

"This is great!" the veteran judge said, a broad smile crinkling his deeply lined cheeks. "Maybe we can have a part in stopping this nonsense!"

"Or at least slowing it down," Melissa suggested. "It asks for an injunction to stop the repeal of the gas tax."

"Yes, I can see that. I was hoping someone would come forward to challenge this disgrace."

"It will need to happen fast," Melissa prodded.

"That shouldn't be a problem," the judge assured her. "In fact, do what you can to push back everything else on my calendar. This is important. I want to deal with it as soon as humanly possible."

"Yes sir!" Melissa said as she turned to leave the judge's chambers. "I'm sorry, do you mean the docket, or your appointment calendar."

"My calendar. We'll do this *ex parte*, in my chambers, for now. Once the I've issued the restraining order, we'll notify the US Attorney and have a hearing."

Melissa nodded, knowingly. It didn't surprise her at all that the judge had already made his decision.

* * *

The wedding was now only a month away, and to Jonesy's relief, Amber was taking a semester off from college to give her time to establish her new home. Her fiancé would graduate in June and she wanted to devote her full time to him and their new life together. She planned to resume college in the Fall.

Jonesy was glad that the hemorrhaging of cash to the university had slowed for a while. The tab for the wedding would soon rise north of $40,000. While that was not much by some standards, it was a fantastic amount of money for the Jones' budget and every dollar was borrowed.

But for the family he kept the face of the doting father of the bride. And it wasn't deception. He was very happy and proud of his first-born. His happiness was just necessarily tempered by his increasingly desperate financial position.

* * *

George Donaldson had never been to the Federal Courthouse in St. Louis, although he had lived just a few miles from it all of his life. As he and his attorney, Blake Reardon, were ushered into the waiting room for the District Court for the Eastern District of Missouri he was a little overcome and had to stuff down the impulse to run back out the front door.

"It won't be long now," Reardon said. Donaldson was reassured by Reardon's confidence but, at the same time, unsettled by the unfamiliarity of it all.

Just then a woman came through and wide, polished wooden door and announced, "Judge Walker will see you now."

Reardon was on his feet and heading for the door immediately. Donaldson struggled to keep up.

They went through an outer office with four desks in it, which Donaldson assumed belonged to various judicial assistants, although he knew nothing about what those jobs would entail.

From there, they were ushered into the judge's chambers. Reardon strode up to the large desk and extended his hand to the man sitting behind it.

"Judge Walker, thank you for seeing us."

"Reardon, good to see you again," the judge answered.

"Allow me to present George Donaldson, representing the Aquarian Community."

Donaldson reached out, shaking the judge's extended hand.

"Please, have a seat," the judge said, sitting himself before the visitors could settle into the overstuffed, leather chairs in front of the desk.

Donaldson then noticed a woman sitting in one corner of the room with what he recognized from TV as a court reporting machine. *So, this is being taken down word-for-word?*

"So, tell me about your petition," the judge said to Reardon.

"Your honor, it is the feeling of the Aquarian Community, and I dare say many others across the country, that the Petroleum Independence Act, passed by Congress and signed into law by the president last year, has served well to reduce the use of gasoline which will lead to a reduction in pollution, especially greenhouse gases which are shown by science to cause the Global Warming currently happening in the world.

"Since the new Congress has been sworn in, a new, reckless law has been passed to repeal the first law and its tax, which has been the primary instrument to reduce the use of gasoline across the country. My clients feel this repeal of the Petroleum Independence Act will once again increase greenhouse gas emissions to dangerous levels.

"I don't think I need to educate Your Honor about the dire effects on the Environment of allowing the prodigious use of fossil fuels to continue."

Reardon finally paused, and the judge spoke.

"Yes, I understand the issues, all right. Mr. Donaldson, tell me about the Aquarian Community."

Donaldson had to clear his throat before he could answer. "Well, we formed the group more than 40 years ago, after the first Earth Day, because we realized the importance of taking care of the planet."

"In what types of activities has your group been involved?"

"Uh, well, we had sit-ins and helped stage demonstrations back in the day. We also organized a trash pick-up drive and sponsored a stretch of Interstate 70 back in the 80s. We haven't been as active in recent years. We're not getting any younger," Donaldson said, with a weak smile. The fact was that the group had been most active more than 30 years ago and few of those still around had been willing to gather for this new campaign.

"Your Honor," Reardon continued, "The Aquarian Community feels strongly that the Congress has acted rashly and the process needs to be slowed down so that cooler heads can prevail. The sooner it is stopped the better."

"I have read your petition and I must say I have been concerned as well about the unthinking way that Congress has proceeded in this matter," said the judge as he began making notes on a legal pad. "I have to say I'm inclined to concur with the Aquarian Community's concern, so I am going to issue a restraining order to immediately stop the repeal of the Act."

"Thank you, Your Honor," Reardon said, and he looked at Donaldson and winked.

* * *

"The temporary injunction leaves the Petroleum Independence Act in place. A hearing must be held within 20 days, but no date has been announced for a trial."

Jackie was in her car when she heard the news on the radio: a judge in St. Louis had issued an injunction to stop the repeal of the gas tax. She didn't wait to arrive at Axiom headquarters before calling Marcus Williams to ask about the legal ramifications. *How could one judge hand down a decision that would adversely affect the lives of millions of people, contradicting the representatives of The People?*

"Marcus, have you heard? What does it mean?"

"Well, it means the repeal is effectively stopped for now," Axiom's Vice President for Legal Affairs said on the other end of the line in his unmistakable bulldog voice. "This is an *ex parte* injunction, which means the judge considered it so important he didn't notify any of the affected parties, but there will have to be a hearing within 20 days. We'll have to scramble, but I'll try to get a seat at that hearing."

"Yes, please move heaven and earth to have us included."

"I will, but it may not be easy. The injunction is aimed at Congress and the president, so the court may not think we figure in at all."

"But we're one of the parties that will suffer the most!"

"Yes, I'll have to make the court see that. If the judge lets the injunction stand after the hearing, there will be a trial to make the decision about whether the injunction is permanent or not."

Permanent!? It was too horrible to contemplate, so Jackie said, "How long will that take?"

"Who knows? It probably won't even start for several weeks."

Jackie's heart sank. It seemed doubtful that they would get relief from the gas tax any time soon with this development. She gripped the steering wheel and her mouth became a thin, tight line as she considered this new reality.

* * *

He had been on the phone for half the day, but Marcus was finally getting close to the person he needed to reach.

"Assistant U.S. Attorney Talbot is in court," said the crisp, business-like voice on the other end of the phone.

"Could you tell him it's urgent that I speak to him about the hearing in Federal Court next week?" Marcus pleaded. He had no idea whether the Assistant U.S. Attorney's executive assistant could be trusted to pass the word along, but what choice did he have?

"Certainly, I will – Oh, wait! He just came in."

Marcus heard a muffled conversation as the executive assistant explained the situation with her hand over the mouthpiece of the phone.

"Hold for Mr. Talbot," she said finally.

"Thank you!"

Talbot was soon on the line.

"Talbot here."

"Mr. Talbot, thank you so much for talking to me. I know how busy you must be," Marcus began, knowing he needed to get right to the point. "I'm Marcus Williams, Vice President for Legal Affairs for Axiom Oil Incorporated. You are defending the United States against the restraining order about the bill to repeal the Petroleum Independence Act, are you not?"

"Yes."

"I'm calling because my company is especially desirous that this injunction not become permanent and that the Act and its tax be repealed as voted by Congress."

"Yes, I imagine so."

"So, I have to ask if there's anyway I can be present and perhaps be called as a witness or submit a "friend of the court" brief or something? Anything?"

There was silence for a couple of seconds on the other end of the phone, then Talbot answered.

"Well I don't know. The restraining order is directed at Congress and the President, not the private sector. Anyway, I'm reluctant to be seen as carrying water for the oil companies."

"I can understand that, but could you look at it as representing the will of the American people in this matter, because I believe that the desire of the American people is very much aligned with our desire to see the Act repealed."

"Hmm. Let me ask you this," Talbot answered. "Would you supply facts and figures that would buttress my arguments?"

"I can give you facts and figures all day long, plus case studies of suffering under the higher prices due to the tax."

"Well, perhaps you *could* help me. You said you would be willing to testify?"

"I'll do anything you need."

"All right, could you put together a brief I can present to the judge and be there in case he'll let you testify at the hearing?"

"I've already started a brief and I'll be there with bells on!" Marcus heard nothing but silence on the other end of the phone. *I guess this government attorney doesn't have much of a sense of humor.*

CHAPTER SEVEN

The petitioner's attorney, Blake Reardon the Third, swept into the court room and set his ostrich-leather briefcase on the table to the right side of the courtroom. George Donaldson followed, tentatively looking this way and that.

Reardon quickly raked a slender, tanned hand through his longish, graying blonde hair, then pulled the wooden chair back and sat down, indicating the other chair to George with a nod.

The attorney could feel the people in the court room watching him as if the manner of his arrival would be crucial to the judge's decision, but also, they watched because it was difficult not to, he was so striking. He reveled in their attention, even as he pretended not to notice.

For Reardon's part, he was accustomed to courtroom theatrics and drama, and had cultivated his every move to serve the purposes of his clients, but ultimately, he was serving his own interests. He could hold a court gallery, not to mention the jury, in the palm of his hand and had managed more than once to pull a dog of a case to victory by sheer force of his charisma.

But this hearing was different. There would be no jury to romance, only an assistant U.S. attorney with which to argue and a judge to impress. It was a simple request: just stop the implementation of a law. And since the law that this law repealed was profoundly unpopular, he was unsure how it would play on the public stage.

While he had entered exuding confidence, he saw that the seats were filled with members of the press. *Keeping it quiet is not on the menu,* he mused. Then again, he would never pass up a chance to step up to the microphone.

He glanced at the defendant's table and saw a short, thin man with black whisps of hair struggling to cover a bald head. This assistant U.S. attorney did not look very formidable.

"All rise!"

At the bailiff's cry the occupants of the courtroom, including Reardon, rose to their feet, then just as quickly, the judge came in and allowed them to sit again.

"Court is now in session; the Honorable Judge Everett Walker presiding."

"Mr. Talbot, I presume?" the judge said, looking at the assistant U. S. attorney.

"Yes, Your Honor, for the Justice Department."

"Yes, how are things in the nation's capital?"

"Uh, fine, I guess."

"Fine." Then the judge looked at Reardon. "Mr. Reardon..."

"Yes, your honor."

"...Representing the Aquarian Community. This hearing is to determine the issues regarding the temporary restraining order I issued not quite three weeks ago at the request of the Aquarian Community to stop the repeal of the Petroleum Independence Act. So, go ahead. Let's hear it."

"Thank you, your honor," Reardon began. "If it please the court, I'd like to enter into evidence the EPA research of the effect of carbon emissions and an estimate of the decrease in such emissions, thanks to the Petroleum Independence Act, which Congress has now reversed." The brief with the EPA research was already in the judge's hands. He scanned it as Reardon continued.

"My client's petition for a permanent injunction is to prevent the implementation of the bill which repeals said Act and to perpetuate the original Act, which has had the effect to limit gasoline sales and therefore the harmful emissions that result from the greatly increased motor-vehicular activity that will follow the repeal of the original Act and its tax."

"So, your client believes the original law, which imposed the tax, was beneficial," the judge interrupted, "and repealing it would be harmful to the environment?"

"That's right, your honor."

"And your client has requested that this court issue a permanent injunction to prevent Congress and the President from implementing the act that repeals the original law?"

"Yes, your honor."

* * *

Marcus Williams thought the argument by the lawyer for the petitioner was pretty thin, although the man was obviously impressed with himself. He was glad when it was the government's turn.

"Mr. Talbot, you may answer," the judge said when Reardon was through.

"Your honor, the United States government holds as sacred the legislative process, because it reflects the will of the people through their elected representatives. While the turn around may be surprising in this situation, it is the legitimate expression of the process our founders created when they formed our constitutional republic.

"It is the position of the United States, therefore, that bill 115-832, which repeals the Petroleum Independence Act, should be allowed to stand as passed by both houses of Congress and signed into law by the president, and the Petroleum Independence Act should be repealed."

"Are you unconcerned at all by the issues raised by the Aquarian Community," the judge asked, "that the repeal of the

Act will bring about a rush of pollution that will ultimately bring about the death of the planet?"

"Your honor, neither I nor the elected representatives of the people are unconcerned for the welfare of Planet Earth, for we live here too, but those predicted effects are supposition and there are more pressing concerns: namely the hardships brought on by the Petroleum Independence Act.

"With your honor's permission, I'd like to call a witness: Marcus Williams, Vice President for Legal Affairs for Axiom Oil Incorporated."

"Um, very well," said the judge.

Marcus stood and walked forward to take the stand.

"Mr. Williams, be reminded that this is merely a hearing, not a full-fledged trial," said the judge.

"Yes, your honor."

Talbot walked over to face the witness box.

"Mr. Williams, can you tell me about the experience of your company's customers and their attitudes toward the Petroleum Independence Act?"

"It has created great hardships for them."

"What kind of hardships?"

"Working people on tight budgets find it difficult to afford to go to work and the shortage of diesel fuel, caused by the artificially inflated price, has meant shortages of all kinds of consumer goods because of it has been more difficult to get goods to market."

"And what can you tell the court about the difficulties your company has experienced since the Act was passed?"

"The Act was calculated to hurt our company and other energy providers like ours, by forcing us to pay the extra two dollars per gallon in tax, one dollar of which we have to absorb. This has made it impossible for us to make a profit."

"What are the implications for the company?"

"Quite simply it means that we will have to lay off employees. We have put that off as long as we could, but if this injunction is made permanent and the Act is not repealed, I don't know if we can survive."

"What do you mean by 'you're not sure you can survive'?" Talbot asked.

"I mean Axiom could go out of business entirely. Tens of thousands would be out of work and thousands more would lose their investments."

"I'm sorry, Mr. Williams," Judge Walker broke in. "How can you say that your company, the largest supplier of gasoline fuel in the country, could go out of business? Aren't you stretching the truth a bit?"

"Not at all, Your Honor. Even the biggest companies don't have bottomless buckets of cash. If we go too long with our expenses being greater than our revenue, we eventually would run out of options and have to cease operations."

Marcus paused only briefly before forging ahead to make the point he had hastily traveled to St. Louis to make: "With all due respect, your honor, this restraining order was filed *ex parte* so the petitioner really should have been required to post a bond."

"I beg your pardon?" the judge said.

"When the court issues an order such as this, the petitioner is usually required to post a bond to cover the damages expected to be caused by the injunction."

"Axiom Oil Incorporated is not the object of the injunction under discussion today, Mr. Williams."

"But Axiom, our employees, our stockholders and our customers are the ones who will suffer; we are the 'affected parties' the law talks about. According to my figures, the petitioner should have posted a bond somewhere in the neighborhood of two billion dollars!"

Marcus looked over at the plaintiff's table and saw the attorney scowling and Donaldson, the petitioner, looking like a scared rabbit.

"Again, Mr. Williams," said the judge, "Axiom is not the object of this injunction, so the law does not require a bond to be posted to compensate you. I allowed you to testify as a courtesy, but you are close to the line of abusing the privilege!"

"I assure you that was never my intention, your honor," Marcus answered.

"Those are all of my questions, Your Honor," Talbot said after a tense moment, nodding to Marcus, who stepped down and returned to his seat. Talbot then returned to the lectern.

"Your Honor, in closing I would just say that the people of the United States have spoken through their elected representatives and they deserve the relief they have demanded. I ask that you rescind the restraining order and do not let the injunction become permanent. Thank you."

Talbot walked back to his table and sat down.

"Mr. Reardon, your rebuttal."

"Thank you, your honor," Reardon said as he rose and went to the lectern once again.

"Your honor, the petition that is before the court is about much more than money, which seems to be the primary concern of the government and its witness."

Marcus was certain he heard a bitter tone when Reardon said the word "witness," referring of course to him.

"The petition before the court is concerned about whether the seas will rise to engulf our great cities, whether the air will become unbreathable and the sun will sear our planet until no one is left alive."

Oh brother, Marcus thought. *He's as melodramatic as a silent movie. What's next? Foreclosing on the family farm?*

"The pollution of our air and water will continue to kill our planet unless something is done," Reardon continued. "The Petroleum Independence Act was that 'something' that needed doing and you, your honor, have the opportunity to save and heal our wounded planet before it's too late."

Marcus looked around at the people around him, most of whom were reporters. It appeared they were enthralled by Reardon. Then he looked back at the judge, who seemed to be just as engrossed in Reardon's theatrics.

* * *

George Donaldson watched the process in amazement, almost forgetting that he was more than just a spectator to the proceedings. Before he knew it, they were wrapping up.

"So, Mr. Reardon, I understand the gist of your request and I have your supporting exhibits," the judge said, "so I will schedule the full trial on this shortly." Then looking at Talbot, he said, "Thank you to all who took their time to be present for this hearing."

"Yes. Thank you, your honor," Reardon said.

"Thank you, your honor," Talbot said as well.

"What's next?" Judge Walker asked the bailiff, who looked at the copy of the docket and called the next case.

"OK, George," Reardon whispered returning to the table and saying to Donaldson, "That's it. Let's go."

Once out in the corridor, George said, "That was quick!" thinking about the fifty thousand dollars he was handing over.

"Yes, these things don't have to take long," Reardon said. "Of course, hopefully the trial will happen soon, so the injunction can be permanent."

"Huh?"

"Right, the temporary injunction stopped the law from being implemented, then a few weeks or even months from now, there will be a trial, where you and I will be the plaintiffs and the U.S Attorney will represent the United States as the defendant to decide if the injunction becomes permanent."

Donaldson gulped. He hadn't really understood until now that he was suing the United States government.

Reardon looked over his shoulder at the main door of the courtroom, where several members of the press were pouring out. They spotted Reardon and immediately started almost running in their direction, microphones and cameras extended.

"OK, George, get ready," Reardon said, facing them while straightening his tie and putting on a big, white smile.

* * *

Marcus Williams took the elevator to the twentieth floor of Axiom headquarters. He had been given the decision of the judge and the news was not good.

"Come!" Jackie said to Marcus' knock and he opened through the double doors.

"So, is it good news?" Jackie asked.

"Afraid not. The judge has scheduled the trial for May."

"No! Three months away? I thought they were in a hurry."

"Well apparently the judge was inclined to agree with the gloom and doom being pedaled by the petitioner's attorney and the restraining order has stopped the repeal, so he doesn't feel like he has to rush."

"So what happens at the trial in May?"

"The judge will hear formal arguments and a range of testimony and will then decide if the temporary injunction becomes permanent.

"What can we do if it becomes permanent?"

"We can appeal. The Eighth Circuit is based in the same courthouse in St. Louis where the Eastern District Court sits and that's where we'd need to go."

"Can you file the appeal immediately?"

"Only after the trial. And it's still not clear we'll have standing. The push-back will be because we are not technically the object of the injunction; Congress and the president are."

"Yes, but we're the ones who are being hurt."

"That's what I told Judge Walker, but I'm not sure it did much good."

* * *

Jason Wood popped the cork on the first champagne bottle himself as the management of his non-profit celebrated the ruling by the judge in St. Louis.

"Today is a great day for Mother Earth," he said into the microphone on the portable podium in the cafeteria at the Champions' Seattle headquarters where his top managers and department heads were gathered.

"A very important brake on the oil companies was preserved, which means less gasoline will be sold, less harmful pollution will be expelled into the air and threat of Climate Change will be lessened. When Congress and the president acted cowardly and voted to repeal the landmark tax, the Federal judiciary came to the rescue of the Earth."

Loud applause and a few whistles greeted these words.

"So, let's enjoy this victory! Enjoy the food and drink before you and tomorrow, the fight continues!" Wood raised a glass toward the room and they cheered again as he stepped away from the podium. Everyone dug in to the plentiful spread hastily catered for the occasion, so they didn't notice Jason Wood slipping aside and punching a number on his cellphone.

"We've got a problem," Wood whispered into his phone. "And we can't wait any longer to deal with it."

* * *

"I'm just as surprised as you are," insisted Patrick, turning so the light would be better in his kitchen during one of his late night "FaceTime®" sessions with Jackie.

"But you must have seen legislation that was stopped by a judge before. How is this possible? The people wanted it, Congress voted it and the president signed it! How can a judge sign a paper stopping it?" Jackie was obviously very exercised.

"Yes, this definitely goes against the will of the people, which is why it's so unexpected. It kind of makes you think something's going on to make this happen."

"You mean there might still be someone trying to hurt us?"

"I don't know, but the restraining order sure happened fast, like somebody was ready with it."

"Well, I wish they would stop. I just don't know what we will do now. I mean, we're trying to appeal, but we're not even sure we would be allowed to appeal."

Patrick could see that Jackie was close to crying. "Yes, I know it makes things difficult. It will be difficult for everyone who needs to buy gasoline."

"It's so stupid! Why can't they see that they're hurting people? I just wish I could find out who's doing this stuff!"

"What are you having to do at your service stations?"

"I just came from a meeting with Benny, my president. He's going to communicate with the VPs of our regions. They'll send out the notices to raise the prices again."

"Bummer."

"You said it!"

"Well, I don't know if this will help, but I've carved out a weekend where I can come to Houston next month."

"Oh, that would be great! I wish you could come right now."

"Me too, but there's a lot to arrange for me to get loose."

"I know. I'm no better."

They talked for another half hour before finally saying goodbye and going to bed in their respective cities. Jackie laid back on her pillow in the darkness with a mass of conflicting emotions weighing down her heart. Talking to Patrick raised her spirits but only so far, because of the heaviness of contemplating the continuation of the punishing gas tax.

CHAPTER EIGHT

The next day, about 250 miles north in Richardson, Texas, another CEO had also received the news of the judge's trial date in May. Gerald Tokalas of Petrocom Energy Limited was more distressed than Jackie, if that was possible. Petrocom hadn't boycotted the gas tax like Axiom had, so it had been suffering with a negative bottom line for about seven months now and had already closed a number of its poorly performing service stations. Even though Petrocom was a major player, going that long without a positive profit-loss statement didn't bode well.

With his sixtieth birthday looming just a year away, Tokalas was determined that his legacy at Petrocom would be to have shepherded the company through this difficult period with wisdom commensurate with his age and experience. He knew, however, that wisdom sometimes meant knowing when to "hold 'em" and when to "fold 'em", like the song said.

Tokalas pushed a button on his phone. "Mary, can you put a meeting on the calendar for tomorrow at ten a.m.? I need Phil and Dave and George. Let them know it's urgent. Thanks."

After he hung up he began to flesh out an idea for a possible way out. He wasn't sure how difficult it would be to sell to his management team, though.

* * *

"I say cut the advertising budget completely out," Phil Snodgrass, VP of Operations for Petrocom said forcefully, his gray head erect and unmoving.

Gerald Tokalas was a bit surprised by this reaction from Snodgrass to his opening remarks about the company's situation since the injunction. Usually, he was a bit of a Polyanna, always sure things would be all right, regardless of the circumstance. *The new reality of the injunction must have had an effect on him.*

"Why would you say that? We need more revenue," Dave Johnson, Petrocom's relatively youthful Marketing VP, shot back. "How will we get that without advertising?"

Petrocom's top management had been going back and forth for about a half hour like this and CEO Gerald Tokalas had mostly just listened. Finally, he decided they weren't getting anywhere, so he spoke.

"There may be another way," Tokalas began, raking a hand through the graying hair on his right temple. "We could propose a merger."

This was met with wide-eyed gasps around the table.

"With whom?" asked George Adams, Petrocom's CFO, the more thoughtful one of the group.

"Axiom."

"Make a deal with the devil?!" Snodgrass nearly shouted.

"We need to merge with a company that's stronger than we are," Tokalas insisted.

"Yes, but to do that with THEM!" Johnson exclaimed.

"That can't be the only way!" Snodgrass insisted.

Then the men around the table looked down at the financial reports in front of them again with sour looks on their faces as they adjusted to the bitter reality that they might have to go, hat in hand, to their competitor.

"Axiom saw that it was impossible to make a profit when we are squeezed between the price cap and the $2.00 tax," Tokalas continued. "They have the infrastructure to absorb this kind of hit." *And their management is in a different class from ours,* he didn't say. That would ultimately make the difference.

"So, we've gone from thinking we could pick up Axiom's market share to surrendering to them?" Snodgrass sneered.

"We wouldn't be surrendering; we'd be thinking strategically. We'd combine our strengths," Tokalas answered.

"What happens in mergers is a lot of fat gets cut," CFO Adams warned.

"Fat will get cut anyway if we stay independent," Johnson admitted, regretfully.

"Heck, the whole cow could die!" put in Snodgrass.

"That's what I'm afraid of," Tokalas looked at the men at the table and saw grim resignation. He knew they would be making a phone call to Houston soon.

* * *

Jim Powers shook his head as he read the directive from his regional office. Did they really have to jack up the prices at the pump again?

As he sat in his tiny, cluttered office in the Axiom service station he managed on a busy corner in New York City, he looked out at the thousands of cars going by and thought how all those drivers were going to be impacted by the reinstitution of the gas tax.

They had had four weeks where prices had been allowed to float back down to normal after the president signed the bill repealing the tax, but now the injunction reversed that and they would go back to having to charge at or near the $6.00 per gallon cap on all their grades of fuel.

He knew this was not the corporate bosses' fault, but he didn't understand whose fault it was. He just knew it was going to cause a lot of pain for his customers.

He had seen the news about the injunction, but couldn't believe they would really go back to the exorbitant prices forced on them by the government.

He wondered what effect it would have on the sales numbers for his store. He took great pride in being one of the few African-American station managers and a manager with one of the highest sales records in the country.

Wearily he got up and started toward the garage to tell one of his employees to change the prices back. The memorandum had said to change the pricing "immediately," so that's what they would do.

* * *

"Well, it was good while it lasted," said assistant manager Tom Keswick.

The normal gasoline prices meant that the trucks from the distribution center in Des Moines were almost back on a normal schedule. The Super Grocery in Schleswig, Iowa, had full shelves again. During the period of high gas prices forced by the gas tax, the trucks didn't come as often and the store often ran low on, or even ran out of, staples.

Keswick's previous job had been at the Petrocom service station in town that had now been closed several months, a casualty of the gas tax.

"Did you say something?"

Tom had spoken within earshot of cashier Tracy McNeal who was putting on her apron getting ready to start her shift.

"Oh, the government is jerking us around again," Pete answered. "Some judge put a stop to the repeal of the gas tax, so now gas will be sky-high again. Distribution will probably cut back on the trucks again."

"People will love that!" she answered sarcastically, then turned and went to her register.

Yes, people will not like it, but what can we do?

* * *

The television was tuned to a local Myrtle Beach station in the spacious lobby of the Harbor Grove Hotel and Resort as franchise owner Dave Martinez reviewed columns of numbers for his hotel on a computer screen behind the lobby desk. It had been background noise intended for the guests coming and going in the lobby, but suddenly his attention was drawn to the screen on the wall as the evening newscast began. The top story featured images of gas stations changing their price signs from the normal prices they had enjoyed for just a few weeks now back to the high prices of the gas tax.

As he watched, a cold fear began at his stomach and slowly moved up to his neck. He couldn't believe what he was seeing; he had heard peripherally about the injunction, but his schedule prevented him from following the news closely.

Last year had been a disaster with the gas tax hitting during the height of the summer travel season. Many of the people he counted on to fill his rooms and restaurant had just stayed home. He had been overjoyed when Congress repealed the tax and was looking forward to a prosperous summer. Now that was out the window, because of one judge.

He had been concerned about the survival of his business last year, but what now? How could he, after last year, survive this? He had already cut his expenses to the bone.

* * *

"I've pretty much hit a wall," said Special Agent Devon Thacker, sitting facing Special Agent in Charge Sam Jorgensen in Washington, D.C.

"Yeah, until Borelli talks nobody has anything to go on. Nothing worthwhile come out of looking at his clients?"

"That's just it. They're all a bunch of choirboys as far as I can tell," Thacker said. "They're all about baby seals and keeping the Environment cleaned up. They're a bunch of self-proclaimed heroes."

"At least they're heroes to some people. Blowing up things and killing people doesn't make them heroes to me, but they're doing a masterful job of keeping up appearances. I know you've followed the money."

"Yeah, with zero results. All the transactions look legit. If it's one of Borelli's clients, they're hiding the money trail well."

"Of course, it's possible that the money didn't come from one of his clients, in which case it's truly a needle in a haystack."

"Yeah, we need a break."

* * *

The wedding was glorious. Everyone present at St. Luke's parish church said so. Jonesy played his part of proud father to perfection. He would not allow his money worries to spoil his baby girl's day. Amber glowed in her elegant wedding dress with its flowing train and every detail of what she was wearing, from her expensive, salon-prepared hair to the white satin heels, had been carefully planned and considered. Jonesy had to admit, she was a vision of loveliness.

The wedding party was resplendent in their expensive, one-use wardrobes, the bridesmaids in robin-egg blue, with pink corsages; their hair coiffed and makeup applied by professionals so each looked as lovely as they would ever look in their lives, except on their own wedding days. Satin pumps matching the dresses completed their ensemble.

The young men attending Ryan were dressed in identical tuxedoes with gray vests and black bowties, looking as awkward and uncomfortable as the bridesmaids were elegant.

The Catholic wedding liturgy was identical to the one celebrated by Jonesy and Margaret so many years ago, and Jonesy saw that Margaret was on the verge of tears the entire time, with occasional lapses into real weeping.

* * *

Later, the reception was as rowdy as the ceremony had been solemn. Jonesy was very conscious of the lavish decorations that transformed the rented Knights of Columbus hall and the open bar from which expensive booze flowed freely.

But it was all a tremendous success and the Jones' friends and family assured them they had done themselves proud.

It was quite late by the time Tobias and Margaret Jones finished cleaning up and gathering wedding presents to take home for safekeeping until the happy couple returned from their Caribbean honeymoon. Their flight had departed two hours earlier, so it would be late indeed when they arrived at their island destination, especially after crossing two time-zones to the east.

* * *

Jonesy was delighted to get home and shed the rented tuxedo and his new, pinching dress shoes. He knew it took time to break in a pair of shoes like that, but he had no intention of wearing them that much.

Dressed in his underwear, he wandered into the dark kitchen and took a beer from the refrigerator. He then went to the living room and sat in his recliner, stretching his weary legs and wiggling his toes to release the soreness.

Shortly Margaret joined him, having also shed her wedding clothes and put on a robe. She sat down and smiled at Jonesy.

"Wasn't it great?" she asked.

"It was really something all right."

"Can you believe our little girl is married?"

"I can't even believe we have children in college."

Margaret leaned back on the couch looking away at nothing in particular. "I just think it was so great to be able to give her such a wonderful wedding! I know it cost a lot, but wasn't it nice to see Amber so happy?"

It took a moment for Jonesy to reply after the mention of the cost, but he recovered. "Yeah, I wouldn't have missed that."

He really meant it. Maybe things would work out after all.

CHAPTER NINE

She was still missing a lamp in her bedroom, so it was darker than she needed it to be. You could have all the money in the world but if you didn't take time to shop for décor you wouldn't have enough light.

Jackie remembered again the night she broke the nightstand lamp over the head of the environmental terrorist who bombed the oil platform. He had broken into her house by shattering a picture window and it was clear he was a few sandwiches short of a picnic. She very well could have died that night. Two police officers were shot, one of whom died in her hallway and the other fell wounded out on the lawn, and it could just as easily have been her.

She shuddered and put it out of her mind. Reliving that night served no purpose. He was now convicted of multiple felonies and would spend the rest of his life in prison.

Jackie was sitting on the king-sized bed in her Frank-Lloyd-Wright-style, stone house in her gated community, sipping hot chocolate and looking at a printout of the far-flung operations of the company her grandfather had founded and her father had grown to its current domination in the retail gasoline market through expansion and mergers. There were drilling operations in four countries besides the USA and refineries in six states. There were offshore operations in the Gulf of Mexico, the Bering Sea and the North Sea. There were retail stores in 33 states and district offices across the country.

She didn't want to close any of them, but she knew that wasn't realistic. Impulsively, she sputtered and threw a pillow across the room where it hit an overstuffed chair and fell harmlessly to the expensive wood floor.

It wasn't like it had never happened before. During the 1970s, when OPEC had its embargo and the resulting supply crisis, her father had shuttered a refinery in Oklahoma. It didn't reopen until the late 1980s.

But she still didn't want to do it. When she had been Vice President of Operations, in attempting to visit all of Axiom's far-flung installations, she had spent time at many of the locations on the list, often staying a few days working alongside the men and women who received Axiom paychecks every two weeks. She had the recommendations of Axiom President Benny Tyson and Derek Jenkins, her incoming Vice President of Operations, plus Dennis' scrupulous reports, showing which operations were the least efficient. Even Wayne had supplied her with supplemental information to which she would barely refer because the detail would just postpone the inevitable.

None of this made it any easier.

Finally, she placed X's beside three significant installations, then put down her pen and stared at the far wall. After a bit, she hopped off the bed and went to her kitchen.

Once there she put on a pot of coffee and sent a text. Presently the doorbell rang.

She hurried to the door and opened it, knowing who would be there.

"I'm making coffee, Bill. Come in."

"Thank you, Ms. James. Is something wrong?"

It was her bodyguard. She never felt she needed one before, but after the break-in by the eco-terrorist, at the urging of her top management and the board, she decided to hire professional protection. It was true that she was well known across the country now and fame sometimes brought out the crazies, so she contacted an agency and hired a bodyguard to park outside the house at night. This supplemented the security guards employed by the gated community. It wasn't always Bill that the agency sent over, but it often was.

"Oh, it's nothing but the stress of the job," she said with a wave of her hand.

Though the bodyguards were supposed to just park outside, Jackie often invited them in for coffee until she went to bed, so she got to know their names and backgrounds.

"Shall I lock up, Ms. James?" Bill asked as he downed the last gulp of coffee from the china cup.

"Yes, Bill. Good night," Jackie said, thankful for the small talk and human contact on this stressful night.

"Good night."

Bill was still in his 20's and had been in the Army Rangers. He was tall with very big arms and broad shoulders. She felt even smaller than usual beside him. She trusted him with her life, obviously, and he knew her routine and made sure the house was secure when she turned in each night.

The only thing she didn't like about Bill was that he called her "Ma'am" or "Ms. James" and treated her like she was a lot older than him. *I'll still be 38 for a few more days, after all.*

* * *

Jonesy withdrew his time card from the time clock after the clunk-clunk that began and ended every day. After he clocked out, he turned to see Buck Donner, a fellow pipe-fitter, standing there with a hang-dog look on his slender face.

"Buck, who died?" Jonesy asked through a smile. "You look like the world is ending."

"It kinda is," Buck replied. "They're closing the plant, Jonesy. Shutting it down. We're all out."

Jonesy stared at him, looking for a sign he was being put on.

"You don't believe me? Look at this," Buck pointed to a poster on the bulletin board that Jonesy had overlooked.

"We regret..." the poster began, and it was signed at the bottom "Axiom Oil Corporate Management." The text in between blurred as Jonesy scanned it, but he was able to digest enough to see that Buck wasn't joking.

The refinery would be shut down and he, with everyone else, would be laid off indefinitely, effective in just 45 days.

Jonesy made a beeline for his boss in his makeshift office in a two-sided cubical on the plant floor.

"Hey Minetti, what's this about a shutdown?"

"Yeah, corporate's decided we're on the chopping block since gas tax is still on."

"Yeah, well, what am I supposed to do?!" Jonesy demanded. "I'm 55 years old. Who's gonna hire me?"

Minetti didn't have an answer, so he handed Jonesy an envelope with his name on it. Jonesy immediately tore it open. Inside was his copy of the notice.

"I'm sure your record here will look good on a resume," Minetti attempted to console his soon-to-be-former crew member. "And you can get unemployment pay."

"Easy for you to say!"

Minetti had a degree and a lifetime of working for the company. He would be taken care of, but men like Jonesy were just being turned out. Eight hundred or more would soon be competing for jobs elsewhere, and two thirds of them were younger than him.

As he trudged to his pickup, Jonesy cursed the Axiom brass, the judge and the whole lot of politicians who caused this personal disaster for him.

Unemployment pay is never as much as what you've been making. What am I going to do now?

* * *

"What's this?" Jackie asked Doris as she returned to her office from lunch. She held out a stack of messages.

"I've been fielding a lot of calls this morning from news people; local and national. They want a statement about the plant closings," Doris said with a sideways smile.

"Ugh. Could you ask Charlene to come to my office. I want her to coordinate this if we are going to have another round with the press."

"Yes, ma'am."

Jackie went on into her office feeling like she might be sick. She hated to think about being in the spotlight again. She decided she should see if anything was already being reported. She picked up the remote and flipped on the big flat-screen TV in her office and tuned in one of the 24-hour news channels.

She didn't have to wait long before there was a panel discussion about the closures.

"Axiom Oil Incorporated has announced that it is closing three plants and laying off an estimated 3,000 workers," an anchor began turning to a guest commentator. "What do you think of this move, Randall?"

"They may have thought they needed to do this, but this is just one more instance of mammoth companies putting their workers last. Why should hard working people be made to suffer, just because the company's profits are down?"

"Could it be because the company can't pay the people if its profits are down?" Jackie knew the people on TV couldn't hear her retort, but she said it out loud anyway. The cluelessness of some in the media was growing tiresome.

* * *

"So, we're working the angle of the judiciary's involvement in thwarting the will of the people?" Ann Falk was nothing if not direct. She and young coworker Jeff Dodd were sitting in Patrick's office for a spur-of-the-moment meeting. With her jet-black, spiked hair and odd makeup, she was a bit unorthodox, but was an invaluable part of Patrick's team.

The Axiom cutbacks were big news. Patrick saw the articles in the Business section of the *Washington Herald* and on CNN, but it wasn't something his political team had to worry about.

Judicial overreach, on the other hand was a recurring topic of stories he wrote or had others write for the *Herald*.

"Yes, that about says it," Patrick answered.

Ann had been on his political team for a couple of years now. No one had better instincts than she, so Patrick was giving her the assignment of writing what would undoubtedly be a long, technical article about the relationship of the Federal judiciary to the legislative branch.

This kind of back and forth between the Congress and the Federal judiciary happened all the time, but Patrick had always been a bit uncomfortable with it, because a single judge could reverse a vote of Congress, the representatives of the people, assuming Congress' legislation reflected the will of the people, rather than the squeaky wheels on K Street. That definitely conflicted with his Libertarian instincts.

While the judges were supposed to be objective and even-handed, Patrick knew from experience that judges were people too, subject to many of the same prejudices, preferences, and peccadilloes as anyone else.

In this case, Patrick knew the injunction had to be hard on Jackie. She had talked of little else but the repeal of the gas tax. He had assured her that it would happen, and he had been right. He was not particularly surprised that there was a challenge, but had been surprised by how quick the judge's injunction had been.

"And Jeff," Patrick said, turning to the newest member of the political reporting staff, "I need you to come up with some salient historical nuggets that illustrate that relationship, noting especially instances where a judge has ruled against the will of the people."

"Do you want me to focus on legislation or popular referendums?"

"Whatever jumps out," Jeff Dodd seemed very bright for someone just out of journalism school. "And whatever shows the tension between the branches of government. It may go in a sidebar or we may mix them into Ann's research."

"Got it," Jeff answered.

"And research some specifics about the Eastern District of Missouri and especially this Judge – Walker, is it?"

"Right."

The politicians and members of the press who had favored The Petroleum Independence Act and its punishing tax seemed to be struggling with a Jekyll-Hyde schizophrenia. On the one hand, they were ecstatic that the judge had issued the injunction to keep the gas tax in place and Axiom was being forced to cut operations, but on the other hand, they were outraged that "working people" were losing their jobs. Patrick found it curious that they could applaud the judge's decision and not understand that the very action they had championed had forced the layoffs.

"Okay, this is for day-after-tomorrow's edition, so better get to it."

"Yes boss," Ann said as they got up and breezed out the door of Patrick's office.

* * *

"Yes, thank you, that is good news," Marcus Williams said. "See you in May."

He hung up the phone after hearing from Assistant U.S. Attorney Talbot that he would be called as a witness at the trial in St. Louis. It was now less than two months until the trial date of May 19, so he would get right to work on a brief for the court and a proposed strategy for Talbot to use during his testimony.

But first, he would go to the office of the CEO and give Jacqueline James the good news.

CHAPTER TEN

The March sun had sunk below the horizon when Jonesy stamped his time card and headed for the door that led to the parking lot of the Axiom Oil Refinery. He had been able to get approved for an extra two hours of overtime per day and he was feeling the weariness that came with it. It did make a difference in his take-home pay, though, and would allow him to pay down the credit cards faster. Even though most of the money he had put on the cards to make the wedding of the century possible had been through introductory zero-percent-interest offers, he knew the promotional period would end and the murderous, real interest rates would kick in too soon. And he only had a few weeks before his regular paycheck would stop.

Once he drove out of the lot, he flipped on the radio as he did every day after work, to check the news and traffic, but today there was some kind of emergency.

." . . are sketchy, but nothing has been heard from flight 825 for more than an hour," said the serious network radio reporter. "The flight departed St. Maarten this morning bound for Miami...."

Hmm, Jonesy said to himself. *St. Maarten is where Amber and Ryan...*

He caught his breath. Today was when they were flying back!

"What airline?! What airline?!" he shouted at the radio as the reporter continued with so little information she was already repeating herself.

"Again, if you are just joining us, American Airlines flight 825 from St. Maarten to Miami. . ."

American was the airline that Amber and her new husband had taken. Jonesy knew because the charge had gone onto one of his newest credit cards.

His throat tightened even as he gave a weak "No!"

Then, his mind spinning, he tried to tell himself that it couldn't be their flight. *Plane crashes happen to other people, not my little girl; not my Amber!*

He knew he would have to find out for sure if it had been Amber's plane and if she had actually been on it. His heart was about to explode and he could barely see to drive, but he made his way home. When he got there, he didn't have to ask

Margaret if she had seen the news. She was standing on the front porch, her eyes red and her face puffy. Jonesy shut off the pickup and ran to her. She collapsed into his arms and began sobbing again.

* * *

For Jonesy, Margaret and Leslie, the flight to San Juan was interminable. Puerto Rico was where the FAA and NTSB had set up a command and information center about the crash.

There was virtually no hope of finding the bodies, but how could they not go?

Once on the ground, they followed GPS to the location at the airport where they had been told to go. It turned out to be an airplane hangar where an American Airlines staffer introduced herself as soon as they entered the cavernous building.

"Hello, I'm Grace Fulton of American Airlines," said a tall woman in a sharp blue uniform and bright white blouse. "I'm here for any questions you have. We are very sorry for your loss. We have an information session at two this afternoon."

"I'm Toby Jones and this is my wife Margaret. We're Amber Jones' parents and her sister Leslie."

Fulton referred to a passenger list on her clipboard and looked puzzled. "I'm sorry I don't see an Amber Jones."

"Oh, that's right," Margaret said. "Check last name 'Peterson'. She had just gotten married."

Fulton apparently understood immediately and looked up at Jonesy and Margaret. "Oh, I'm so sorry. Yes, I see it now. Travelling with Ryan Peterson?"

They nodded. Jonesy hadn't thought until just now that the Petersons would likely be coming too. They hadn't talked to the other family because they barely knew them.

"I'm so sorry. Can I answer any questions?"

Jonesy hesitated but then said, "Where did the plane — where did it happen?"

"The site was a couple of hundred miles to the north of here. Puerto Rico was the nearest and most convenient place from which to base our investigation."

"Have they determined what caused — it?" Jonesy asked.

"We don't have definitive word. The only thing we know is that radio transmissions before the accident indicated a problem with an engine. Because it happened soon after takeoff it could have been birds being taken into the engines."

Jonesy felt his stomach tighten as he thought that maybe his baby daughter was gone because of a damn seagull!

"Have they found — anything?" Margaret's voice broke.

"Not too much unfortunately. What we have found is over there," Fulton said, pointing to a row of folding tables holding several hundred random, water-logged personal belongings. "You are welcome to look through them and identify any items you find that belonged to your loved one. I'll record the ownership and, once the investigation is complete, we will send your loved one's effects to you if you like."

"That would be nice, I guess," Margaret said. "Have they found any – anybody?" The last word was an octave higher than the others and Margaret clapped her hand over her mouth to stifle a sob. Jonesy saw that Leslie's eyes were brimming with tears, which were beginning to run down her face.

"I am so sorry, but in a water event like this, it is unlikely that we will find anyone. We are still searching the area. Would you like to look through the items that have been found?"

For a moment, the Jones family just looked at one another; they didn't move and didn't speak. Making simple decisions like this made Jonesy's head hurt. Finally, he said, "Yes, let's go see what's over there, Margaret," then to Fulton, "Thank you."

They went to the end of the row of tables closest to them and began looking at the items that had been recovered as Fulton followed a few steps behind. It was a hodge-podge of personal items, not much intact luggage, but mostly items that would be buoyant. He didn't say anything to Margaret, but Jonesy realized from looking at what they had found that the plane had broken up when it hit the water. That was why they weren't likely to find any bodies. For a moment, he looked away at the light streaming through the high windows of the hangar.

Beyond the first row of tables was another row of folding tables with computers and telephones on them and men and women at work on the investigation into the accident, Jonesy assumed. They were largely unconcerned with the the Jones family and the other forlorn friends and relatives of the victims filing past the pitifully small collection of belongings that had been found in the vast Caribbean Sea. Beyond them was a large roped off area where a few parts of the plane were laid out in roughly the positions those parts would have occupied when the plane was whole. A few people were examining them.

The Joneses were almost through looking through the items on the tables when Leslie exclaimed, "Mom and Dad, look! It's Amber's wrist bag!"

Jonesy looked and indeed saw the designer leather bag that he had thought was too expensive. Now, if he could have Amber back, he would buy her 10 of them; 100 if she wanted.

Margaret was softly crying as she zipped open the small clutch. She reached inside and pulled out a few soaked bills and Amber's driver's license. She looked at her husband and the three of them collapsed in each other's arms, sobbing.

CHAPTER ELEVEN

"I just got a strange call," Axiom President Benny Tyson said, as he sat down in front of Jackie James' massive oak desk. He had sat in front of this desk many times when "Junior" James, Jackie's legendary father, had managed the company.

"From whom?" Jackie asked.

"Phil Snodgrass at Petrocom."

"What'd he want?"

"He called to say that Tokalas wants to meet with you."

Jackie's eyebrows went up and then the left one arched higher. Jackie didn't need to ask who Snodgrass and Tokalas were. Petrocom competed with Axiom head-to-head in several markets. She knew the top brass at the Richardson, Texas, company well, at least by the industry press. "What for?"

"To talk merger."

"And he called you?"

"Yeah, that surprised me, too. I should think they would have called Dennis." Trask was Axiom's Chief Financial Officer.

"No, it makes sense they would start in administration," Jackie said. Then she pushed the speaker button on her phone and dialed a four-digit extension.

"Dennis Trask," the voice on the line said after one ring.

"Dennis, Jackie. Benny is here with me. Petrocom has made an overture to him about meeting to talk about merger."

After a pause, Dennis answered, "Can't say I'm surprised. They have to be really hurting." Dennis didn't sound too sorry.

"So, what's your gut reaction?" Jackie asked.

"I suppose we can see what they have to say," he began slowly. "But their sheet probably looks worse than ours right now. I don't know if we could prop them up or if they would pull us down."

"Normally, I'd see this as a real opportunity," Jackie said. Her father had built Axiom through mergers and acquisitions.

"But this is hardly a 'normal' time," Dennis finished her thought softly.

* * *

Waco wasn't really halfway between Houston and Richardson, but it was the best place for the two groups to meet in order to have adequate meeting space. It was also just out of the way enough to not attract attention. At this delicate stage, secrecy was vital. Any news getting out could easily scuttle the whole deal before it got started.

The delegation from Petrocom arrived at the Hilton Hotel in Waco first because they had made the arrangements and had the most direct route, straight down Interstate 35. Gerald Tokalas had driven his Lincoln Navigator, carrying two others who had been at the meeting where they decided to propose the merger: Phil Snodgrass, VP Operations and George Adams, Petrocom's CFO. The chairman of Petrocom's board of directors, Charles Holland, came with them as well, because it was, of course, a decision that would require board approval.

Holland had spent 40 years in the banking industry and he was as dignified as Phil Snodgrass was brash. Phil didn't sit on the board, so they hadn't really crossed swords before, although Tokalas could imagine they would have difficulty finding common ground. *But*, Tokalas thought as he approached the hotel's front desk, *you play the hand you're dealt*.

"Gerald Tokalas," he stated to the young woman behind the desk. "I reserved a meeting room."

"Yes Mr. Tokalas. You will be in the Chaparral Room," the woman answered. "It's all set up for you. Go right down that hall and to the right and the room will be on your left."

The men obediently went down the hall, sweating in their dark business suits in spite of the chill outside, each one carrying a briefcase filled with reports that he had been charged with generating for use when the conversation required them.

They entered the Chaparral Room to find two skirted tables arranged to make a square with 10 chairs on the four sides.

"How many are coming from Axiom?" Snodgrass asked.

"Five, I think," Tokalas answered.

They got settled on one side of the table and waited in near silence for the Axiom group to arrive.

* * *

It was only five minutes later when the contingent from Axiom entered the Chaparral Room. Jackie entered first and strode to where Gerald Tokalas was sitting.

"Jackie James," she said, introducing herself.

"Gerald Tokalas. It's a pleasure," he said, quickly standing and shaking her extended hand.

Each of them then introduced their teams around the circle as the Axiom men each claimed a chair at the table.

"We created name signs for each of us," Snodgrass said, taking nine folded pieces of paper from his briefcase. He began passing them around the table. "Put the card with your name on it in front of you so we all have to think as little as possible."

Good natured laughter met this instruction as Jackie and the men did as they were told. They engaged in some polite banter about everything and nothing: the Rangers and the Astros, the Cowboys and the Texans, things men talk about, even though Jackie was the de facto highest ranking person in the room.

"Well, I guess there's nothing left to do but get started," Jackie said, looking at Tokalas during a lull in the sports talk.

"Yes, I don't think I need to tell you how difficult the past few months have been thanks to the Petroleum Independence Act," Tokalas began. Nods all around indicated agreement.

"Our companies have been competitors for a long time," he continued, looking at Jackie. "I admired your father a great deal. He built a great company, obviously."

"Thank you, and thanks goes as well to Bud Eldridge," Jackie said gesturing to Bud, Axiom's chairman of the board, dressed in a western suit, string tie and cowboy boots. "He and my father worked closely together for many years."

"You deserve credit as well, for 'Operation Backlash,'" Tokalas answered. "Wish I had thought of it."

"Well I'm not sure it had lasting impact, since here we are." Jackie knew she didn't have to reference the court's injunction. All the men at the table were all too aware of it.

"Yes so, in light of where we are now, we should see whether there might be a wedding in our future," Tokalas joked, hoping to lighten the mood, but looking at his side of the table he saw expressions more appropriate for a funeral. Looking then at the Axiom side of the table, he saw crossed arms and downturned mouths. This would not be an easy meeting.

* * *

The meeting had gone on for two hours. The participants had been civil, but the atmosphere was pretty icy in the room. They had begun by exchanging and signing NDAs, Non-disclosure Agreements. Now they were in the midst of actually showing their hands.

"What can you say," Bud asked, leaning his chair back on two legs and looking at Tokalas, "that will make me feel better about this idea? It's pretty clear that you're here because you see the handwriting on the wall."

"Sure, we're hurting, just as you are, as evidenced by your plant closures," Tokalas began, brushing back a stiff gray hair on the side of his head. He was acutely aware that Axiom held the best cards, and they likely knew it, but he resolutely went forward with his rehearsed pitch.

"Each of us brings strengths to the table. We compete head-to-head in quite a few markets. That would end. We also have a presence in some markets where you don't."

"And vice versa," Bud bellowed. "In fact, we probably have more territories where you DON'T sell."

Tokalas bit his tongue and continued. "Yes, we may want to look at our respective maps as these discussions proceed. I'm just saying that we've both been weakened by the government's actions and I firmly believe that if we combine our efforts we would both benefit."

"If it didn't take us both down," Bud muttered bitterly.

"Hey, we're not excited about it either!" Snodgrass shot across the table.

"Pipe down, Phil!" George Adams of Petrocom almost shouted. "This isn't comfortable for anybody, but we're here because of factors beyond our control. Nobody likes the position we are in, but this is where we are and we have to deal with our real situation and not what we wish it was."

The rebuke of one Petrocom executive by another calmed everyone down. Tokalas sat silently and Bud looked down at the cowboy boot on his crossed leg.

"Okay, we're all on edge because we see everything we've worked for slipping away," Jackie said, determined to get the discussion back on track. "But we have to figure out if the suggested merger will benefit us both and let us move forward."

She looked at her own executives and saw them nodding.

"All right, Mr. Tokalas. . ."

"Call me Gerald."

"All right, Gerald, have you given any thought to how this would happen structurally?"

* * *

"We should just buy them out," Bud said petulantly, on the highway back to Houston in Jackie's Range Rover.

"We can't afford to buy anything right now," Dennis argued. "We don't know how long we're going to be in this position."

"But an equal merger is insulting. We've got a much bigger market share than they do."

"We can certainly structure the deal in our favor," Dennis said, "Once we get down to discussing specifics."

"Unfortunately, nothing can happen fast, anyway," Benny said. "The boards and stockholders of both companies have to approve it after the terms are worked out."

"If we both last that long," said Jackie grimly.

They continued on toward Houston in silence.

CHAPTER TWELVE

"Hello Doris."

"Mr. Garrity! So nice to see you. Go on in, she's expecting you," Jackie heard Doris answer from her office.

Patrick pushed open one of the tall, polished-wood doors and entered Jackie's office. She immediately and sprang from behind her desk, running to him.

"Patrick!" she said as she ran into his arms.

"It's been too long," he said setting down his small bag. He had insisted on taking a taxi from the airport, because he arrived in the middle of the afternoon, even though Jackie would have picked him up.

She didn't answer but instead lifted her face to his and kissed him for a long moment. Then they just stood holding each other and Patrick wondered why he had not found a way to come sooner.

"It's been way too long," Jackie agreed when she finally pulled away. "How was the trip?"

"Oh, you know flying. Uneventful is what you aspire to."

She drew him over to the couch and they sat close to one another with her hands folded into his.

"It's so good to see you, in person, that is. I've missed you."

"Me too," Patrick answered. "Technology helps, but there's no substitute for – touch."

Jackie felt her face flash hot. It had been a long time since she had been touched the way she knew Patrick meant. She was both thrilled and frightened by the possibility. But instead of going further down that road, she surprised herself by changing the subject.

"So, how's the new crop of politicians coming?"

"Well, as you know there are a lot of them!" He appeared to like her change in the awkward direction the conversation had been headed.

"I know it's got to be a tremendous overload for you after the fruit-basket upset in Washington!"

"Yes, we're getting a handle on it though. I've got a great staff. Small, but they're really good. How about you. How're you and your staff holding up?"

"The strain is showing. Since the injunction – which you didn't warn me about, by the way – we've been trying to figure out what to do now. We're boxed in pretty good.

"But enough about bad news," Jackie exclaimed with a wave of her small hand. "Where do you want to go for dinner?"

"Hey, I'm at your disposal. Your town, your call."

Just then, her desk phone rang with Doris' distinctive ring.

"Oops, that's Doris. I'd better get it; she wouldn't interrupt us if it wasn't important."

Jackie hopped up and skipped to the desk like a school girl, grabbing the phone. Patrick involuntarily rose and followed her to stand by the desk watching her expression as she answered.

"That's all right, Doris. What's up?" she paused, listening. "OK, no problem. I'll come out there."

After hanging up, she told Patrick, "I need to approve a news release so it can get there by the deadline. You know all about that," she laughed. "Charlene Washington is right outside. I'll just be a second."

Patrick nodded as she went through the door. He smiled and looked around the large room. He once again thought about the huge empire she ran and marveled at the ability wrapped up in the small, cute woman he had grown so fond of.

He looked at the top of the desk with its orderly stacks of papers and files. He fingered the corner of one stack, wondering if he even would understand what was in the files.

Then he focused on the label on one of the files. In printed block letters, undoubtedly created by the supremely efficient Doris Maxwell, it said "Petrocom Merger."

What? Merger?

He looked back at the door. She had not come back. Gingerly, he opened the file and looked at the first piece of paper inside. At the top in all capital letters it said,

CONFIDENTIAL

PROPOSAL TO MERGE PETROCOM ENERGY LTD. WITH AXIOM OIL INC.

DO NOT COPY OR DISTRIBUTE

Patrick's reporter curiosity was running at full gallop now. Conflicted, he began scanning the page, but knew that would take too long, so on an impulse he took his iPhone® from his pocket and snapped a picture of the page, then closed the file. He reasoned he could read it later.

He then turned and walked slowly back over to the couch and sat down to wait tensely for Jackie to come back.

"OK, that didn't take long," Jackie said when she returned, "Are you hungry?"

"Actually, yes. Remember, it's an hour later for me."

"I know a great seafood place where I haven't taken you yet."

"Great."

* * *

Jackie chose an upscale surf-and-turf restaurant for their dinner, not so much for its food as for its atmosphere. Wall sconces provided most of the soft, warm light in the dining room, besides candles in centerpieces in the middle of bright, white tablecloths.

"So, what do you think of the place?"

"I just know I love the way your dark eyes sparkle in the candlelight."

Jackie blushed and looked down at her fish and vegetables artistically arranged on the large white plate.

"You don't know how wonderful it is to hear something like that," she said, her voice catching. "You're very thoughtful."

"Oh, good," he said, appearing relieved. "I'm really rusty, so I'm probably as clumsy as a schoolboy."

"It's been a long time for both of us, so I guess we should allow one another some slack."

Patrick sliced through his filet, but before putting the slice in his mouth said, "I just don't know how I got so lucky to be sitting here with you. A year ago, I never would have guessed this could happen."

"That's the way it should be; you shouldn't be looking for – it." Jackie's last word hung in the air. She didn't define "it", but she knew he knew what she meant.

For a moment, she was seized by a desire to take him home for the night, but her upbringing stopped that thought and brought her back to her senses.

* * *

That night in his hotel room Patrick basked in the glow of the evening with Jackie, especially the long goodnight kiss she had let him have. The thrill of holding her in his arms was equaled only by the longing that made his heart ache.

He felt so fortunate, yet inadequate, being with someone so wealthy and powerful, but she was down-to-earth and seemed to care for him. *I can't believe how great my life is right now.*

He decided to check his email, so he took his phone, but suddenly remembered what he had seen earlier, so he brought up the photograph he had taken of the page in the folder on Jackie's desk. He had to hold it in landscape and "pinch" the image to read it easily. What he saw excited him.

The page he had photographed appeared to just be a cover page for a document that resulted from a meeting. Yes, it gave the date and place of the meeting and the participants: four from Petrocom and five from Axiom. It seemed from the paragraphs on this page that what followed was minutes from the meeting and a letter of intent toward a merger of the two companies.

He looked up from his phone and considered the implications. The date of the meeting revealed that it had happened after the injunction, so the corporate bosses at Petrocom must have decided that the company wouldn't make it if the gas tax continued. They had apparently approached

Axiom about a merger. *Or more likely a buyout*, Patrick thought, reading between the lines.

In light of everything that had happened, with the injunction just being the most recent problem facing the two companies, this was big news, however it was obvious that the companies didn't want the news to get out.

Patrick felt his dinner all go to one knot in the middle of his stomach. He hated being in this position right now. In other cases, he had run stories like this without giving it a second thought. The name of the game was getting the scoop; being first with the big story.

But this was different. This time he not only knew one of the subjects of the story, he loved her.

He hadn't actually told her that he loved her or even admitted it to himself, but he realized that it was true.

He went to bed, but his sleep was easily interrupted.

* * *

The iPhone® in Shelby Golden's pocket vibrated, which irritated him, because he was just beginning his day and was immersed in analyzing a computer screen of up-to-the minute New York Stock Exchange data. Golden tugged at his bow tie and struggled with whether to check his phone.

As business editor for the *Washington Herald*, he was always on a deadline and today was no different. Email, the web, phone calls and texts were vital to doing his work but they were also distractions. A few seconds several times a day could put him behind and interfere with the quality of his reporting.

But the tug of curiosity was too great, so he took his phone from his pocket and swiped it open. There was a text from Patrick Garrity at the political desk. What could he want?

There was an image attached to the text. He tapped it to enlarge and saw a photo of a letter. He only needed to read a few lines before understanding why Patrick had sent it to him.

* * *

On Saturday, Jackie and Patrick went to Galveston in her Range Rover. They spent the day lounging on the beach with their hands intertwined and eating whatever and whenever they wanted. It was still too cold for swimming or sunbathing, but a day at the beach was always a good day.

Patrick seems a little quiet though, Jackie thought. *Maybe he's just relaxed.*

After sightseeing and browsing a few beach souvenir shops, they ended the day by strolling on the beach as the sun went down, arms linked as they watched the show that God put on everyday but they each only rarely took the time to enjoy.

They drove back to Houston in the twilight. Tomorrow Patrick's plane back to D.C. would leave very early, so they sat in the car a good long time talking and touching before he got out and went to his hotel room.

* * *

"What happened! Did you talk to the press?"

"What are you talking about?" Jackie replied to her first phone call on Monday morning.

"I just got a call from the *Wall Street Journal* asking for an on-the-record statement about our merger talks," Gerald Tokalas shouted at his phone. "We were supposed to keep this quiet!"

"I swear," Jackie insisted on the other end of the line, "I haven't talked to anyone about our discussions."

"Well, somebody did. We're at a very delicate stage. Who knows what will happen if it gets out now?"

"I'll talk to my staff, but I don't think anyone would have talked."

"Yes, and I'll do the same. I didn't tell the reporter anything. I didn't confirm or deny, which is as good as confirming it for these vultures," Tokalas exclaimed. "I'm sorry for accusing you. I just don't want anything to wreck this so early."

* * *

The next morning, Axiom CFO Dennis Trask brought his copy of the *Wall Street Journal* to Jackie's office.

"How do you suppose this happened?" he said, laying the opened paper in front of her.

The headline of a one-column article said, "Axiom and Petrocom in Merger Talks."

Jackie sighed. "Tokalas called me yesterday saying he got a call from a Journal reporter. I said I would check with everyone who was at the meeting to see if they talked to anyone."

"What about your reporter friend?"

"I didn't say anything about this to him!" Jackie insisted, but the seed of doubt was planted. Patrick had arrived back in D.C. yesterday.

"I'll go to the other guys and see what they have to say for themselves," Dennis said. "You don't worry about it."

After Dennis left, she sat at her desk just staring straight ahead. Then she looked down at the neat stack of folders at her left elbow. The stack got shuffled all the time, but the second from the top was her file clearly labeled "Petrocom Merger." She quickly laid it open in front of her and could see that nothing had been removed or the contents reordered.

She then opened her own copy of the *Journal* and read the article closely. She looked again at the letter of intent on the top of the paper-clipped sheaf of papers in the file and she whispered, "Oh, no!" covering her face with her hands.

Then her desk phone buzzed with Doris' ring.

"Yes, Doris what is it?"

"Well, it's the Houston Chronicle. They want a statement about the merger. What should I tell them?"

Jackie lowered her head. It was starting again.

"Transfer it to me. I need to get ahead of this."

"Are you sure?"

"Yeah, I can't run from it."

"Ms. James, this is Jane Consedine, Houston Chronicle," the voice on the other end of the phone said after Doris transferred the call. "What can you tell me about the merger with Petrocom that was reported in the Wall Street Journal this morning."

"I cannot comment at present," Jackie said, *because no one was supposed to know about it.* "I'm preparing a statement and I'll make sure you get notified as soon as it's ready."

"Can't you give me something for your hometown newspaper?"

"I wish I could, but I'm not prepared. Now if you'll excuse me I need to get started on that statement."

Jackie hung up without allowing the reporter to ask a follow-up question, which she knew would come. She called Doris into her office and told her any more calls from reporters should be deflected with a promise of a statement to be issued later. She then called Charlene Washington to alert her to the requests that would soon be flooding Axiom's Public Relations office.

* * *

"Patrick! Was it you?" Patrick heard Jackie's voice trembling with anger on his voicemail. "It looks like you saw something in my office and passed it on. I'm not going to say what it was because it is confidential. If you did, we are through!"

Patrick didn't need Jackie to tell him what she was talking about. He called her back immediately.

"Please let me explain!"

"OH! That's all I need to hear! How could you?!" And she ended the call.

Patrick laid the phone down and put his hand over his mouth. His conscience was already bothering him. He had thought he could obscure the fact that it had been him that leaked the news about the merger meeting, passing it to Shelby Golden who agreed to forego the scoop for his own business section and pass it on to a friend at the *Journal*.

Still, Patrick knew Jackie could put two and two together. He had been in her office, alone with the file. And the only information in the Journal piece was taken from the single page he had photographed.

Patrick didn't know how he could make it right. His reporter's thirst for getting the scoop had been too much for him. Would Jackie ever forgive him? He decided he would call and ask. Tomorrow.

He suddenly felt a pain in his chest and his throat convulsed.

CHAPTER THIRTEEN

"Did you see the article in the *Wall Street Journal*?"

"Yes. Maybe it's a good thing?"

"It's a doggone disaster!" Heath Wellingsworth the Third had little doubt, unlike his friend on the other end of the phone.

"But, Heath, mergers can be good. Heaven knows the news about our Petrocom stock hasn't been good in a long time."

"That's ridiculous! Leaks like this are always bad!"

"Are you opposed to the merger?"

"I don't know! We didn't get to hear a plan, did we?"

The young, supremely confident Wellingsworth and his friend, Chad Dunn, were both heavily invested in Petrocom stock and they had taken a bath over the past few months, with the stock price on a steady downward path.

"I'm a good mind to sue to put a stop to this."

"Now Heath," Dunn cautioned. "Shouldn't we wait to see if it turns out to be good. What if the market is happy about the prospect of a merger?"

"I don't know. I just think it's a bad sign," Wellingsworth said as he hung up the phone. He immediately got up from his desk in the dark paneled study of his conspicuously old-money house and went down to his four-car garage where he brought his classic Ferrari to life and roared down the street toward his lawyer's office.

* * *

Jackie was dreading making the call, but she knew it had to be done. She had put Gerald Tokalas' phone number in her cell phone contacts because she had figured they would be talking a lot. Now she wasn't sure.

"Tokalas," the voice on the other end of the phone said.

"Gerald, this is Jackie at Axiom. I am calling to apologize."

"Oh?"

"Yes, I'm sorry to say, I found the leak."

"Who was it? Was it Eldridge? I thought he wanted to scuttle the deal!"

"No, it wasn't Bud. It was my friend, Patrick Garrity."

"Who's that?"

"Well, he's the Political Editor of the Washington Herald."

"What! How is HE your friend?!"

"Well, we were sort of seeing each other," Jackie said quietly. *Wow this is even harder than I thought!*

"You told him! How could you tell a reporter?!"

"No, I didn't tell him anything. He was in my office and he happened to see the memorandum."

There was silence on the other end of the line for a few seconds, then Tokalas spoke. "You'd better hope this doesn't cause problems; it could force us to stop the negotiations!"

Jackie thought, *Hey, you called us. We didn't ask for this!* But she said, "I know, I'm very sorry. I'm already getting requests from the press for statements."

"As am I. I'm telling them as little as possible, but the cat is out of the bag!"

When Jackie ended the call, she just let her iPhone® fall to her desktop and she buried her head in her hands.

* * *

Patrick ended the call on his cell phone before Jackie's voicemail message ended. He had heard it five times today and had left messages which she had not returned. He laid his cell phone on the counter in his modest kitchen and grabbed a cola from the refrigerator, popping the can open in the near darkness of evening.

He wondered what he would have to do to be forgiven. Right now, he didn't see a way, and if she wouldn't answer or return his calls, he couldn't find out what it would take.

He thought of buying a plane ticket and flying to Houston and forcing her to listen to his pleas for forgiveness, but he knew he might not get past the receptionist and building security. Doing that would be impulsive and his work schedule hardly allowed for impulsive behavior.

During the height of "Operation Backlash", he was sent to Houston for his job and could invent reasons for additional trips, but those assignments were not being offered now.

His pain was part ire at himself for what he had to admit was a betrayal of Jackie's trust and part fear that he might never see her again. But there was also his abuse of his access to a newsmaker and that was a problem for his career and professional ethics.

* * *

That night, after a day at work in which Patrick could barely concentrate on his tasks that were made more urgent by the daily looming deadline, he arrived as usual at the Blue Ribbon Grill, his favorite after-work place, and was able to get his favorite booth. *But that is the only thing going my way,* he thought sullenly. How could he have been so – so what? Committed to his profession? Eager to get the scoop? All those things had not caused him a moment's hesitation before.

But this time, he had hurt someone he cared about, maybe irreparably. And he knew that others could be hurt as well because the news of the potential merger got out prematurely.

Getting to know Jackie had given him a window into the lives of people who made up a corporation: the employees, the stockholders, the customers, all of whom depended on the success of the enterprise for the food on their tables and clothes on their backs.

In the past, he had seen corporations as big, cold, impersonal machines that would run roughshod over people in pursuit of profit, cheating their customers and exploiting their employees. As a journalist, he had seen it as a badge of honor to humiliate and expose the activities of corporate management; as a sort of public service, to reveal the nefarious goings-on behind boardroom doors. He realized that was the default attitude toward business among most people in his profession and it had been his belief until not too long ago.

So, revealing secret merger talks was a scoop to which he and his fellow reporters aspired and for which they won awards, but this time it was personal. He knew many of the people affected by the leak, at least on the Axiom side of the merger talks, and he reasoned that the same kind of people were on the Petrocom side as well. Yes, the executives were paid well, maybe overpaid, but, thanks to getting to know Jackie, he realized it was likely they were doing the best they could for everyone depending on them in a bad economy.

He felt a pain in his chest once more as he remembered the hurt in Jackie's voice the one time he had talked to her since his trip to Houston. She hadn't answered his subsequent calls.

Remembering the silence on the other end of those calls only amplified the pain of his heart.

Just then a familiar waitress appeared at his elbow.

"Hi, Mr. Garrity, can I start you with your usual to drink tonight?" Jenny said, her dark blonde hair pulled back behind her ears. She casually rested her slender hand on the table, waiting for his answer.

Patrick looked up and started to nod, telling her to bring his standard iced tea order, but then he stopped.

"Jenny, bring me a Sam Adams Boston Lager."

The waitress' eyebrows went up and her eyes grew wide. Patrick knew he had once told her of his battle with alcoholism and she had never known him to order anything but iced tea and an occasional coffee.

"Are you sure, Mr. Garrity?"

"I'm sure. Get me a beer, please."

She turned without a word and walked toward the kitchen. While she was gone, Patrick's mood grew darker as he thought about his betrayal of Jackie and how alone he felt.

Jenny returned presently and set the tall draft glass down in front of him on an embossed paper coaster. She didn't leave, but stood stone-still, looking into Patrick's eyes. Patrick looked down to avoid her gaze and finally she turned and left.

He put his right hand on the cold, sweating glass and lifted it slowly. He looked at the amber liquid with its small bubbles floating to the foamy top. It had been a long time. He held the

118

glass midway between the table and his mouth for several seconds, his mind a jumble of competing thoughts.

On the one hand, he longed to down the glass in one long chug and then order another. He knew from long experience that this one drink would only be the beginning of a binge that might last for days, but he felt he deserved it. He NEEDED to dull the pain and this would certainly accomplish that.

But the other side of the coin was that he knew, in spite of himself, that crossing this line would solve nothing and would bring its own special pain. Pain that he had worked very hard for many months to avoid on the road to sobriety.

As he considered his hard-won victory long ago, and the record of being "clean and sober" that he was so proud of, he set the glass back on the table, but continued looking at it.

Soon the desire to dull his pain surged again and he lifted the glass once more. Then he saw Jenny looking at him from behind the bar. He looked at the glass, lowering it again.

Immediately he was angry at himself for caring what a waitress thought of him. She knew nothing of his situation: of the pressures of his profession, the relentless deadlines, the dog-eat-dog competition. She also didn't know how his heart was hurting right now; how utterly alone he felt.

Angrily, he jerked the glass to his mouth and let the cold, amber brew flow down his aching throat.

* * *

"Have you seen the stock ticker this morning?" Gerald Tokalas asked his VP of Operations, Phil Snodgrass, who had just entered the CEO's office.

"Yeah, what do you make of it?"

"Makes no sense to me. I was sure the price would fall when the merger talks were leaked."

"Apparently, the market approves of a merger of Petrocom with Axiom."

"I guess, but what does that say about the market's confidence in us?"

"The market hasn't shown a lot of confidence in our whole industry since the Petroleum Independence Act."

Just then the intercom on Tokalas' desk phone buzzed.

"Yes?" Tokalas said after pushing the speaker button.

"A courier just dropped off a letter. I think you'll want to see it right away."

"OK, bring it in."

Tokalas' administrative assistant was through the door into his office immediately, handing the envelope across the desk.

"Thank you," Tokalas mumbled as he tore open the envelope and removed a single sheet of paper. He read just a few lines before almost shouting an obscenity.

"We're being sued to stop the merger!"

"What? Who?" Snodgrass asked.

"Wellingsworth."

Tokalas didn't have to tell Snodgrass who Wellingsworth was. He was at all the stockholders' meetings and was always the first to the microphone when they had question-answer sessions. He was a large stockholder, one of the largest that wasn't an institutional investor, and he could make a lot of noise.

Tokalas then read the entire service letter to Snodgrass.

"Well I guess we need to call legal," Snodgrass remarked sourly.

* * *

A huge thunder cloud loomed to the East of Jackie's BMW roadster as she drove the short – for Texas – drive to the family's Hempstead ranch. She had the top down and her dark hair was flowing in the wind. This was her version of executive nine holes of golf on Wednesday afternoon.

While her Type-A personality usually had her working long hours, today she simply couldn't stay in her office. Too much that was happening was beyond her control anyway. She sped the final mile to the ranch and swung the little green Z4 through the gate with the wrought iron "Bar-X" over top and zipped toward the stables.

"Hello Ned," she said when the caretaker welcomed her as she raised the top on her convertible. Although she didn't feel like it today, she made small talk with the man, another of her employees, who must be lonely on the huge acreage few people visited anymore. Eventually, when she was able to excuse herself, putting on her cowboy hat, she hurried to the barn.

"Hey, baby. So good to see you," she said to Sable, her favorite horse. She caressed the long, regal face and powerful neck before slipping a bridle onto her head and letting the reins lay on her mane.

"Can I help you get saddled up?" Ned asked, having followed her to the barn.

"Oh, no thank you. It's part of my therapy," Jackie answered with a wave and forced a laugh as she laid a red, blue and yellow Navajo-patterned saddle blanket on Sable's back.

"How's your mother?" Ned asked, seeming to need to talk.

"She's doing pretty well. I convinced her to sell the estate and get a more manageable place. She's moving this weekend."

"Does she need help?"

"It's very kind of you to offer, but if I know my Mama, she'll have marshalled an army of professional movers. I'll help her with a few personal things, but she's got it covered otherwise."

"Downsizing, huh?"

"Yeah, it's time."

Jackie could see that Ned observed her with a concerned look on his face as she turned to throw a small saddle over the horse's chestnut back.

"Well, have a good ride," he said as he walked away.

She acknowledged his "goodbye" and her mind turned to the reason she needed to come here today. Patrick's betrayal had been a crushing blow and had damaged Axiom's budding relationship with Petrocom. But the dashed dreams of a future with Patrick was a personal hurt and was the hardest on her. Tears ran down her cheeks as she cinched the saddle and mounted Sable and guided her out of the barn. It only took a nudge and Sable began trotting out onto the wide pasture.

This was where Jackie came when things got to be too much. When she was young, her most vivid childhood adventures played out here at the Bar X on the back of an old, quiet mare. Later, she learned real horsemanship mounted on a spirited cutting horse. Now she came to relieve stress, and there were so many things weighing her down.

Out in the pasture, with the prairie grass and bluebonnets of the huge ranch, she let Sable have her head and allowed the tears to come hot and heavy as she rose and fell with the rhythm of the horse's gallop.

Her mind was idle as the raw emotion poured out. Hurtful sorrow was followed by anger, and then by a stab of grief once more. Twice she turned Sable away from the wall of willows lining the creek bank because she wasn't ready to stop. She wasn't ready to grapple with what had been weighing her down.

The thunder cloud was over head now and the sun's warmth was replaced by cool shade. Finally, she let Sable go to a stand of cottonwoods among the willows and climb down the bank to drink from the creek just as the rain began to fall.

She dismounted and looked up through the trees at the darkened sky. The trees provided scant shelter from the rain, so her western shirt and jeans began to get wet, but she ignored it.

She sat down on an outcropping of red sandstone, letting her cowboy boots hang over the ledge above the stream. Her crying subsided and she wiped her eyes with her sleeve as rain pelted her cowboy hat.

Finally, she allowed herself to think. She immediately was angry that Patrick had betrayed her like he had. She now saw that he was a reporter first. He had previously held back publishing a story when she asked him to, but that was early in their relationship, if that's what it had been.

This was different. Though they hadn't been together much, they had moved their relationship forward as best they could long distance, so Jackie had thought they had a bond. *Why didn't I see that his work came first?*

Now Jackie directed her anger at herself for not knowing that would be the case. Part of her also realized that she was not much different. Her work was a huge priority for her, but right now she wasn't allowing herself to think about what she would do if the situation were reversed. Right now, she was focused on her anger and hurt because of what Patrick had done.

But when that emotion was spent, it was replaced by despair. Despair that she would always be alone. Despair that she would never have children. *It's lonely at the top*, she thought bitterly.

How often she had heard those words, but now they were literally true for her.

And it didn't help that she was turning 39 on Saturday!

The rain was steady now and Jackie looked up at the dark cloud through the bowing willow branches and majestic cottonwoods. She began to weep again and silently prayed.

She prayed first for an end to the pain, even as she knew that grief was a process that couldn't be hurried. Her thought-prayer was rambling and incoherent, but she believed God understood. Didn't the Bible say something about the Holy Spirit interpreting "groanings"? Yes, something like that.

She then prayed for her mother and that brought another stab of grief as she was reminded of the now-empty place her father had occupied for her whole life. She wondered if she needed help working through the grief she felt about the loss of her father. She had stayed so busy since he died. She figured a counselor would tell her she had "work to do", if she found time to go to a counselor.

She also wondered if his loss figured into her attitude toward Patrick. She decided it didn't because they were nothing alike.

She gradually transitioned to praying about all the hurting people, suffering because of the gas tax: her employees, especially those she had laid off; her customers, who had difficulty affording gas to get to work, and Axiom's stockholders, many of whom were retirees who depended on the health of the company for their fixed incomes.

She realized that those three categories included millions of people. By extension, millions more, in fact the whole country, were being adversely affected, as long as the tax was in place.

All because one judge handed down an injunction.

Jackie didn't mind challenges and obstacles if she could act to solve the problems, but this was completely out of her control. So, she prayed some more that a solution would present itself.

Vaguely she realized that the judge's injunction would have to be met in court, but her mind was such a jumble, the thought could not completely form.

She was startled by the sound of thunder and she looked up to see that the storm had developed lightning. Knowing she shouldn't remain under the trees that could attract thunderbolts, she stood up on the outcropping and mounted Sable again. She took off at a gallop, the rain stinging her face, but she didn't care.

CHAPTER FOURTEEN

Jonesy's wife, Margaret, was in such a dark place of grief after the death of Amber and her new husband that she didn't seem to see what was happening to Tobias Jones. Back home in Indiana, they didn't talk much. Maybe that could come later. He had told her that he would be without a job soon of course, but there would be unemployment pay, so with all that had happened, it seemed to Jonesy that she didn't want to think about that right now.

For his sake, Jonesy was numb. With the help of a steady diet of alcohol, he was descending into a despondency that was darker than anything that he had experienced before. Though he was aware of it, he was powerless to stop himself.

He spent each evening with a glass or bottle in one hand and the other hand balled into a fist, sitting motionless in his favorite chair. His mind was a jumbled collage of delinquent bills, a beautiful, brunette bride, planes crashing into the sea, cold-hearted suits in the corporate headquarters and the face of the judge who prevented the gas tax from being lifted that caused his career to end.

Each time a bill came for some aspect of the wedding, it wounded Jonesy afresh, as he realized that he must pay the bill, but his baby girl would never grow old with her new husband; would never give him grandchildren.

Eventually he was drinking before going to work as well as after and spiking the coffee in the thermos he kept close by all day. Morning blurred into afternoon blurred into midnight. Each time going through the steps that brought him to this point always ended at the same place: Judge Everett Walker.

In the evenings, he began to go online and read everything he could find about the Axiom plant closings. He had never learned to use the Internet very well, being more inclined to mechanical pursuits, but now he was motivated. Soon he knew more than he had ever known before about the enviro-terrorists who attacked the Axiom drilling rig, the gas tax that boxed the company in, the surprising upsets in the election, the Congressional bill that would have repealed the tax, and the injunction that kept the profit-killing tax in place.

Even in his alcohol-induced fog and depression, Jonesy knew that Amber's death was not anybody's fault. The closing of the plant that would compound his financial desperation:

perhaps that could be laid at the feet of Axiom's top executives, but there was no doubt that the judge had forced their decision.

He continued to go to work until there was just one week left until the plant closing. Production had stopped a week earlier; the employees of the Gary Axiom Refinery were in shutdown mode. Jonesy went through the motions on autopilot, doing what he was told and what his experience told him to do, with his conscious mind continuing to brood on the dark collage.

A couple of nights before the plant's closing day, Jonesy was at his lowest point, feeling completely helpless to control his own life. About one a.m., he decided he had to do something.

* * *

Patrick had managed to communicate with his office a couple of times, even though he had called in sick. Now it was evening and he had convinced himself that he had things under control. It wasn't hard to do. A steady supply of cheap liquor and cheaper beer allowed him to talk himself into anything.

Vaguely he realized that he needed to get himself together enough to go to work tomorrow. Being gone two days in a row just wasn't done. He had worked sick many times and he didn't know if he could lie well enough to convince his managing editor that he was so sick as to miss two days in the same week.

He stumbled over to the kitchen trash can and dragged it to the table, where he swept the eight or ten empty bottles into it, never thinking that he would ordinarily recycle them.

He sat down heavily in a kitchen chair and with great difficulty realized that he needed to eat if he was to be in shape to go to work tomorrow. He felt a wave of shame as he struggled to organize his thoughts into a plan of action. He had known this feeling many times: the feeling of failing again; of disappointing people who counted on him; of being powerless in the face of addiction.

He wondered if he had anything in the house to eat. Stumbling to the cupboard, he found an old box of corn flakes, but there was no milk in the refrigerator. He proceeded to eat them by the handful straight from the box, standing over the kitchen sink, barely realizing how pathetic it would look if anyone saw him.

Even in his state, he realized he needed to not drink again. This much he knew from his 12-step meetings. You couldn't "cut down"; you had to cut it off. He figured there were still two or three bottles left in the refrigerator from the second 12-pack he'd bought on the way home last night. Immediately the familiar battle began raging in his dull mind.

He could get rid of those last bottles by drinking them, which made perfect sense to him in his current state, but another voice in his head said now was the time to stop and he should get rid of those bottles if he was to recover his responsibilities.

But thinking about his responsibilities and how they had brought him to this only made him want another drink. Slowly his frustration and anger grew and eventually he turned his disgust upon himself. Suddenly he stood to his uncertain feet and hurried to the refrigerator, jerking open the door and gathering the remaining bottles with a loud clanking and threw them in the sink.

One by one, he twisted the caps off each bottle and let the cold beer and whiskey in turn run down the drain. He mourned it as he watched, unable to know if he had done the right thing.

* * *

The morning of his last day on the job, Jonesy said goodbye to Margaret like he always did, with a peck on the cheek, then stopped and gave her a bear hug before going out the door. He carried his lunch box out to the pickup as usual, knowing he was leaving for the plant for the last time. However, he also knew he wouldn't be coming back to Margaret and their home.

What Margaret didn't know is that he had already stowed a duffle bag in the bed of the pickup and he would stop to put it in a secret place before going to work.

* * *

At the refinery, Jonesy's fellow workers were subdued. Some had blown off steam in the lunch rooms over the past 30 days, cursing Axiom management, the gas tax, Congress and the judge who handed down the injunction, but today they went about their final duties with a fatalistic silence.

At noon, the lunch whistle sounded and all the men laid down their last few chores and gathered in little knots to munch whatever they had brought for the last time. Except Jonesy.

He had his lunch box in his hand, but today there was nothing but strong coffee in the thermos. Instead of sitting with his buddies to eat, he made his way through the cavernous building to an outside door near the huge gasoline storage tanks, which looked like gargantuan sardine cans sitting one beside the other.

By the end of the day they would be empty. Ever since the announcement that the refinery was closing, a convoy of tanker trucks had come in and out of the yard. Each one was gradually filled with refined product and headed out to service stations or other storage facilities that had not received the ax.

Jonesy had checked at his mid-morning break, so he knew which of the few remaining tanker trucks was pretty much filled. He strode toward it, with his employee's picture-badge conspicuously visible. It would be similar enough to trucks he had driven years ago when he worked for Axiom as a driver.

He could see that the driver was nowhere to be seen, waiting until the tanker was full before returning to drive it away. The large, ribbed hose was still attached and fuel flowing, although the refinery employee assigned to that storage tank was over in the shade of the tank in a folding chair with a couple of other men, his attention totally on lunch and conversation.

Jonesy didn't pause when he got to the driver's door but swung it open and, with some difficulty made the three giant steps to climb into the cab, landing his stocky frame on the driver's seat. The keys were in it as he knew they would be and he rapidly brought the huge semi-tractor to life and slammed it into gear. Before the man in charge of the tank could rise out of his chair, Jonesy stomped on the accelerator and sent gravel and cinders flying from the tractor's eight rear wheels.

As the truck sped away, the hose ripped loose from its aluminum coupling and gasoline spilled across the curved, mirrored side of the tanker and splashed onto the ground. Flying gravel from the spinning wheels sparked and the airborne gasoline burst into flame. On the gravel-covered earth, petroleum residue from years of activity, ranging from refined motor fuel to crude oil to brake fluid leaked from a thousand trucks, ignited creating a field of fire, stopping the men who tried to pursue the rapidly departing semi. The fire immediately spread to include wooden work tables and equipment racks. Other men nearby noticed and went for fire extinguishers.

An alarm sounded, alerting the entire facility to the developing emergency, although no one could react quickly enough. Jonesy kept the "pedal-to-the-metal" and soon the plant's front gate was in sight. The massive chain-link gate rode on a track and was opened when trucks needed to pass through, but Jonesy was not about to wait for the operator to open the gate for him. He saw the guard's wide eyes in the shack and his upraised hand in a futile attempt to say *Stop!*

The massive flat radiator and broad bumper on the front of the Peterbilt tractor ripped the gate from its frame and the truck was soon careening to the left as Jonesy drove it down the plant road toward the Interstate 90 access road.

* * *

Jonesy had first headed the tanker truck toward the Interstate highway and that was where Indiana State Police cars were speeding, sirens screaming, to intercept it. Jonesy heard the radio news say they already had his description. He knew plant management would know he was absent.

But Jonesy had thought his plan through so that, instead of getting on the Interstate, he was at that moment parked on a dirt road with tall oak trees on either side so the truck would be visible only partly from the air. It was a sparsely populated area, so the houses were far apart.

Climbing down from the cab, he hurried over to a tree where an inconspicuous cardboard box sat near the trunk, partly covered in dry leaves from the previous fall. Pushing the box aside he picked up a large black garbage bag and from it retrieved the stuffed, green duffle bag from the place he had carefully hidden it earlier that morning. He slung it over his shoulder and headed back to the truck, where he set it on the ground and unzipped it, taking a toolbox from inside.

Quickly he climbed into the cab and lay on his back under the dashboard, using wire cutters from the duffle bag to sever the wires that connected the GPS and dispatch computer to the onboard cellular link. Next, he cut the wiring on the GPS tracker on the front of the trailer. This would not prevent him from being found but it would make it more difficult.

With that done, he also took his personal cell phone and turned it off, finally popping out the battery because he had heard that a cell phone can be tracked even if it's turned off, unless you remove the battery.

Finally, he got out of the cab and climbed to the top of the tanker. He disconnected the coupling with its torn hose and reconnected the cap which was dangling on the end of the chain. Having secured the fuel, he returned to the cab.

Jonesy then just sat and waited more than half an hour, knowing that it was risky to stay so near the refinery, but reasoning that law enforcement would be looking for a speeding truck trying to get away and would probably be several miles away by the time he moved again. A truck driving at normal speeds an hour later would not be noticed, or at least would be less likely to be stopped.

When enough time had elapsed, Jonesy started the engine once again and eased the truck into gear, slowly moving forward until he reached U.S. Highway 41 and turned south.

CHAPTER FIFTEEN

News of the theft of the tanker and the resulting fire reached Axiom headquarters almost immediately and barely before the news media began to disseminate the story.

Doris came into Jackie's office with Vice President of Operations Derek Jenkins. They looked like they had bad news.

"What now?" Jackie said wearily.

"Just got a phone call from the Gary refinery," Jenkins began. "There's been an incident."

"What kind of incident?"

"An employee stole a tanker and there was a fire."

"Oh no! Was anybody hurt?"

"No. It's a miracle though."

"Thank God! Do they know who took the truck?"

"Yes," Jenkins referred to a handwritten note. "Tobias Jones. He's a pipefitter."

"Where is he now?"

"The state police are looking but haven't found him yet."

"Can we track him?"

"He must have defeated the GPS and Satellite comms," Jenkins said. "The truck has gone completely dark. The cops don't even have a cell signal."

"Not far to Illinois," Jackie mused, knowing that it meant nothing. He could be headed anywhere.

"Why would he steal a tanker truck?" Doris asked.

"Maybe just to get back at the company for shutting the refinery?" Jackie hoped this was unnecessarily pessimistic. "This is the last day for that plant."

"Let's hope that's all it is," said Jenkins as the two women regarded him with question marks on their faces.

* * *

Patrick Garrity was in his office at the *Washington Herald* when news about the theft of the tanker came on as an "Alert" on CNN. He unmuted the TV and watched the report, thin though it was so far. He knew there would be more later.

He called Jackie, but knew it was futile. She hadn't answered any of his calls for some time now. He left a message anyway.

"Hey, I just saw the news. I'm happy to help if there's anything I can do. 'Bye."

An unexpected pain in his chest accompanied the end of the call. He closed his eyes briefly and found another number in his contact list and pushed "Send."

"Hey, you got a second?" Patrick asked his AA sponsor.

* * *

That night, Patrick sat slumped on his old sofa in his non-descript apartment. He hadn't gone to the Blue Ribbon Grill, so as to avoid temptation. He was holding on for dear life as he got sober again. He was reluctant to think of Jackie because it might cause him to want to take refuge in drink again, but he couldn't help thinking about the new crisis and how Jackie must be reacting.

Reviewing all that had happened, he remembered a conversation in which Jackie had said she wished she knew who was doing this to them, referring to the gas tax and the injunction. He wondered if it would be possible to find out. *After all,* he thought, *I AM a journalist.*

He was sure he could find who petitioned for the injunction, but that might not be who was really behind it. He opened his laptop and first quickly reviewed the articles the *Herald* had run about the injunction, but he already knew everything that was in them. Then he went to the website for the biggest St.

Louis TV station. He used the site search to find articles and video clips about the petition.

He soon found a video interview with a peacock of a lawyer bringing the petition and standing beside him was an older man who was introduced as George Donaldson of the Aquarian Community. The guy looked like he didn't have the gumption to originate a petition like this, nor did he look like he had the money. He watched the video and saw that the lawyer, named Reardon, was finishing Donaldson's sentences for him.

To Patrick, Donaldson looked like a pawn. He decided he needed to know more about George Donaldson.

* * *

"Mrs. Jones, you'll have to come with us."

When Margaret answered the knock at her front door, she was already feeling bewildered. She had just seen on the evening news how Toby had apparently stolen a tanker truck from the refinery on his very last day. He still hadn't come home and she was desperate to know what was going on.

Three men with very serious expressions had briefly shown badges, then demanded she come with them. She was so confused she had a hard time finding her purse and locking the front door.

"Where are you taking me?" she thought to ask only after they had ushered her into the back seat of a large, black and white SUV.

"We just need to ask you some questions about your husband Mrs. Jones," answered one of the men Margaret now realized were police detectives.

"Do you know where he is?"

"We'll ask the questions, Mrs. Jones."

* * *

Margaret was taken to a windowless room at a precinct of the Gary, Indiana, Police Department, where she was told to be seated at a table, then the men left her alone. She became more and more apprehensive as she waited. She could see her reflection in a glass across the room and she decided it must be one of those two-way mirrors like they have on police TV shows. That meant someone was likely watching from the other side, which made her even more uncomfortable.

Eventually, one of the detectives returned and sat across from her. "Sorry about the wait, Mrs. Jones. We just have a few questions about your husband."

"Okay."

"Why did he steal the truck from the refinery?"

"I – I don't know."

"You don't know?" the detective asked sternly. "He must have said something, or there must have been something that set him off."

Margaret looked at the officer with wide eyes. She hadn't thought about it, but of course something had happened that could have set him off. She couldn't stop the tears now. "Well, he lost his job. And our daughter – died. She was killed…"

"Your daughter?"

"Yes, Amber. She had just gotten married. She and her husband…" she sobbed, unable to continue.

The detective looked uncomfortable as he watched her, apparently gauging her sincerity.

"They were both killed? How were they killed, Mrs. Jones?"

"Their plane crashed."

The detective had a pained look on his face and almost appeared sympathetic.

"Do you think that caused your husband to do this?"

"How should I know?!" Margaret shouted through her tears. "He didn't say anything to me. This morning he said goodbye to me just like he has every day for thirty-three years."

"Nothing had changed?"

"Everything had changed! Our daughter was killed! How could anything be the same?"

The detective made a note on his legal pad. "Do you have any idea where he would go?"

Margaret shook her head and tried to regain her composure.

"Any relatives or friends in another part of the state or out of state he might go to?"

"He has a brother in Chicago, but they don't talk much. I doubt he'd go there."

"Have you called your brother-in-law?"

"No."

"What's his name?"

"Thomas. Thomas Jones."

The detective added the name to his notes. "Do you have a phone number for him?"

"Not with me," Margaret answered, dabbing her tears.

"Are you sure you didn't have any idea Mr. Jones was going to steal that truck?"

"No," she said quietly. "No idea whatsoever."

* * *

It was dark now and Jonesy had begun to wonder if staying off the Interstate was a good idea after all, because his progress was much slower on the two-lane state highways and he was in a hurry to get to his destination. It was now his only reason for living. Still, he knew instinctively that, assuming no one knew where he was headed, fewer people would remember seeing a tanker on the back roads.

But the going was more difficult at night, what with the road curving and occasional stop lights and 90-degree turns in some of the small towns. At least it kept him awake, Jonesy thought.

He had a plan and, so far, he had followed it rigorously. Though he had been undisciplined in the days since Amber's death, he was now possessed of a purpose that had awakened in him the training he had received in the military. Few of his friends were aware of it, because he didn't brag about that part of his life, but he had been a demolitions specialist in the army. That meant he knew all about bombs; everything from dynamite to incendiaries. It was the latter that had inspired the theft of the tanker truck. He had been able to find most of the materials and equipment he would need in his garage before he left and he had a tanker load of flammable liquid behind him. What he lacked could be found at any hardware store.

As his wheels hummed on the asphalt, he thought of Margaret and was momentarily saddened. Yet, his plan was the only way he could right the wrongs that had been done to him. It would set things right, and that was what he must do, in spite of the pain it might cause.

* * *

Margaret Jones had not known that her grief could go deeper. She had to turn off the TV to avoid seeing the video of the fire at the refinery and her husband's driver's license picture being shown over and over on the local news.

After she was questioned by the police yesterday, reporters began calling, but she had managed to avoid talking to many of them. She was becoming a virtual shut-in.

The phone rang. She was afraid to answer it. *What if it is a reporter? But what if it is Toby?* Finally, she answered.

"Hello?"

"Mom, what's going on? I heard something on the news."

It was Leslie, calling from college. *Thank God,* she thought.

"Oh honey, I don't know what to do!"

"Mom, I'm coming home right now. I can be there in a little over an hour."

"Thank you," Margaret said, her voice breaking. "Drive carefully." She hung up the phone, sat down and wept.

* * *

"I've put something together for the calls that will certainly come." Charlene Washington had called Jackie's office to request an emergency meeting. Jackie took the press release from her Public Relations officer and scanned it.

"This looks good. I hope the press will finally see us as more of a victim in this situation."

"Don't be surprised if some members of the media make the tanker theft about the plant closures."

"Yes, I can see that they might do that. I just wish we could catch a break," Jackie said. "Do you have everything you need on Tobias Jones?"

"Yes, we've got his employee records and I've called and talked to his supervisor to get some personal information. One thing I discovered is that his daughter was recently killed in a plane crash returning home from her honeymoon."

"Oh, no!" Jackie exclaimed. "That is truly terrible. So, you can almost sympathize with him. He has a wife?"

"Yes, her name is Margaret," Charlene checked her notes.

"Let's find out what we can do for her," Jackie said.

"Uh, Ms. James," Charlene appeared reluctant to speak.

"What is it?"

"Well, I just think you need to be careful."

"About what?"

"About appearing too sympathetic. He did commit a crime, after all, stealing and vandalizing company property, and we don't know the extent of her knowledge or involvement."

Jackie thought for a moment. Charlene's instincts were very good. That's why she was such a great public relations officer.

"Well, I doubt his wife was involved," Jackie answered, "and now she's probably devastated. I guess we should check with someone local to get a read on her. If she's innocent, I'd like to do something for her, if we can without creating problems."

"Yes, ma'am. I'll see what I can find out."

"Thanks. Good job, as always. Let me know if we get any blow-back."

"Yes, ma'am."

* * *

"Hello, George Donaldson?"

"Right on! You got me!" said the voice on the phone.

"Uh, this is Patrick Garrity of the *Washington Herald*."

"Oh. Another durned reporter!" said Donaldson, laughing. "What the heck? What do you want?"

"Uh, well, I just wanted to get some background on your petition for the injunction to stop the repeal of the Petroleum Independence Act."

Patrick then heard Donaldson take the phone away from his mouth and howl with laughter. *Is this guy high?*

"That was somethin,' wasn't it? Like a hot knife through butter!"

"What do you mean?" Patrick asked.

"I mean it was so easy, like it was all figured out. 'Nothin' to it but to do it.'"

"Yes, it did happen fast. Was the Aquarian Community the only plaintiff?"

"Uh, yeah. Sure."

"Did the Aquarian Community have the funds for legal fees?"

"Oh, yeah, absolutely!" Then Donaldson went off into gales of laughter once again.

Yes, definitely high, Patrick decided.

"I guess that means you didn't have the money for the legal fees? Where did it come from?"

"Oh, that's a secret," Donaldson said in a low whisper. "Yeah, they want to be anomyna..., anomyna..., anom--"

"Anonymous?" Patrick said. Then, reasoning that if Donaldson was indeed high he might fall for a trick question, asked, "Who wants to be anonymous?"

"Why the lawyers, of course."

"But the lawyer was in the courtroom with you and it was covered by the press. He's hardly anonymous."

"No, I mean them lawyers that gave me the money."

Patrick carefully considered his next question. "Were these lawyers from Washington?"

"Yep. Bellingham, I think he said. How'd you know?"

Oh, Patrick thought. He had been asking about Washington, *D.C.*, but Bellingham was a city in Washington *state*. He wondered how much further he could push his luck.

"What was the name of the law firm?"

"Durned if I know. It was on the check." Then Donaldson mumbled, "I have the check stub somewhere. Gosh, I never seen such a big check before!"

"How much was it?"

"A hundred thousand big ones! Yes sir! Said we could keep half if we'd give the St. Louis lawyer the other half. Then I just had to sit in court with him and he did all the work. 'Nothin' to it but to do it!'"

"Well, thank you Mr. Donaldson, you've been very helpful."

"How do you think I can afford this weed? It's prime, too!" With that Donaldson dropped the phone laughing again.

Patrick hung up. He looked at the far wall of his office thinking about the surreal conversation he'd just had.

So, a law firm in Bellingham, Washington, went to Missouri, and paid a loser like Donaldson to play the part of plaintiff to get the injunction handed down. Someone was trying to cover their tracks, but who?

How many law firms could there be in Bellingham?

A quick web search gave him a list of websites featuring law firms of various sizes and specialties. He figured the injunction was desired by one of these firm's clients, not the firm itself. And the fact that they had petitioned for the injunction in Missouri instead of Washington meant they REALLY didn't want to be found.

He looked at a few of the websites and wasn't getting very far, then he had a thought: *If this is part of the larger plot, the client would likely be an environmental group.*

The outfit in Texas that bombed the Gulf Pride oil platform had been an environmental group of some kind, and they had received the money from a Washington, D.C., lobbyist. It made sense that the injunction to keep the gas tax in place would be something an environmental group would want. Patrick knew that the FBI didn't feel like they had found the mastermind behind that attack. The lobbyist they had arrested didn't seem to be the one who was actually funding it. *And George Donaldson isn't the mastermind of anything,* he thought with a grim smile.

He started focusing on the client pages of the law firms that specialized in nonprofits, because that's what environmental groups usually were. When he went to the client page on the website for Fischer-Williams, the first name on the list was Champions of Mother Earth, headquartered in Seattle.

Where do I know that name from? he asked himself. It took a couple of minutes but then it hit him. The lobbyist's brochure!

He frantically began looking for Marvin Borelli's brochure he had picked up in Congressman Kellerman's office. *What did I do with it?* he thought.

Then he found it, together with the notes he had made on the vote for the House bill to repeal the Petroleum Independence Act. He opened it, then flipped it over and found it on the back panel under "A Few of Our Prominent Clients."

Champions of Mother Earth was the first one on the list.

That can't be a coincidence, can it? he thought.

*   *   *

The bright spring day didn't match Jackie's mood at all. It was moving day for her mother and also Jackie's thirty-ninth birthday. She was dressed down in jeans, a loose-fitting shirt and running shoes, with her hair tied back.

It wasn't that her mother had forgotten her birthday; she actually seemed to think if Jackie helped her move, it would be a good opportunity for them to be together.

Of course, there wasn't much to do. The professionals were doing all the heavy lifting and her mother's household staff would do most of the settling in. But there were a few items, some heirloom lamps and delicate antiques, her mother didn't trust to the movers, so Jackie drove her Range Rover over to the estate house and together they loaded it with those items.

It only took a couple of leisurely hours before they had unloaded the few precious items at her mother's new place, which was a hive of activity, with the professional movers and the staff of the old house crossing paths everywhere as they moved in the furniture and carefully unpacked boxes.

Jackie's mother gave clear directions to a few members of her staff about where certain things were to go and then turned to Jackie.

"So, shall we go have your birthday lunch?"

"Okay," Jackie answered, struggling to smile. Just then her iPhone® rang. She looked at the screen. It was Patrick. She silenced the ringing and put the phone back in her pocket.

"Aren't you going to answer that?" her mother asked.

"Nope. Let's go eat," Jackie said heading out the door.

* * *

Patrick wasn't surprised that Jackie didn't answer the phone, but he figured, since it was her birthday, he had to try. He had thought maybe she would be off-guard on a Saturday, or even would cut him some slack since it was her birthday.

He had sent her a present; a relatively inexpensive necklace, but he couldn't afford anything better. Now he felt like it was probably a waste. She probably wouldn't even acknowledge it. She could afford jewelry 100 times as costly, if she wanted, but

Patrick realized she rarely wore a lot of jewelry; all the more reason his gift would likely be ignored.

He did think she should know about his conversation with George Donaldson and what he had been able to determine about the connection to Champions of Mother Earth. He would have to find a way to communicate that information to her, whether she wanted to talk to him or not.

* * *

It was raining in Seattle, as usual. In his penthouse office, Jason Wood was reading an account of the Axiom tanker truck theft and smiling from ear to ear. He could hardly believe his good fortune. His earlier attempts to hurt the oil company through bad press had backfired, largely because of the boycott and how it was seen as a populist cause. But this tanker theft was unexpected. Perhaps there was a way to exploit it to finally hurt the company that was so indifferently hurting the Earth.

He quickly sent emails to a few key people in the media that he could count on to shape the news. If he could turn the public against the oil companies, they would be glad to see them go as he activated the second part of his plan. But to do that he would have to leave his plush headquarters and dress down a bit.

* * *

The warehouse was in a part of town that had been bustling with commerce a few decades ago, but had fallen on hard times with the real estate bubble. But that was good for Jason Wood, because it meant there would be few occupants of other buildings to notice his comings and goings.

The lease was in the name of a holding company called Consolidated Services Inc., that was in turn owned by Amcor, LLC, that was itself a subsidiary of a company which he had created, but put in the name of his wife's cousin, without his knowledge. That way it couldn't be readily linked to him.

He had found various uses for the holding company, distanced as it was from his public persona as CEO of a philanthropic organization. Whenever he needed to do something that shouldn't be associated with Champions, he did it through Consolidated.

The warehouse was empty except for old dusty boxes and broken pallets scattered around. However, the main office space was scrupulously clean and well-lit, as well as equipped with a robust Internet connection and powerful computer.

Jason Wood sat down in the comfortable chair that appeared out of place in the rustic surroundings and quickly went to a website that he used for investing. His familiarity with his secret brokerage account meant it took virtually no time for him to find what he was looking for.

On the screen were several stocks in which he was secretly invested, but the largest holdings were in two companies: Petrocom Energy Limited and Axiom Oil Incorporated.

He zeroed in on Petrocom.

CHAPTER SIXTEEN

Gerald Tokalas groused under his breath about the colossal waste of time this trial was. Why would one of Petrocom's biggest stockholders sue the company because of merger talks? If Wellingsworth was intelligent or reasonable at all he would wait to see what the plan was. *He might like it,* he thought.

He shifted on the uncomfortable wooden bench and listened to the proceeding, just getting underway.

Petrocom's lawyers were ahead of the wooden railing and its swinging gate at the defendant's table. At the other table was Wellingsworth, the plaintiff, and his attorneys.

Wellingsworth was a thorn in Tokalas' side, but until now he had just been an annoyance at stockholders' meetings. This suit had potential to scuttle the deal with Axiom and, for all his supposed interest in his investments, Wellingsworth didn't understand this merger might well be Petrocom's only lifeline.

As a large personal investor, Wellingsworth should have been more aware and concerned with Petrocom's situation, but he appeared too busy thinking about how it slighted him that he hadn't been notified.

What's so bad about merging with Axiom? Tokalas pretended to ask the plaintiff at the table across the room, even as he remembered his top management's negative initial reaction to the prospect.

Their pride had been hurt by approaching Axiom to "save" their company. It was an admission of failure, Tokalas realized, and maybe Wellingsworth was motivated by pride as well.

Unfortunately, this trial meant that the second meeting with Axiom management that had been agreed upon at the first meeting in Waco had now been put on an indefinite hold, pending the outcome of this proceeding, and Tokalas had no idea how long to expect this to take.

"Your honor, the bylaws of Petrocom Energy, LTD., clearly state that a merger must be approved by a vote of the stockholders," intoned Wellingsworth's lead attorney. "The company flouted this requirement by meeting with the representatives of Axiom Oil Incorporated."

We would have put it to a vote, had we been allowed to get that far, Tokalas argued in his head. His legal team, patiently waiting their turn at the table had made this very clear in their pre-trial meetings: the company was required to take a vote of the stockholders to proceed with a merger, but the suit came so early that they hadn't gotten far enough with their negotiations to put it to a vote. *Now we may never get to that point,* he complained in silence.

"Petrocom's management moved forward with their plan to merge with Axiom Oil Incorporated and my client and his fellow stockholders had to find out through the news media."

We hadn't gotten to the plan! Tokalas continued arguing, knowing that the company's legal team would argue better than he could, but the arguments practically made themselves. What did Wellingsworth think he would accomplish?

Tokalas felt stomach acid curdling his breakfast as his frustration grew and the burning climbed up his throat.

Tokalas' one comfort was that Texas judges tended to abide no nonsense and, to Tokalas, that's what this suit was.

* * *

Yikes! What's going on?

The next morning, Gerald Tokalas was shocked by what he saw on the stock ticker in his brokerage account. He always had Petrocom's stock price displayed so he could check it immediately when he logged in. Today, he was about to leave his office to go to court when he decided to see if the stock was still being buoyed by the revelation of merger talks, but instead it had fallen by a third from its value the day before.

"Wellingsworth!" he shouted in anger in his empty office. He felt certain the lawsuit was to blame for this turn of events.

* * *

"Have we communicated with his wife?"

The topic was Tobias Jones and the theft of the tanker as several of Axiom's top management sat around the small conference table in a corner of Jackie's office with Doris taking notes. They had already discussed the news coverage, the insurance concerns and the activities of law enforcement. Now Jackie was wondering about the family.

"Well, I'm sure the police have talked to her," Derek Jenkins, V.P. of Operations said, seemingly unsure what his boss meant.

"I mean have we offered her any support in the wake of her husband disappearing?"

Derek at first looked at her blankly and then began writing something on the pad in front of him. "I'll make that call as soon as we get out of this meeting."

"Good. I know we wouldn't have to, but, unless she's an accomplice, she needs to know she's supported. Her husband, even though he's committed a crime now, did give a lot of years of his life to the company."

Doris looked at Derek and back at Jackie with a wry smile.

"Talk to Charlene. She was going to learn more about her and evaluate the public relations pitfalls of reaching out to her."

"Yes, ma'am," Jenkins answered.

* * *

It had been a week. Living in the cab of the truck was not a hardship. Jonesy had done it before when he was a driver. He had also been in much worse situations in Iraq.

If he had not been so single minded, he would have felt guilt. Guilt for leaving Margaret without a word. Guilt for stealing the truck, guilt for stealing the car he was now using to track the Judge to his house.

It hadn't been hard. He had seen the judge's picture multiple times in news reports and online, so he just waited until the judge left the courthouse in his limo and followed him home. Then Jonesy drove back to where he had hidden the truck on a lonely road outside of St. Louis and worked to perfect the device he had built.

Over the past week in St. Louis, he had watched the Judge's daily pattern. It was as predictable as the sun coming up in the morning. He rose at 6:00 a.m., collected the newspaper from the porch of his grand house by 6:15, had breakfast and showered by 7:15. The car arrived at half past. Traveling to the courthouse took anywhere from 45 minutes to an hour, giving the judge 45 minutes minimum to review cases before a nine o'clock gavel on the first case, Jonesy surmised.

Jonesy had followed the limousine enough to know the route and to know when it would be at any given point on the route. That would be very important to his plan.

* * *

He decided to do it on a Tuesday because it was exactly a month since his Amber's plane had crashed returning from her honeymoon. No one else might know, but Jonesy knew.

The night before, he slept almost not at all, but used the time to double- and triple-check his mechanism. He decided it was perfect. Before he went to sleep, he took a clear plastic blister pack out of a sack. Earlier in the day he had purchased a prepaid cell phone. He now used his pocket knife to cut it out of the rigid plastic packaging and switched it on.

Jonesy knew that Margaret would not be awake, if she was following her usual pattern. He didn't want to talk to her anyway, because he knew she would try to talk him out of his plan. So, he was calling late enough to have to leave a message.

"I'm sorry Margaret," he began when the home phone answering machine finished its message in his own recorded voice. "I had to do something to set things right. This judge's decision forced the plant closing and that put me under with our finances. I'm sorry to leave you with this mess but maybe my life insurance will fix it. Goodbye Margaret, I love you."

He hung up and waves of emotion washed over him. Thinking about her and Leslie, thinking about Amber, remembering the humiliating mountain of debt. Tomorrow he would get the only justice available to him.

* * *

The phone on Lieutenant Tyrone Gomez' desk rang. He glanced at the clock on the Gary, Indiana Police precinct wall as he picked up the phone. It was twenty minutes after midnight.

"Gomez."

"Sir, this is Tyler. Got a hit on the tap at the Jones' house."

Gomez leaned forward and picked up a pen, hovering over a pad on his desk. "What did you get?"

"Jones called and left a message for his wife."

"From his cell?"

"No, he likely used a pay phone or a burner."

"Do we have a number?"

"Yes. We're running it now. The area code is Missouri."

"Missouri? If we confirm that, the FBI will definitely get involved." Gomez didn't have to tell his junior officer that the FBI was already looking at the theft of the tanker themselves.

"Let me know what you find," Gomez said, lowering the phone slowly. *What are you doing, Mr. Jones?* he mused.

* * *

Agent Callie Strong hung up the phone, brushed aside a dark lock of her short hair and walked the 35 feet to her boss' office.

"Come in," said Special-Agent-in-Charge Darren Wheeler of the St. Louis field office of the FBI.

She entered and wordlessly handed him a note.

"What's this?" Wheeler asked.

"That guy who stole the tanker truck in Indiana: he's in Missouri."

"Where?"

"Don't know, but he called his wife, evidently using a burner. Gary PD picked it up from a tap on the wife's phone."

"Tobias Jones," Wheeler read from the note, stroking his chin. Then to Callie: "He's driving a dang 18-wheeler. Put out an APB. Somebody must have seen it."

"Will do, boss."

* * *

The next morning, very early, Jonesy started the tanker truck's huge engine and eased the vehicle out of its hiding place and onto the Interstate toward the city.

Soon he exited and pulled into a large strip center parking lot and parked where he could see a long way down a wide boulevard. For an hour, he patiently waited as the sun rose and the sky changed from dawn pink to early morning yellow.

Presently, he saw what he had been waiting for: the black Town Car was right on time. Jonesy put the truck in gear and pulled out into the traffic, ahead of the limo.

It wasn't long, though, before the Judge's car passed the large truck just as Jonesy wanted it to do. He shifted and pushed the accelerator, changing lanes to move beside the limousine on the left. Without looking at it, he picked up a small aluminum box that had a cheap two-position switch mounted on it and two wires streaming away from it. Then, just as he nosed past the Judge's car, he jerked the wheel to the right and slammed on the brakes, downshifting as he braked to bring the heavy truck to a stop. He smiled as he heard the large black car's tires scream on the asphalt, as the driver struggled to stop before hitting the tanker.

But there was no impact. That surprised Jonesy, but it didn't matter. He lifted the little box and flipped the switch.

Instantly the tanker trailer exploded in a fireball that lifted the tractor's rear wheels off the ground for a couple of seconds. Burning fuel washed over the windshield of the truck in front of him and immediately burned away in black smoke.

Surprised, Jonesy realized that he was still alive and unhurt. The cab had shaken horribly but apparently the sleeper cab behind him had absorbed the blast. He had expected to end his life in this one magnificent act of justice, but it was not to be.

He looked at the right rear-view mirror seeing the limousine in flames. *No one could have survived that*, he exulted.

Now he realized he shouldn't stay because the cab would rapidly be engulfed in flames, not to mention that the scene would soon be swarming with police and reporters, so he grabbed his duffle bag, jumped from the cab and ran as fast as his short legs could carry him to a row of businesses that looked like they had been built during the forties, including a liquor store and pawn shop. He found a gap between two dilapidated buildings and was able to squeeze through. This had not been part of his plan, but, as he moved away from the "accident" down a deserted alley, he was pretty sure he hadn't been followed. All the bystanders' attention was likely focused on the engulfed limo.

He knew he needed to get far away from there and fast. But how? His one vehicle was sitting in the middle of the road quickly turning to a charred wreck. The car he had stolen was several miles away, hidden on a lonely rural road.

He took a right turn down a side street to put more distance between himself and the scene of his crime, walking as fast as he felt he could without calling attention to himself. He idly wondered if he could catch a city bus, but he had no idea where he could catch one going where he needed to go and besides, that would just give a bus full of people an opportunity to recognize him. Then he noticed the street was lined with parked cars. He began checking the drivers' doors of each one he passed. Eventually he found one that was unlocked: a small Japanese sedan.

The keys were not in the ignition. *That would have been too easy,* Jonesy thought. It was not a problem, though; Tobias Jones had known how to hot-wire a car since he was a teenager.

Soon he was driving down the side street, rapidly putting distance between himself and the scene where he realized police were gathering, because he could hear sirens.

CHAPTER SEVENTEEN

It took less than half an hour before the St. Louis TV news coverage of the tanker explosion became national news, as police and reporters put the facts together and someone realized from the license plates that a Federal judge had been in the limousine. When that became known, the national news outlets took notice and quickly put it together with the tanker theft in Indiana. Fifteen minutes after that, Jackie's office phone rang in Houston.

"Ms. James, someone from the FBI is on the phone asking for you," Doris said. "It's about the tanker truck."

"Thanks, Doris. Put them through." She reflexively stood up and pushed her chair back from the desk.

"This is Jacqueline James."

"Ms. James, this is Special Agent Darren Wheeler of the St. Louis, Missouri, office of the FBI. The tanker truck that was stolen in Indiana has turned up here and exploded. Another vehicle was involved. Two people were killed."

"Oh no!" Jackie could hear noise in the background and guessed that Wheeler was at the scene.

"The other vehicle was a Federal Government car being used by Judge Everett Walker."

"What? Oh, my!" It took a second for it to sink in. *That's the judge who stayed the repeal of the gas tax!*

"We don't have forensics yet, so we aren't sure, but it appears the judge is one of those who was in the car. It was very badly burned."

Jackie couldn't respond, so Wheeler continued.

"I'll keep you apprised of the progress of the investigation. We may have questions for you or other company personnel."

"Of course. Let me know how I can help."

After she hung up, she sank back in her chair and just stared straight ahead.

Oh no! What about the trial?

She grabbed the phone again and dialed Marcus Williams' extension.

* * *

Special Agent Darren Wheeler, 43, with close-cropped hair and the build of a Rams linebacker, had only just ended his call to Jacqueline James in Houston when he was called over to the cab of the recently extinguished tanker truck by Agent Callie Strong, a 10-year veteran of the FBI who, though she might be considered attractive off the job, was all business when on duty. He had to step carefully to avoid debris and the foam used by the firemen to extinguish the blaze.

"Somebody had been living in this truck for quite a while," Strong said, pointing to piles of junk food trash. There was no obvious damage to the inside of the cab, unlike the sleeper behind it. "And we found this."

Her latex-gloved hand held a small, shiny metal box with a simple switch on top and two wires running away from it.

"Bag that and get forensics over here to go through this cab!" Wheeler ordered. He started to walk away and then turned back to her. "And get the explosives guys down here to see what this guy used inside the tanker to blow this thing."

He turned away and dialed a single speed-dial number on his government-issue, secure cell phone.

"Justin, I need you and two more down here," Wheeler commanded another of his agents. "Jones blew the tanker with some kind of trigger and it looks like he walked away. We have a fugitive to find."

* * *

Fox News' St. Louis affiliate was first on the scene and Patrick Garrity was watching the 24-hour news channel in his office at the *Washington Herald.* The footage showed firemen battling a blazing Town Car and tanker truck, then, cutting to when the flames were extinguished, the charred, twisted metal of the two vehicles.

"Well, now we know what happened to the stolen tanker truck," Patrick said aloud. Then a file picture of Judge Walker went up and the anchor reported that the judge had been a passenger in the car.

"Holy--! An Axiom tanker killed the judge that killed the gas tax repeal? Oh, wow!" he exclaimed, realizing the implications.

Next the image of Tobias Jones appeared on the screen. Patrick had seen him before of course, since it was known almost immediately that he had stolen the tanker, but he had successfully evaded the police, unfortunately for the judge.

* * *

He had really been off his game today. His handball opponent, on the other hand, had been on fire. So, after his early morning game and shower, Jason Wood left the gym where he began at least four mornings per week before starting his day at the Champions of Mother Earth headquarters disappointed with his performance. He felt that his day wasn't getting off to the good start he had planned.

When he got in the car, it was just about eight o'clock and he turned on the radio. It was time for news, but he wasn't in the mood, so he was reaching to change the station when he heard something that made his hand stop in midair.

"A Federal judge in St. Louis was killed in a collision with a gasoline truck this morning. Judge Everett Walker had been Federal Judge in the Eastern District of Missouri for..."

The report ended shortly after with very little detail. Finally, he snapped off the radio. His mind raced as he just sat in his car without starting it. There would be an investigation. It was a Federal judge, after all. Reporters as well as police would be all over it. In fact, the FBI would certainly be involved.

What did the report say? "A gasoline truck"? *Was it – could it have been – THAT gasoline truck?*

Wood had no trouble connecting the dots from the judge's injunction, to the Axiom plant closing, to the truck theft and now to the judge's death. He knew the investigators could connect the dots, too. How long would it be before they asked who provided the money to the Aquarian Community?

He would have to do something drastic to keep that last dot from being connected to him.

* * *

That night, Jackie was at home in her Frank-Lloyd-Wright-style home in her gated community. She was pretty stressed with all that was going on. To divert her mind, she snapped on the TV. Not liking what was on the first channel, she flipped the remote up a couple of times and laid it on the foot of the bed.

Unfortunately, she stopped flipping channels on a 24-hour news channel, which shortly had an alert about the death of the judge in the fiery crash.

"The judge was apparently killed by an explosion of an Axiom Oil Company truck. Is it a coincidence that Judge Walker issued the stay that kept the Petroleum Independence Act in place? And what did the management at Axiom know about what Tobias Jones would do with the truck?" the anchor asked rhetorically. "Perhaps time will tell, but you have to wonder, don't you?"

"Oh, for Pete's sake!" Jackie exclaimed. *Do news people have nothing better to do than spin gossip and innuendo?*

After her initial disgust with the plastic anchor's baseless insinuation, Jackie had a chill of concern run through her, remembering how the media had refused to hear anything but the story they had decided on during "Operation Backlash."

* * *

Jonesy hadn't expected to survive the explosion, but the sleeper had taken the brunt of the damage and shielded him from injury. He was thankful to be alive, but his plan had not extended past getting justice in the fireball in St. Louis.

He was driving his stolen car aimlessly on backroads, going generally southwest, away from St. Louis, away from Indiana, away from home, away from Leslie, away from Margaret.

The car he had stolen would soon be out of gas and he knew it would take a lot of money to fill it up with the gas tax still in place. He mentally did the calculation and figured if the tank was 15 gallons, the cheapest gas he could find would cost $75.00 to fill it. He hadn't brought much cash. He didn't figure he'd need it. He would have to get more soon somehow. He had a wallet full of credit cards, but knew if he used them, the police would certainly know and then they could find him.

Suddenly he felt a severe pain; not a physical pain, but an emotional one. He burst into tears and bellowed as he wept bitterly, struggling to keep the car between the lines on the two-lane road. He had been focused on getting his revenge on the judge and had assumed his pain would end in the fiery explosion, but here he was, still alive and utterly alone.

He wept for Amber, for the home she would never build, for the children she would never have, for the long life of which she had been deprived. But he also wept for Margaret, who had no warning of what he had decided to do; who likely would be questioned endlessly by police, Federal agents and reporters. She was not equipped to handle that.

Now that the deed was done, he realized that it had solved nothing, but instead had made things so much worse. Margaret would now learn how desperate their financial situation was and he was not there to go through it with her. Instead she would suffer through not knowing if he was alive or dead or whether he would ever be able to come home again.

There could be no doubt that the police knew he had stolen the truck and that he had used it to kill the judge. It wouldn't take any time for them to figure out why he had done it, but it wouldn't matter. The injustice of the judge's decision would be eclipsed by Jonesy's murder of him.

Where am I going? Perhaps he should go to Mexico. Yes, that might be the right thing. But he didn't have his passport with him. Of course, if he did have his passport and tried to use it at the border he would likely be arrested. They would almost certainly be watching the border for him. He put it out of his mind. Perhaps an answer would occur to him later.

He was not even really sure where he was. He vaguely remembered crossing the Arkansas state line several hours ago. Then, he had crossed an Interstate highway with signs pointing East to Little Rock, so he must be in Southern Arkansas. The road seemed to be angling West through heavily wooded and mountainous country. Shortly he saw signs that indicated he was entering Hot Springs. He looked down at his gas gauge. He would have to think of a solution soon.

CHAPTER EIGHTEEN

It had been years since he had paid much attention to the news, but, since he had now been on TV news himself, involved in what turned out to be a major story, he had been tuning in more regularly and watching more closely.

George Donaldson was getting familiar with the local reporters as he watched the TV news, not just to see his story but to see what else was going on in the world. After all, life couldn't just be about pot and '70s rock, could it?

He also remembered why he had stopped watching local news in the first place. It was boring. Well, at least it was repetitive. How many times could you see reports of automobile accidents, political scandals and celebrity puff pieces? But recently there was a story that stood out.

"A fiery accident today took the life of Federal Judge Everett Walker and his driver. . ." the reporter said.

What? That's MY Judge! Donaldson thought.

He watched the rest of the report, then switched channels to another local station to see if they were reporting it too. Eventually he learned that the gasoline truck that was used came from a refinery that was shut down because the company cut back after the injunction; the injunction for which HE had petitioned this very judge, who was now dead.

What the heck is going on? Maybe I should have asked more questions before accepting that $50,000.

* * *

"Boss, I think we may have something on Jones," Agent Callie Strong informed Special Agent Wheeler. They had scoured St. Louis looking for the truck-thief-turned-murderer, but so far had found no trace of him.

"Yeah, what's that?"

"A car was stolen off a side street about the time of the gasoline truck explosion that killed the judge."

"Well, get an APB out on it!"

"Already done."

"What are you thinking Jones will do now?" Wheeler asked.

"I'd like to think he'd go back toward home, but I don't think we can count on that."

"No, he's got to know we're on his trail, so he's probably going the other way."

"Yeah, but does he have a support system going south?"

"As far as I know all his family is in the Midwest."

"So, somebody will spot him or he'll mess up and we'll find him," Strong commented optimistically.

"Yeah, but the circle of places he could be gets bigger with every passing hour."

"True that."

* * *

Because it was the middle of the night, no one was around as Jonesy parked as far from street lights as he could. This meant he was about 300 yards from his destination, to which he immediately began walking briskly.

It felt good to stretch his short legs in the night air after so many hours in the car. He wanted to get there and back to his car and on the road as fast as possible. Yet he didn't think running would be a good idea. He couldn't afford to do anything to call attention to himself. Finally, he saw what he was looking for: a home with a garden hose in the front yard. He watched the house for a couple of minutes but saw no lights and no signs of life, so he entered the yard and picked up the end of the hose, pulling it over under a tree where he would be shaded from the moonlight.

He took his pocket knife, opened it and quickly cut off the threaded brass connector on the end of the hose, then cut a length of hose about a yard and a half long and dropped the rest of the hose to the damp grass. He was turning to leave with the newly cut length of hose, when he noticed something else. It was a bucket of fertilizer with a garden trowel in it. He went over to it, quickly and quietly dumping out the fertilizer and the trowel. Then he paused. The bucket was dirty and he couldn't have that. He knew he was taking a huge chance, but he took the bucket toward the house, following the hose until he found the water spigot in the dark. He turned on the water and went back out to the cut end of the hose and thoroughly rinsed out the bucket.

He dropped the hose and looked back at the house as the water continued to flow out of the cut end and decided not to risk returning to the house to turn the water off. So, he returned to the street and walked back to his car.

He then drove until he saw the next thing he had decided he needed to find: a big-box-store parking lot where a few cars were parked some distance from the building. At this hour, they could only be cars belonging to employees still at work inside or people who had simply left their cars in the lot overnight. He looked up and down the street. No one was around.

He went from car to car until he found one that didn't have a locking gas cap or cover. He then returned to his stolen car and drove it over near the car with the open gas cap. He set the bucket down and put the hose deep into the gas tank. He sucked on the other end of the hose until the siphoning action pulled the precious gasoline into the bucket. Using an improvised paper funnel, he then poured the gasoline into his stolen car's tank. He was able to repeat this process six times before there was no more fuel to be had. He looked at the bucket and decided it would hold about two gallons, so he figured he now had between 10 and 12 gallons. In this fuel-efficient, foreign sedan, he could get a long way down the road with that much fuel.

He put the bucket and the hose in the trunk of his stolen sedan. He was about to get back in the car and drive away when he had another thought. He looked around at the few scattered cars in the lot and, taking a screwdriver from the toolbox in his duffle bag, he removed the license plate from "his" car. He then walked over to a car that was more or less similar to the Japanese sedan he had stolen in St. Louis and went down on one knee at the rear of the car. He laid the stolen car's license plate on the ground and took the screw driver to the license plate on the other car.

Soon he had the license plate off the car and had replaced it with the plate from the rear of the stolen car. He sucked in a lung full of the humid night air, and slowly got up again, his knees creaking. Then he began briskly walking back to his car, where he quickly installed the plate from the other car. Grimly he smiled, satisfied that he had sufficiently confused things by switching the plates that he would be more difficult to find. The police would be looking for the stolen car, but its plates were on an Arkansas car now. And, unless he missed his guess, the owner wouldn't notice that his plate had been switched for quite some time.

* * *

Agent Peter Gersich still wasn't sure how he ended up at the FBI. He was an accountant by training after all. But the FBI needed forensic accountants and Gersich had been one of the youngest CPAs around, which appeared to have hurt him on his first several interviews at Fortune 50 companies. So, when the offer came from the FBI, he took it. The weapons training had been unnerving, but he had managed to barely pass so he could remain in the program.

He also wasn't sure how he was chosen to go to Washington, D.C. He assumed agents with the most experience were sent here, even if it was the field office, as opposed to the J. Edgar Hoover building. Yet here he was and he had been called to the office of Special Agent in Charge Samuel Jorgensen himself.

He gave three timid taps on the door.

"Come in," Jorgensen said with his booming voice.

Gersich slipped his slight frame into the chair in front of Jorgensen's desk and pushed his glasses up on his nose. "You needed to see me, sir?"

"Yes, I'm hoping you can help me with something. Several of us have been looking at something from all angles, but we can't seem to break through."

Gersich listened as Jorgensen outlined Marvin Borelli's activities, with his history of financing violence.

"So, someone had to have provided the money, and we naturally figure it's one of his clients, but we haven't been able to shake anything loose."

Jorgensen slapped a stack of papers down on his desk in obvious frustration. As Jorgensen paused, Gersich asked, "So what would you like me to do?"

"I need fresh eyes to follow the money. So far Borelli won't talk, but there's got to be a paper trail."

"Are you sure it was one of his clients, or is that just the operative theory?"

"No, we're not sure, unfortunately. I know it may sound like I'm asking for a miracle, but we've just looked at it every way we can and I thought maybe you could take a look; see if you see what we didn't."

"All right, I can do that."

"And if there's any way for you to cyber-search or whatever, maybe you can find something that way." Jorgensen handed over a fat manila file. "Here's the information we have. Start with Borelli and go out from him, I guess."

"Yes, sir. Do you have any likely suspects?"

"Again, no. They're all squeaky clean as far as we have been able to tell, but someone gave Borelli the money and maybe others as well, like politicians who got contributions for voting for the gas tax bill."

"Yes, sir."

"And, while you're at it, I want you to explore a pet theory of mine," Jorgensen continued, though Gersich had assumed he was through. "I can't shake the feeling that the injunction in St. Louis is connected to the oil platform bombing. Again, I don't have any proof – yet – but I just think somebody's intent on keeping the gas tax in place. The bombing was the reason for the passing of the tax in the first place and the injunction was to keep the tax in place, so they just seem like they're both accomplishing the same thing."

"All right, sir."

"Thanks. Keep me apprised."

"Yes, sir."

As Gersich left Jorgensen's office he wondered where to begin finding what experienced agents had seemingly given up on and the perpetrator had likely gone to great lengths to hide.

* * *

"You're not my attorney."

"I didn't say I was YOUR attorney," Robert Thorne replied into the prison phone as he looked through the visitors-room glass at Marvin Borelli in his orange jumpsuit. His own attorney hadn't visited him since the FBI put him in Federal prison without explanation.

"So, what do you want with me?"

"You're in a very delicate situation and I'm here to get a read on your loyalty."

Borelli's face was one big question mark. "Loyalty to whom?"

"To the Cause. And to your employer."

"I work for myself, so I don't know who you mean, but I doubt I still have any clients." Borelli hadn't heard from any of his lobbying clients since his arrest.

"As I said," Thorne continued dispassionately, "you are in a delicate situation. Why do you think the FBI has moved you to Federal prison without setting a hearing date?"

Borelli scowled but said nothing. He was wondering that himself. Being in the general population at a Federal prison somewhere in 'Podunk,' Virginia, was many times worse than being held in FBI custody in Washington, D.C.

"They want you to talk. Our mutual employer needs to know if you are going to be strong or you'll fold."

"'Our mutual employer?' Like I said, I work for myself."

"Just know this," Thorne's voice deepened and got quieter. "If you talk, it may be Friday the thirteenth."

Borelli at first looked at the lawyer blankly, then comprehension dawned and he gasped involuntarily. When Thorne saw that, he hung up the phone, rose and turned to leave. It was several seconds before Borelli got up and asked a guard to take him back to his cell.

*　*　*

"Boss, we got a hit on that APB for Jones' stolen car," Agent Callie Strong informed Special Agent Wheeler as she entered his office without knocking.

"Where?"

"Hot Springs. Local PD found it abandoned in a parking lot."

"So, he's going south, like we thought."

"I guess. What do you want to do?"

"I want you to run down to Hot Springs and see if you can get any evidence from it."

"Yes, sir."

"I can't spare anybody to go with you, but I doubt you'll run into Jones. He's probably got another way to travel by now or he wouldn't have ditched the car. Meanwhile I'll alert all law enforcement departments south of Hot Springs, assuming he's continuing that direction."

"Yeah, I'll let you know what I find out," Strong said, turning to leave Wheeler's office.

*　*　*

The impound lot was in an industrial area of Hot Springs and Agent Callie Strong was accompanied by a young cop who appeared fresh out of the academy. She drove her car and he came along just to show the way and point out the stolen car.

"There it is," the young man said, pointing to a small import.

"Thanks," Strong said. She first looked at the tag on the rear of the car and compared it to the tag number on the stolen vehicle report of the car that was stolen in St. Louis. Sure enough, it was a match.

Even so, something seemed off to Strong, but she couldn't identify it, so she decided to continue investigating to confirm that Jones had been in the car.

She returned to her car and took a small forensics kit from her "go bag." With it she would do a preliminary analysis of the evidence and if she decided he had indeed stolen this car, she would have it hauled to St. Louis for a detailed forensic examination and she would be done for today.

She opened her kit and took out a fingerprint brush, then stopped. "Wait a minute, the stolen vehicle report says the car is gray," she said looking first at the young police officer and then at the printed report. "This car isn't gray! It's blue!"

"Well, I guess it could be blue-gray," the officer said.

Strong then walked quickly toward the front of the car

"There's no front license plate."

"Don't need 'em in Arkansas."

Right, Arkansas doesn't require front plates, Strong thought. "But the car Jones stole was a Missouri car. It should have a front license plate."

The young officer's face was blank.

Agent Strong then went to look at the VIN plate under the windshield in front of the driver's seat, comparing it to the report. "It's a different Vehicle Identification Number! This is not the same car!"

"It's not?"

"He switched the plates! This is not the car he stole at all. He's still driving it."

She paused for moment, then had a revelation. "The VIN will tell us whose car this really is and what the license number is," she exclaimed as she scribbled the VIN of the second car on her stolen vehicle report. "We need to get back to your precinct, get the tag number for this VIN from your DMV database and do a new APB!"

"Why?"

"Because that's the tag number on the car Jones is driving!"

* * *

Another day had passed and Jonesy had spent it sleeping in his stolen car somewhere in the mountains south of Hot Springs. His gas tank was not empty, but his stomach was. He had to do something soon.

But he also had begun to feel like he needed to ditch the car. It was bound to have been reported stolen by now and its proximity to the time and place of the gas truck explosion would make it easy for the cops to think he was the one who took it. Maybe he was just being paranoid, but he feared the ruse of switching the license plates wouldn't be enough if they were looking for this car.

A couple of hours after the sun disappeared through the pine trees to the west, Jonesy once again started his stolen sedan by hot-wiring it; something he had become expert at doing. As darkness descended on the Ouachita Mountains, he eased out onto the state highway, with only an occasional oncoming car meeting his with its headlights on bright. The remote area was exactly what he needed.

Then he saw it: a farm house that was dark except for a dim light on a pole. Jonesy wasn't sure what kind of farming could be done in these hills and pine forests, but he stopped anyway. There were several buildings behind the house and vehicles to the side. Jonesy reasoned that out here, people probably still didn't lock their doors.

After turning off the highway onto a dirt road a few hundred yards from the house, he slowed and, turning off his headlights, found an opening in the barbed-wire fence that lined the road on both sides. He pulled the sedan off the road and across a cattle guard. There was a low stand of trees along the barbed-wire fence and he pulled the car under one of them. He hoped there would be enough brush cover to prevent the car from being found for a while. Now he had to go see if he was right about country people locking their doors.

Before leaving the car, he gathered up his meager belongings, and, as an afterthought, removed the license tag from the sedan. Removing it would maybe slow down its identification and it might come in handy later.

He walked as silently as he could down the gravel driveway onto the farmhouse property, looking intently at the house and still seeing no activity. *People out here likely go to bed early*, he thought. Then he turned his attention to the vehicles.

There was a sedan, similar to what he had been driving; too similar, he decided. Next to it was a flatbed truck. It would be too distinctive, he told himself. Finally, there was a late-model pickup. *That would be perfect*. There would be scores like it on the road in the same color. Now if he could just get into it and get it started.

Moving to the driver's side of the pickup, which happened to be away from the house, he tried the door and found it unlocked. That was half the battle. He threw his duffle across the bench seat and climbed inside, checking the steering column for the ignition in the dark. There was no place for a key. *But wait! A lot of vehicles don't have keys these days*. He felt around the dashboard. There was a round button. He pushed it and the engine roared to life!

But the headlights and the radio came on as well, blaring some god-awful country song. He frantically searched for the switches to turn them off. After what seemed like an age, he located first the lights, then the radio and was once again in darkness except, for the light from the gauges on the dash. With a quick glance at the still-dark farm house, he slipped the truck into gear and slowly moved it down the driveway onto the country road, cringing at the noise of gravel crackling under the large tires, and headed back to the highway.

Only when he was a mile or two down the road did he think to look at the gas gauge and was gratified to see that it was at almost three-quarters of a tank. Next, he would find food. He still had enough cash for that, since he hadn't had to put out money for gas. He was sure there would be a truck stop ahead; the kind he had patronized many times in his years on the road, where the food was manly and portions were generous.

* * *

The phone on Patrick's desk rang insistently. Patrick ran into his office, just getting back from an editorial board meeting to snatch the receiver from its cradle.

"Garrity, this is your friend in the Justice Department," the voice on the other end of the line said. Patrick didn't need to ask the caller's name. He got periodic tips from this anonymous source, whom he had cultivated for years. They hadn't met face-to-face for a long time, to keep the source anonymous.

"What is it?"

"I thought you'd want to know: Former Senator Nathan Taylor is being officially indicted tomorrow."

"No joke? What's the charge?"

"Conspiracy and bribery."

"Really? Was there money other than campaign contributions?"

"I don't know about that; I've told you all I could find out without raising suspicion."

"Okay. Thanks. Will there be a press conference?"

"No, because he was a long-time Senator, they are trying to pick him up quietly."

"Tomorrow?"

"Yeah, bright and early."

Patrick hung up and immediately dialed another number. He had to wait while a receptionist transferred his call.

"Jorgensen."

"Sam, Patrick Garrity."

"What do you want?"

"Just checking: where are you on the investigation into Nathan Taylor?"

"Who said we were investigating Taylor?"

"Well, I know that the attack on Axiom's oil platform was a conspiracy and Taylor used it to pass the Petroleum Independence Act. Stands to reason he knew something."

Special Agent Samuel Jorgensen said nothing for several seconds and Patrick let him think of what he would say next.

"I'm not going to comment on this at all."

"You can't tell me where you are on the investigation?"

"I didn't say there was an investigation."

"Come on, Sam. I didn't just arrive in this town. Give me something."

"Sorry. Can't help you. Goodbye, Garrity."

"Just let me have something so I know where to look."

But there was silence, then a dial tone, on the line.

* * *

The next morning, Patrick and his photographer, Sanjay, drove to the Georgetown neighborhood where former Senator Nathan Taylor lived with his wife. They parked about a block away from Taylor's house. It was 5 a.m. and still dark.

"Okay, hopefully we're early enough."

"Oh, we're early enough," Sanjay yawned and raised his camera, peering through its long telephoto lens. "Nobody's stirring yet."

"Okay, we may have a long wait, but I doubt it. I figure the FBI will show up pretty soon, so they'll be sure to catch him home. Until we see something we can enjoy our coffee."

"Right, boss," Sanjay answered, taking his to-go cup from the cup holder in the center console.

They only had to wait about half an hour.

"Look. What's this?" Patrick said.

Sanjay sat up and looked through his telephoto lens again. "Yep, that's an Fed SUV if I ever saw one."

"Okay, let's go. I want you to get a good shot of Taylor being brought out."

Patrick took his mini recorder from his pocket, ready to fire questions at the soon-to-be-disgraced former Senator in the early-morning light.

They were walking on a sidewalk in front of the townhouses, trying not to call attention to themselves. Luckily, the FBI agents were focused on their mission and didn't pay any attention to the two men on the sidewalk.

As Patrick and Sanjay got close, the agents went inside and Patrick realized they had to stay close so they could ambush the agents and Taylor when they came out, but needed to continue not being noticeable.

"Let's sit down here," Patrick said, gesturing to the front steps on the stoop of the adjacent townhouse. "Try to appear casual," Patrick smiled and Sanjay put his camera with its flash and long lens in his lap, trying to make it as small as possible.

It took another ten minutes and then the front door opened again. Patrick watched briefly to let the first agent emerge, followed by another agent holding Taylor by the elbow.

"This is it!" Patrick said. "Let's go."

Sanjay stood and immediately pointed his camera and clicked the shutter. The flash lit up the early-morning shadows and Patrick sprinted toward the three men, who stopped their walk to the SUV and turned, surprised.

Patrick held his recorder in his extended right hand. "Senator, Patrick Garrity, Washington Herald. What do you say to the charges being made against you?"

Taylor's eyes landed on Patrick with confusion, then flashed with anger, but he said nothing.

"Stand back! Out of our way!" said the first agent.

"What are the charges against the Senator?" Patrick asked him without standing back or getting out of the way.

"No comment!" Taylor said, finding his voice.

"Did you accept bribes, Senator? Is that why you introduced the Petroleum Independence Act?"

Taylor's eyes shot daggers and the FBI agents were obviously no happier with Patrick and Sanjay, who continued firing his camera, capturing every angry facial expression and the dark suited men leading the former Senator away.

Finally, the agents got Taylor into the SUV and sped away.

"Okay," Patrick smiled at Sanjay, "Show's over. Good job."

Sanjay smiled back and began clicking through some of the digital shots on the screen on the back of his camera.

* * *

Patrick's front-page article about the arrest of Senator Nathan Taylor shocked the nation's capital and there were whispers of gossip, but also nervous, strangely quiet politicians who knew they might also have accepted money in exchange for their vote on the gas tax bill.

The Justice Department could not be as discreet as it had planned about the indictment, after all. A spokesman was forced to give a press conference in which he faced a press pool angry that Patrick had scooped them and that Justice would have kept the indictment quiet if they could have.

Patrick attended the press conference but didn't ask any questions; he had his scoop. And the Justice Department was still trying to be tight-lipped, giving out as little as possible.

* * *

The news of Senator Taylor's arrest was shocking. Jason Wood read the article three times, not knowing how the FBI could have enough evidence to call for an indictment.

They had covered their tracks very well, or so Wood thought.

Yet Marvin Borelli had been picked up and now Taylor! There were beginning to be too many loose ends; too many people who knew too much. Taylor himself didn't know specifics about Wood, but Borelli did. And Wood couldn't be sure how much George Donaldson knew. He could be a real problem. He probably wouldn't hesitate to spill everything he knew to save himself.

Something would have to be done, and soon.

* * *

Agent Callie Strong had been back to St. Louis only a couple of days when her APB with the revised tag number paid off. The car was found on a country road in southern Arkansas. There was no tag on the vehicle, but the Vehicle Identification Number matched the car that was stolen in St. Louis the day Judge Walker was killed.

"So, he's changed vehicles again," Special Agent Wheeler concluded when Strong gave him the news.

"Yes, and we know what vehicle he's using now," Strong said triumphantly. "A 2015 Chevy Silverado with a crew cab. It was stolen just a few yards from where the other stolen car was found, in a rural area in southern Arkansas. Here's the VIN on the truck," she said, handing him a stolen vehicle report. "It appears he's still going south, so we need to revise the APB. No telling what tag he's got on the pickup by now, but at least we know what he's driving."

"Okay. If he crosses into Texas or Oklahoma, we'll need to get the Dallas field office involved." Wheeler said. "Go ahead and give them a head's up. I figure he's going into Texas."

CHAPTER NINETEEN

A light rain was beginning to fall in Dallas; a welcome respite from the dry heat that was already beginning in April and would last until the end of September. In the northern suburb of Richardson, Petrocom Energy's headquarters was one of the tallest buildings in town. The appearance of prosperity was far from the reality, however. The boom days were long past. Today, the company was beset on every side it seemed.

Where regulation didn't hem it in, taxes did. When the volatile stock market went in his company's favor, lawsuits did not. The creases in CEO Gerald Tokalas' worried brow had become permanent, since there was no respite from the grinding gasoline tax.

The hope for repeal of the Petroleum Independence Act had evaporated with the injunction and Tokalas could see no rescue. The lawsuit by their stockholder was dragging on and the outcome was in doubt. He hated that his lot might be to manage the company's decline and death.

Sitting at his desk as he did every morning he wasn't travelling, he reached for the Dallas Morning News business section and scanned the tiny type of the stock exchange listings, gravitating naturally to his own company's stock with its daily dwindling value.

But what he saw stunned him. The stock price had plummeted 30% overnight! He was accustomed to seeing a steady, slow decline in the valuation of his company since the Act was passed and again with the lawsuit, but this was shocking. He immediately picked up the phone and dialed the number for his CFO.

"George!" he fairly shouted into the phone. "Have you seen the stock price this morning?... Well, get up here. We need to figure this out!"

Tokalas leaned back in his executive chair, fearing this might be the beginning of the end.

* * *

Dennis Trask was on his way to Jackie's office on the twentieth floor of Axiom headquarters.

"Good morning, Doris?" it sounded like a question.

"I suppose," Doris answered with uncharacteristic solemnity.

Dennis made no comment but motioned for Jackie's door and Doris waved him inside without rising.

When Dennis entered through the huge varnished-wood, double doors, he saw Jackie standing by the floor-to-ceiling window. The drapes were closed except for the section where she stood, leaving the room darker than it usually would be.

"Well, it's happened," Jackie said without turning around.

"I'm sorry. What's happened?"

"Petrocom is gone. They filed bankruptcy this morning."

"Bankruptcy? Chapter Seven?"

"Yep," Jackie answered in the colloquial Texan twang her father might have used.

"Whoa!" Dennis sank into one of the leather chairs in front of Jackie's desk without being bidden. "What happened?"

"Their stock tanked. Overnight. Not sure why."

Jackie finally turned to face Dennis and walked to her own chair behind her father's old desk and sat down.

"I guess we dodged a bullet," Dennis said, knowing he didn't need to reference the attempted merger.

"Well we dodged THEIR bullet. Don't know about our own."

Dennis rubbed his chin for a moment before answering.

"There's always a reason for a precipitous drop in the stock price if it's not in line with the rest of the market. Something has to cause it."

"It wouldn't happen if people just lost confidence? People all decide to sell at once?"

"Yes, that would do it, but it doesn't usually happen unless something drastic happens to trigger it, like a scandal or the death of a 'key man'. Let me make some calls and see what I can uncover. I'd bet the longhorns on Bud's El Dorado that there were some hijinks behind the scenes."

Jackie felt the warmth of a welcome, rare smile at Dennis' joke at Bud Eldridge's expense. Axiom's chairman of the board didn't really drive an El Dorado with longhorns on the hood, but it was a fitting caricature of that quintessential Texan.

"OK, let me know what you find out. If something underhanded is going on, we need to see it coming."

"Will do. Anything else?"

"No. Let's find some good news. I don't regard Petrocom's fate as good news, even though they were a competitor."

"No, it's not good news at all," Dennis said as he rose. "I should be able to know something by tomorrow."

"Thanks."

As Dennis softly closed the large door behind him, Jackie considered what he had said. Had someone done something to take down Petrocom? If so who? And why? She had no trouble thinking of who might want an oil company to fail. They had been dealing with the falling dominoes from the attack on the oil platform for a year now.

So much had happened, but it was all far from over.

How she hoped her own company would not end in bankruptcy court like her competitor.

* * *

A mud-caked pickup lurched to a stop on a hilltop near the little town of Paul's Valley, Oklahoma. The two men in the truck's crew cab just stared ahead at an idle drilling rig for a couple of minutes before one of them broke the silence.

"I guess we have to tell the men," Mack McElroy said softly.

"It's a cryin' shame," answered Kinsey Long, his partner in Sooner Partners, LLC, an independent oil exploration firm which had exclusively contracted with Petrocom Energy. They had been waiting for Congress to repeal the gas tax so the big refiners and gasoline retailers would be able to afford to resume buying crude oil.

"We can find another buyer," Long said absent-mindedly.

"Who's buying right now? Everybody's on hold 'til the tax is lifted," McElroy replied. "We can't pay men to stand around waiting for the government to get its act together."

"Yeah, but if we lay them off they can get unemployment."

"That doesn't help us," McElroy pointed out. "As owners and employers, we can't get unemployment. I've got to put clothes on three growing boys. I don't know how long I can hold on."

"Yep, me too. Sure glad we got rich in the oil bidness!"

They laughed bitterly before falling silent.

* * *

The sound of dishes, coffee cups and silverware on the lunch counter on a lonely road in Eastern Colorado echoed through the room as several large men sat perched on chrome and vinyl stools, eating large, fat-laden, bacon-and-eggs breakfasts and talking like old friends, because that's what they were. As truck drivers, they had seen one another periodically, if haphazardly, for years, often in far flung cities. They all spoke the same language of diesel fuel and long hours on the road.

"So, what're you doing now that Petrocom's goin' down?" asked one.

"I guess I'll be looking for a new gig, since my company has been hauling for almost nobody but them. I'm sure they'll try to find other loads, but I don't think they can get enough new business to keep going."

"Really? Is it that bad?"

"What're they going to do? It's not like this is a great economy to be completely changing our business."

"Yeah, but haulin' is haulin,' and there are other things to haul besides gas."

"Well, I heard a couple of suits talkin' yesterday in the depot and they seemed to think the company was gonna fold."

"Lord, Lord!"

"I guess that's where we are. Your company need drivers?"

"I can check."

* * *

"Sue, where is everybody?"

The question came from Larry Botski and was directed to his wife and business partner as they looked out the window of their food truck. The vehicle symbolized all their family's hopes and dreams as small-business owners. It was after noon and usually by this time they were mobbed by scores of hungry workers from the Petrocom storage and distribution facility in Olive Branch, Mississippi.

They had been too busy preparing the burgers and nachos that were their staples to notice that cars had been streaming out of the facility shortly after arriving all morning. Finally, one of their regular customers approached the truck.

"Hey, Larry, Sue," he said nodding to each of them. "They closed down this morning. No warning."

"What?!" Larry and Sue exclaimed in unison.

"Yeah, the whole company is going down. I guess the gas tax did it in. So, I'll buy one more burger and soda, but I guess it will be the last time."

After their lone customer left, Sue looked at Larry. "What are we going to do?"

"I guess we'll need to find another location that needs a food truck." Larry answered with the most hope he could.

The price of fuel had made it hard enough to make a profit in their business, but now, they might not have a business.

* * *

There were five screens in the office of Axiom's CFO, Dennis Trask. The 40-inch, High-Definition TV screen could display whatever was on his computer for viewing in small meetings at his small conference table or it could be switched to cable TV for seeing news or a business channel. His computer had two monitors, so he could compare spreadsheets or view any number of investment sites. A laptop and tablet rounded out the total of five, but that didn't count his smart phone.

He was sitting with his nose just six inches from one of the computer screens, close enough to see individual pixels, studying a graph of Axiom's stock price on an investment website. The trend was down, which was no surprise, with some upticks occasionally, but the overall trend was definitely down.

He knew the profit-loss statements for the past few months by heart, or at least close enough. The gas tax had necessitated watching every expenditure very closely. There was no profit to be had; his job was just a project of trying to make the loss as small as possible. The company couldn't continue like that for long. Closing down plants helped with payroll costs in the short run, but in the long run, shutting operations would reduce revenues as well.

That was the nature of business: keep revenue above expenses and put as much distance between them as possible. That was the only way to guarantee that product could be delivered to customers, employees could keep their jobs, and that stockholders could receive a return on their investment.

Dennis idly wondered why some people demonized "profit", as if there was a choice about whether to try to have one or not. Companies that consistently failed to make a profit went out of business, people lost their jobs, investors lost their investments and consumers didn't get served. In the case of Axiom, many of the investors were also employees, through the profit sharing program, and Dennis knew they didn't have the money to lose. Most of them had children to feed, clothe and send to college. Others were retired and depended on their investments in 401ks that rode the stock market rollercoaster. That some people thought the corporate "profit" the employees counted on was a bad thing was incomprehensible nonsense to him.

It was these small investors he was thinking about as he studied the downward staircase representing Axiom's stock price on the graph. His own portfolio had lost value, of course, but he was responsible for a lot more than just himself.

Suddenly, he zeroed in on a particularly precipitous drop in the price about three days ago. Clicking to look closer, he could see a lot of stock being sold at once. He switched to the adjacent screen where he had another web browser open showing a graph of the price of Petrocom stock over a couple weeks. He let out a low whistle as he compared the dates. Both companies had the same dramatic sell-off and drop in value the same day.

CHAPTER TWENTY

"Naked Shorting."

"What?" Jackie looked back at her CFO blankly.

"It's called 'Naked Shorting,'" Dennis Trask repeated. He had phoned ahead before asking for an impromptu meeting in Jackie's office with several members of Axiom's management that were available on short notice, including Legal V.P. Marcus Williams and President Benny Tyson.

"That sounds obscene."

"Well, in the world of investing, it IS kind of obscene."

"So, I know what it means to sell 'short,'" Jackie continued. "When a trader pays a fee to 'borrow' a stock and sells it, counting on the stock price falling so he can later buy it at the lower price, return it to the owner from whom it was borrowed and pocket the profit."

"Right, that's legal and nobody has a problem with it. 'Naked Shorting,' on the other hand, is when the trader doesn't follow through to buy the stock, so the unsuspecting buyer of the 'borrowed' stock doesn't ever receive the stock they bought."

"And you think that's what's going on with our stock?" asked Benny Tyson.

Dennis pointed at a line of numbers and symbols on the large flat-screen monitor to the right of Jackie's desk where he had called up the figures for Axiom's stock performance. "Look at this record of the past week. See what's happened to our stock price?"

"Yes, it's fallen like a rock," Marcus said bitterly, "But it's been falling for months."

"All too true, but why do you think there would there be a dramatic fall now?"

"The injunction and plant closures?" Jackie suggested.

"No doubt those things hurt our stock price," Dennis continued, "but they happened weeks ago. The market usually reacts within hours of an announcement like that."

"So, you think someone sold a lot of our stock without actually owning the stock?" Benny asked. "I can understand why someone would try to manipulate the stock price to earn a profit, but why wouldn't they then buy the stock at the lower price and reap the profit?"

"There could be a couple of reasons," Dennis replied. "One reason people usually do Naked Shorts is because they then keep the entire higher price of the sale, so their profit is 100 percent. It's the same as if you stole a car and then sold it for the blue-book value."

"But I sense that you think something else is going on," Jackie said, reading between the lines.

"I actually started to think about this when I saw what happened to Petrocom. The other reason for Naked Shorting is to manipulate the market. It's the dark underbelly of trading, where the traders drive a company into bankruptcy so they can profit from its demise."

"So, you think someone is purposely trying to drive our stock price down to put us out of business?" Marcus asked, appearing to bristle at the idea. Jackie could feel her own ire rising as she gradually comprehended the implications.

"It wouldn't be the first time."

"But wait, I don't understand something," Jackie said. "Why don't Federal regulators reverse the fraudulent trades when the 'naked shorters,' or whatever they're called, don't follow through and buy the stock. Isn't there a time limit?"

"Yes, there is. Three days. But the SEC sees billions of trades in that amount of time on the various exchanges, so it can't usually analyze a single trade to enforce the rule. It can eventually charge habitual offenders, but individual trades usually go through without the government doing anything."

"That's outrageous!" Jackie exclaimed as she leaned back and crossed her arms. *Someone could be trying to put us out of business and the regulators who are charged with watching things wouldn't even try to stop it?!*

Dennis shrugged as if to say, *what are you going to do?*

"So, if someone sells a 'borrowed' stock," Jackie continued, "and never actually buys the stock to replace the borrowed shares, that means the stock they sold never existed?"

"Exactly. And that's how it manipulates the market. If someone is able to borrow and sell enough shares of stock which never get returned, those become phantom shares, which increases the number of outstanding shares being traded beyond the actual number available."

"The market is flooded and value is diluted," Benny put in.

"Right again. If the number of phantom shares being traded is a large enough percentage of the total shares available before the phantom shares were created, simply increasing the number of shares reduces the value of the real shares. And when that happens, real stockholders get nervous and begin selling their real stock, which drives the price down further."

"So, what do we do, if the SEC isn't likely to do anything?" Jackie asked, frowning.

"Well, you know people at the FBI, right?"

"Yeah. You think this is malicious?"

"Wouldn't that fit with what we've experienced the past several months?"

"Yes, but what can we do in the meantime? It could take the FBI months to find out who's doing it."

"There is something we can do," Dennis said, looking around the table. "Buy back our stock. That would show that we have confidence in our company."

"I suppose that might inspire confidence," Jackie mused, "but would it be enough to stop the slide into oblivion?"

"It might be the only way."

"But if the stock is going to take a dive, is it wise to go all in?" Benny asked.

"That's when we SHOULD go all in," Jackie said. "Dennis how much stock is likely to be involved in this manipulation?"

"It might only be five percent, but it could be enough to start a panic."

"Then, here's what I want to do," Jackie slapped the table, causing the men to start, and stood to her feet to lend herself more authority. "I want us to buy all the stock we can get our hands on. If somebody's out there selling, we need to snap it up to show there's no reason to panic!"

"Ms. James, that seems risky," Benny began.

"Everything is at risk here, Benny! You saw what happened with Petrocom. If this is malicious, it means we're next. This demands decisive action now!"

Then she looked at Marcus. "Is there anything in the bylaws that limits our ability to buy back our own stock?"

"There is a limit without a vote of the board, but I don't know off the top of my head what it is."

"Then here's what we are doing: we're going to buy all we can get right up to the limit and if we need to do more, we'll call an emergency meeting of the board."

She looked around the table and then added, "And here's another thing: I have a diversified personal investment portfolio. I'm going to call my broker as soon as we get out of this meeting and order him to sell every stock I own except Axiom and use the money to buy Axiom stock until there's none available," she paused only to take a breath.

"I can't tell you what to do, but if you care about this company and your place in it, I'd advise you to do the same. This is an emergency and we've got to do what we're going to do quick, right Dennis?"

"That's exactly right, ma'am. It is urgent! At least now is a good time to buy. After the gas tax is finally repealed and the stock price goes back up, we can sell and take a hefty profit."

"Okay, then. Dennis, you can place the buys. Get whatever you can. Marcus, you nail down the limit on buying our own stock in the bylaws and let Dennis know when he has to quit. Benny, you put together a notice to the board members about an emergency meeting if we need to have one. We may not but we've got to be ready. We do this today!"

"Yes, ma'am," they said in unison.

* * *

"Do you have evidence?" Special Agent Jorgensen asked.

Jackie had called him because she figured he would be the most likely to know who to reach out to in the Byzantine Federal Government. Because it was potentially stock manipulation, she knew the Securities and Exchange Commission would be a logical place to call, but she didn't know anybody there. On the other hand, the Secret Service in the Treasury Department was in charge of cybercrime and if someone was manipulating the market they were almost certainly doing it over the Internet.

She knew that Jorgensen had been involved with Axiom's investigations almost since the attack on the Gulf Pride platform last year, so he was her best contact.

"No real evidence. We just watched one of our competitors go down the tubes and we are seeing a similar pattern in our own stock performance. My CFO thinks someone is manipulating the market."

Jorgensen paused before saying, "Well, that IS interesting and might fit with something else I'm looking at."

"What's that?"

"I can't tell you that right now, but I will definitely look into it and I'll be in touch."

"OK. Thanks."

As Jackie hung up the phone, she was surprised a call to a government agency might actually be acted upon rather than being kicked to another agency. Jorgensen seemed to already see a link to something he was investigating. Her curiosity was raging about what he knew and who he was investigating.

She just hoped he would find something in time.

* * *

"It looks like it worked."

Jackie was looking at the graph Dennis had pulled up on the large screen to the side of her desk showing Axiom's stock price having stabilized for the past three days.

"I suppose it's too much to hope that the price might start moving back up," Dennis commented.

"I'm just glad it's not falling further," Jackie answered. "That's the best we can expect until our situation changes."

"I'm glad you insisted that we do the stock buyback. I think that may have just saved us."

"Well, I just figure, if we aren't confident in our company's viability, no one else will be."

"I think you're exactly right."

"I just wish I knew who was trying to sink us," Jackie said with worry creasing her brow.

"Maybe the FBI will find something soon."

"It can't be too soon."

CHAPTER TWENTY-ONE

This is a wretched place, Jonesy thought. But this was what he was reduced to: staying in homeless shelters to have an opportunity to sleep in a bed instead of his stolen pickup, which was hidden several miles out of town.

He was in Texarkana, Texas, now. He stopped there because, he had reasoned, it was big enough to have a homeless shelter, but small enough that the law enforcement presence might not be alert enough to spot him.

He was in bed for the night and was looking forward to a good breakfast in the morning. There were other men in the room, some of whom were snoring. The smell of cleaning products was inescapable in the shelter, along with other smells that were not as welcome.

The people who ran the shelter were kind and conscientious; they belonged to some brand of protestant church. Jonesy didn't mind their overt attempts to proselytize the occupants of the shelter. He did, however, mind that they were intent on their "clients" finding jobs. That couldn't happen for Jonesy. He couldn't do anything that would put him on the radar.

The place was "wretched" mostly because of the other occupants of the shelter. Most of them were just pitiful; down on their luck and unable to pull themselves up, even with assistance, but there were a few who seemed like they could be a threat. They were either fugitives from the law like Jonesy himself, or they were addicts of some sort who had let their addiction ruin them. There were a few who were mentally unbalanced, which could mean they were just annoying, but it could also mean they were volatile and dangerous.

This was Jonesy's third night here and he was thinking it should be his last. He didn't feel comfortable staying in one place too long. He figured law enforcement had sent his picture out to agencies and departments all over and he couldn't risk someone recognizing him.

How he missed Margaret and Leslie. And Amber. He buried his face in the pillow so no one else would hear his sobs.

* * *

"Daddy, I seen a truck down by the creek by the highway bridge yesterday and again today," said young Ethan Willis after supper.

"What's so unusual 'bout that?" Tom Willis, Ethan's father, didn't have to ask why he was near the creek. Eleven-year-old Ethan passed that way every day on his way home from school.

"'Cause it was covered up, like somebody's hidin' it."

"Was it on our land?" the farmer asked his son.

"Yep, it was this side of the highway, but it's down by the creek covered by a tarp where nobody could see it."

Tom Willis considered what his son had said. "Let's hop in the truck and you show me exactly where it's at."

Ethan ran out the door of the farm house to get in the pickup, excited for an adventure on a late Spring evening.

* * *

The sun was very low in the west when Tom Willis and his son Ethan pulled off to the side of U.S. Highway 67 east of Texarkana and stopped.

"See it Daddy?"

"Actually, no I don't. Take me down there."

With the waning light, it was relatively dark down by the creek, so Tom retrieved a powerful flashlight from his pickup-bed toolbox. They began the steep descent through tall Johnson grass from the bridge to the creek below, struggling not to be tripped up by the tall grass.

Tom finally saw the dark mass under a Black Oak tree as Ethan continued pointing every few seconds. They approached it cautiously.

"Did you look under the tarp?" Tom asked.

"No!"

Tom could see the tires and part of the body of the dust-caked pickup below the tarp and decided no one could be inside the truck because, in the premature Texas heat, they would be dead. The corners of the tarp were weighted by rocks from the creek bed. Tom rolled one away with his boot and cautiously lifted the edge of the tarp.

Inside the cab, he could see a lot of trash and was immediately struck with the thought that someone must be living in it. They were gone now, but they might come back. He lifted the tarp some more and saw the Arkansas license tag.

"You say this was here yesterday, too?"

"Yeah."

"You did right showing me this. I think we better let the Sherriff know about it. One thing for sure, it don't belong here on our land!"

* * *

The Sherriff's office took its time getting over to see the apparently abandoned truck. It was late the next day when lanky Deputy Lucas LeBrand was dispatched to the scene. He was the youngest and newest member of the Bowie County

Sherriff's department, so he got all the "cat-in-a-tree" assignments. So far, he thought police work was pretty boring.

He parked his department-owned Ford Explorer on the shoulder of U.S. 67 and looked down toward the creek bank. It was getting late and the sun was not much help in the shadows down by the creek.

"This is LeBrand. Just arrived at the scene. I'm checkin' her out," he notified dispatch on his radio.

LeBrand didn't see any tracks but it had been dry and the ground had baked hard and then cracked open in the Texas sun, so a vehicle couldn't be expected to leave tracks. Finally, he spotted it as he climbed down the steep bank. When he got to it, he threw back the tarp. Sure enough, it looked like someone had been living in it.

He nudged his Sherriff's Department cowboy hat back off his forehead, then pulled out his notebook and jotted down the tag number. He then keyed the mic on his radio.

"Found it. Can you check Arkansas tag number SJD-K62?"

Momentarily the answer came back. "That's a 1999 Honda Accord registered to. . ."

"Not hardly. It's on what's gotta be at least a 2012 Chevy Silverado with a crew cab. It ain't no Accord! I do believe we got a stolen tag right here. And a stolen vehicle, too, most likely."

LeBrand then walked around the pickup, shining his flashlight in the bed, which was empty and into the cab, where he saw a duffle bag in the back seat, a rats' nest of snack

213

wrappers and drink cans. He stopped at the windshield on the driver's side and shown the flashlight at the VIN plate.

The officer raised his head. *What was that?* Did he hear something? Now the night was quiet except for the crickets and bullfrogs announcing the darkness descending on the creekbank. *Probably nothing.*

"I got the VIN on this truck, you wanna see if it's in the computer?" he said into the radio.

"Shoot," replied dispatch.

Deputy LeBrand read the long vehicle identification number off and continued examining the truck while waiting for dispatch to come back, thinking, *this is one sweet ride, but it needs a good washing.*

"Lucas, that's affirmative on the stolen vehicle," dispatch said on the radio after a couple of minutes. "I'm sending someone out with a forensics kit. You stay put."

"10-4." This was the boring part. He now had to make sure nothing was disturbed until the lab guy arrived. That meant climbing back up to his truck and getting the crime scene tape and establishing a perimeter for the lab guy to work in.

He looked at the truck once more. *I can see why someone might wanna take it,* he thought. *It's a sweet ride for sure.*

He turned to start back up the hill but was suddenly startled in the dark by a disheveled man with a rock in his hand.

* * *

Jonesy lunged at the Deputy reaching high to slam the rock into the left side of his head as hard as he could. Blood flowed from Lebrand's cheekbone and Jonesy immediately hit him again near the temple.

The stunned Deputy was falling backwards but even as he was falling he was trying to pull his 9mm Glock from its holster. Jonesy tackled him and threw him to the ground, grabbing his right arm to keep his hand away from the gun.

His weight holding the slender deputy down, Jonesy held the deputy's right arm with his left hand and, with his right, struck him once more with the rock right in his face. The deputy went limp and didn't move as blood began trickling out of his nose.

Breathing hard, Jonesy rolled off the officer and tried to think of what to do next. *This Mayberry reject has probably called in the information about the truck.* That might alert all the law enforcement looking for him. And now they could add assaulting an officer to his list of crimes.

He cursed under his breath in the gathering darkness. He had known he needed to get rid of the truck. He had had it too long. And he shouldn't have left it here for three days, but the bed in the shelter was too comfortable.

Now what? he asked himself and cursed silently again.

* * *

It had been a long drive from St. Louis, but at least the government-issue Ford LTDs were comfortable, Special Agent

Darren Wheeler thought. A couple of agents had come over from Dallas and they were all getting the latest from the Bowie County Sherriff's Department.

"How's your Deputy?" Wheeler asked.

"He'll be fine after his broken nose heals. I guess we can't call him green anymore," Sherriff Aldus McKay laughed, then turned serious. "The suspect took his firearm, though."

"I wouldn't have expected anything else. At least he didn't use it. It could have been a lot worse. So, any idea where our suspect went from here?"

"No idea at all. How do you know he's the guy? Lebrand wasn't able to give much of a description."

"Oh, he's the guy all right," Wheeler assured him. "Stealing a tanker in Indiana, killing a judge in Missouri, then stealing a car in Missouri, whose plates end up on a truck he stole in Arkansas. The only thing left is to get the DNA report from the candy wrappers."

"Why do you think he left the truck?" asked one of the agents from Dallas.

"Probably figured it was burned and there'd be a BOLO out for it, which there sure as heck would have been," McKay said.

"So where is he now?" the other Dallas agent asked.

"Keep drawing the line from Indiana through here and what have you got?" Wheeler said.

"Mexico," McKay replied. "But how's he travelling?"

"Either stole another car or stole the money for bus fare," Wheeler said, "That's why we've got to check every bus station and every stolen vehicle report from here to McAllen."

CHAPTER TWENTY-TWO

He supposed he ought to head to bed, but it didn't matter what he did. He had no one to answer to and no one checking on him. George Donaldson was an island of anonymity, in spite of his recent exposure in the press.

He had finished his microwaved supper hours ago and now had finished a joint while downing a series of shots of Scotch, so he was very relaxed. After a false start, he was able to get up off the couch and stumble off toward the bedroom.

He went into the master bathroom and gave his teeth a perfunctory brushing, because it was a habit his mother had made him form early. Besides he preferred a clean mouth.

He stripped down to his underwear and threw back the covers on his never-made bed. He sat rather than lying down and reached over to get a TV remote from the nightstand. He snapped on the new, big-screen and changed the channel to a local station, but realized he was too late for the news. He cursed and snapped the TV off again and threw the remote in the general direction of the night stand, then laid back and turned off the bedside lamp.

He lay still for a bit, then opened his eyes. *Is my mind playing tricks on me?* He thought he had heard something inside the house, but he didn't have pets, so what could have made a noise?

Grumbling, he got out of bed again and walked out into the hall and listened. Hearing nothing, but feeling sure he had heard something, he walked toward the front of the house and entered the living room. He looked around, then reached to turn on a table lamp.

That was the last thing he ever did.

* * *

Special Agent Darren Wheeler knew it was no one's fault that Tobias Jones had been able to enter St. Louis undetected, but the assassination of a Federal judge in his jurisdiction would not make any of the higher-ups in the Bureau consider him for promotion any time soon.

It had only taken a few minutes to put two-and-two together and realize why Jones had targeted Judge Walker. The plant closing and theft of the tanker truck was common knowledge and the St. Louis office of the FBI was one of many on a list that had been keeping an eye out for the truck.

Of course, no one could have known what was in Jones' mind. The only break they had was the night before when he called home and the Gary, Indiana, police picked it up because of their tap. They had let Wheeler's office know that Jones had called from St. Louis but that had been only a few hours before he had killed the judge.

So, it was no one's fault; it couldn't have been stopped. But that didn't make him feel any better.

The fact that it had happened in their jurisdiction was motivating all his agents to now leave no stone unturned as they uncovered more and more information in their investigation. They knew what kind of vehicle he had stolen and were in communication with police, sheriff and state trooper offices throughout a widening circle spreading out first from St. Louis and now from Texarkana.

They believed Jones had killed the judge because the injunction had caused him to be laid off, so they had also subpoenaed the transcript of the hearing which led to Walker's injunction and that's when they found George Donaldson's name. Wheeler had never heard of the "Aquarian Community", so they had a lot to learn from him.

Wheeler sent two agents out to O'Fallon to interview him.

* * *

Agent Callie Strong and her young, lanky partner, Don "Junior" Anderson, pulled up in front of George Donaldson's house in O'Fallon, Missouri, in their government-issue Ford sedan about noon. They exited the car, walked up the cracked concrete walkway between two patches of ill-kept lawn and mounted the steps to the broad porch.

Anderson rang the doorbell, but heard nothing, so he waited a few seconds and knocked.

There was no response, so Anderson knocked again.

"I'll check around back," Anderson said. Callie nodded her understanding of their practiced protocol that he would check to see if Donaldson was home but hiding.

While she was waiting, she knocked again for good measure, then looked through a window to the right of the door.

"Junior, get back up here!" Strong shouted into her comm. "I got a body."

Anderson returned to the front of the house just as Callie was picking the lock on the front door. They went in together, pistols in hand, and Anderson finally saw what Callie had seen through the window: a man matching Donaldson's description was lying on the living room floor in his underwear with a circle of dark blood under him on the carpet.

* * *

Special Agent Wheeler stood on the front lawn of George Donaldson's house watching the forensics team moving in and out of the front door with their equipment.

"Yeah, it's George Donaldson, all right," said Agent Callie Strong. "His driver's license was still in his wallet in his bedroom. And the fact that the wallet still had cash and credit cards in it rules out robbery."

"Nothing was taken? So, what does it look like?" asked Wheeler.

"It looks like someone wanted him dead. Why I don't know."

"Well, hopefully the forensics report will reveal something," Wheeler said, "but a couple of possibilities come to my mind."

"What's that, sir?"

"It's possible that Tobias Jones came to O'Fallon to kill Donaldson. It was his petition, after all, that led to the judge's injunction, which led, in turn, to the plant shut down, which cost Jones his job."

"You think so? The blood looks pretty fresh and we know Jones left Missouri several days ago."

"We'll see what the forensics say, but it might make sense. Our theory is Jones killed the judge because the injunction got him laid off and Donaldson petitioned for the injunction."

"I sense a 'but,'" Strong said.

"Yeah, I don't expect the forensics to agree and I wonder if Jones would've have gone out of his way to kill Donaldson."

"But who then? What's the second possibility?"

"That's just it," Wheeler looked around the yard. "I don't know who else would have wanted Donaldson dead. It's just my gut making me wonder if there's more than meets the eye; something someone needed to hide."

"You think Donaldson was killed to shut him up?"

"I don't know, but it's our job to find out."

* * *

The living room was dark and he hadn't turned on a light because the gloom matched his mood.

Patrick was just hanging on by his fingernails, or so it seemed to him. His lapse into drinking again had shaken him and, though he had managed to pull it together with the help of his AA sponsor, his nerves were raw and his work was suffering.

He was sitting on the couch in his generic two-bedroom apartment, a battle going on in his mind. He had not gone to the Blue Ribbon Grill since falling off the wagon, though he missed it terribly. But it was too easy to order a drink there. It hadn't been a problem for several years, but now he didn't dare go there, at least for a while.

He hadn't gone anywhere else either. He wondered if there was anything decent to eat in his refrigerator. Chances were good the answer was "no."

Rather than check, he decided to watch some news, so he grabbed the remote and turned on the TV, which was already tuned to Fox News.

"...was the plaintiff in the petition for the injunction that stopped the repeal of the Petroleum Independence Act," the female anchor said.

What? Are they talking about George Donaldson?

Patrick kept listening as they showed footage of George Donaldson's home in O'Fallon, Missouri, surrounded by police, FBI, Emergency Medical personnel and news media.

Eventually the anchor came back around to the lead: "If you're just joining us, George Donaldson, executive director of the Aquarian Community, which successfully petitioned in Federal Court for an injunction to stop the repeal of the Petroleum Independence Act was found dead in his home today, the victim of a gunshot wound. Law enforcement has not ruled out suicide, but has said it seemed doubtful.

"It was just last week that the judge who handed down the injunction, District Court Federal Judge Everett Walker, was killed in St. Louis."

Patrick sat back and put his hand on his forehead. *What are the chances?* he asked himself. The judge is killed and now the plaintiff? Wildly different methods, admittedly, but both apparently murdered? Had Tobias Jones killed Donaldson too? That made sense in a way. He was upset about the injunction which cost him his job, so maybe he was taking it out on everyone involved.

He thought about Jackie; was she on Jones' list? He wished she would answer his calls. If Jones had killed again, it would add to her stress that a former employee was on a killing spree.

He knew there was no point in calling, but she needed to know what he had learned about Champions of Mother Earth being a client of both the lobbyist, Borelli, and the Bellingham, Washington, law firm to which Donaldson had pointed him.

He decided he needed to talk to her whether she liked it or not, and that might require doing something extreme.

CHAPTER TWENTY-THREE

"Can we really do that?"

"I think it's the best recourse," Marcus answered Jackie. "The judge died before the trial, so another judge in the Eastern District of Missouri would need to be appointed and a new trial date set. Who knows how long that would take?"

"But to appeal to the Supreme Court?"

"We have to appeal to the Eighth Circuit to let us go right on to the Supreme Court, of course, but I've consulted our outside counsel and they say it's our best shot at a speedy resolution," Marcus Williams sat with Jackie at the small conference table in a corner of her office. His short legs were crossed as he leaned back from the table which had a stack of papers he had brought, in case Jackie needed to see precedents. She didn't.

"Well, we definitely need this resolved quickly. Do you know the process of appealing to the Supreme Court?"

"I had a cup of coffee at the Supreme Court once, but I definitely wouldn't try to do it myself. Our outside counsel has referred us to a firm in D.C. that specializes in representing before the high court."

"Sounds expensive," Jackie said dryly.

"Not as expensive as bankruptcy."

"Yeah, I guess. OK, I think we'd better run this by the board. This is a major step."

"Yes, that's right. I've already put in a call to the D.C. firm that I was referred to. They're available."

"So, get them here A-S-A-P!"

"Will do. By the way, what do you hear from the FBI?" Marcus knew about the potential stock manipulation from the meeting where Dennis had outlined his suspicions for Axiom's upper management.

"Well, it was interesting. I called the agent I know in D.C., Jorgensen, and he's looking into it."

"He didn't pass the buck?"

"No. I fully expected him to send me to the SEC or Treasury, but he hinted that he already had relevant information in his current investigation."

"Hmm," Marcus said. "So, there may actually be criminal market manipulation going on connected to his investigation into our attack?"

"He didn't say."

"That could be important to our case. When will you know more?"

"He said he'd let me know, I guess when he knows more."

"Yes, the more I think about it, the more important this is to getting relief in our situation," Marcus said, stroking one of his several chins. "I'll go right now and make contact with the firm in D.C. and give them this tidbit. The wheels of justice move slowly, but this might just grease the skids a bit."

"I'm sorry, Ms. James," Doris stuck her head in through the double doors. "Sorry to interrupt."

"No problem. What is it Doris?"

"Something just came over the news. The leader of the organization that petitioned for the injunction in Missouri has been found dead."

"What? When?"

"Just today I guess."

"Do they know who did it?"

"They haven't said."

"What on earth?" Jackie said, looking at Marcus, who was obviously dumbfounded.

* * *

"Okay, here's what is going to happen," began Marcus Williams, Axiom's legal VP. "We're going to St. Louis to appeal the injunction in the Eighth Circuit Court of Appeals and petition to appeal directly to the Supreme Court, which would permanently decide the fate of the bill to repeal the Petroleum Independence Act."

Marcus was addressing a group of Axiom management plus Bud Eldridge, chairman of the board, who had gathered in the boardroom on the twentieth floor of the black and gold tower in Houston. His long legs with his signature cowboy boots were crossed with one knee above the top of the conference table and his Cowboy-chic suitcoat was open across his pot belly.

Also at the table was Daniel Moreau, a representative of Sinclair-Roberts-Dubois, the Washington, D.C., law firm Marcus hired to guide them through the maze of Federal judicial protocol, precedent and process. Designated as lead attorney for this petition, Moreau, in his 50s with close-cropped hair and tailored suit, was the picture of a knowledgeable, as well as formidable, Washington, D.C., lawyer.

"Ordinarily, there would have been a trial in the Eastern District of Missouri, which is housed in the same Federal Building in St. Louis as the Eighth Circuit, to decide whether the injunction would become permanent, but there is nothing ordinary about this situation." Marcus saw nods of acknowledgement around the table.

"First, the judge who handed down the injunction is dead. We certainly don't celebrate his death. It definitely muddies the water and, if anything, makes things more difficult. Second, the leader of the organization that petitioned for the injunction is also dead, apparently murdered."

Marcus knew he wasn't telling them anything they hadn't already heard, but he needed to give them the basis of the case they would be presenting in St. Louis.

"Third, the judge's injunction is hurting nearly everyone in the country, not the least of which are our customers, whose lives are made more difficult with the high price of fuel and everything that descends from that.

"And, while we don't have specifics, the FBI has an ongoing investigation based on the theory that the injunction may have been just as much a conspiracy as the oil platform bombing; maybe even some of the same players, especially after the murder of the petitioner.

"In view of all this, we believe – that is I and Sinclair-Roberts-Dubois," Marcus gestured to Moreau. "We believe we could get the injunction lifted by petitioning the Eighth Circuit to allow us to appeal directly to the Supreme Court."

Jackie saw nods of comprehension around the table.

"Question." It was Bud. "Is there any issue of Axiom's right to petition in this matter? After all, the injunction was between some group nobody ever heard of and the Federal government. That's who would have been at the table for the trial, right? If they weren't all dead, I mean."

Nobody felt like laughing at Bud's poorly timed joke.

"That's right," Daniel Moreau answered without standing. "But that trial can't happen now, so unless someone comes forward with an appeal before the Eighth Circuit, nothing might happen, or maybe another judge would take it up a year from now. My understanding is time is of the essence."

"Darn tootin'!" Bud answered.

"So, as I said," Marcus continued. "While we don't rejoice at the judge's death, or the petitioner's death for that matter, it does provide an opportunity. We can show that we are being harmed by the injunction and therefore have reason to come before the court."

"So, will we then be the plaintiff against the Federal government?" Jackie asked.

Marcus looked at Moreau.

"Yes," Moreau answered. "We will be appealing the Federal District Court injunction to the Eighth Circuit Court of Appeals and we will make it plain that, in view of the events surrounding the death of the judge, as well as the murder of the petitioner and the conspiracy that surrounds the whole business, the injunction should be vacated and the repeal should proceed as voted by Congress."

"But can't the District Court just rescind the injunction?" Jackie asked.

"They could, but the death of the judge complicates it and they might not be inclined to overturn Judge Walker's injunction. Plus, if they had the trial and ruled in favor of the injunction, we'd have to appeal it anyway. That's why we need to appeal to the Eighth Circuit to issue a judgment. Then when we go to the Supreme Court, the District Court will be the defendant, defending the injunction that was handed down by the judge in their jurisdiction."

"Can the Eighth Circuit refuse our appeal to go to the Supreme Court?" asked President Benny Tyson.

"Yes, but knowing the Eighth Circuit judges as I do," began Moreau, "I think they will see the need to have this decided by an impartial court. They likely have very strong feelings about the whole matter, due to the fact that one of their own was killed. Technically they could refuse our appeal, yes, but we will be very clear that if the Eastern District hears the case themselves and upholds the injunction, we will appeal anyway. So, we'll say, it would make more sense to go ahead and let the high court hear it."

"Cuttin' out the middle man!" Bud exclaimed. "I like it!"

The Axiom other managers looked at each other, not feeling too reassured.

* * *

"Get on with it!" Special Agent Wheeler was growing impatient. He was now in Dallas, listening to some pretty thin, evidence-free scenarios; conjecture on the whereabouts of Tobias Jones being put forward by agents of the Dallas field office of the FBI. After his brush with the Sherriff's department in Texarkana, he had abandoned the stolen truck and pretty much disappeared.

"Why don't we know more?" Wheeler asked after no one responded. "This guy can't have just vanished."

The Dallas agents looked at one another. They didn't know Wheeler and couldn't gauge how extreme his reaction truly was.

"Special Agent Wheeler, we've got BOLOs out all over the eastern part of the state," said one of the Dallas agents. "If he shows himself, we'll know."

"There's no report of a stolen car near Texarkana," a female agent submitted, "so he's either laying low or taking the bus."

"What did we get from the bus station in Texarkana?" Wheeler asked.

"Well, none of the ticket agents recognized him and, if he bought a ticket, he apparently paid with cash."

"Yeah, he's pretty ordinary looking," Wheeler admitted. "We've just got to think he's going to make a mistake and we've got to be there when he does."

"There's one other possibility," another agent said, timidly. "He could have hitchhiked, in which case we'd be even less likely to spot him."

Wheeler scowled at the scuffed, vinyl-tile floor.

* * *

It had been years since he had ridden a Greyhound bus. The people riding with him gave him a wide berth, because, Jonesy was sure, he looked like a wild man and smelled horrendous. His hair and beard were not too bad, since he had been able to bathe and shave and wash his clothes at the homeless shelter. But that had been a couple of days ago, and he figured he was looking and smelling pretty rough again.

He looked out at the flat, south Texas landscape. He had bought a ticket to San Antonio, reasoning that the police or rangers or FBI, whoever was pursuing him, would expect him to go directly to Mexico. That was his ultimate destination, but he had taken a circuitous route to throw them off his scent.

After his brush with the "Mayberry" cop near Texarkana, he had reluctantly left "his" truck and fled across several square miles of farmland in the dark, often staying in creek bottoms to ensure he would not be seen. When he figured out where he was, he realized he had gone back toward Texarkana and saw this as an opportunity. He wouldn't go back to the homeless shelter, but had walked through a suburban neighborhood in the wee hours of the night and broken into a backyard shed, where he stole some high-dollar power tools. He had hidden them on a vacant lot and, once it was daylight, asked a passerby where he might find a pawn shop.

It had taken most of the day for him to retrieve the heavy tools, make his way on foot to the nearest pawn shop, complete the transaction to get some cash and then walk several miles to the bus station, where he bought a ticket to San Antonio. He figured he couldn't risk stealing another car, because the cops probably had that routine down pat and would be looking for him by monitoring stolen car reports.

Taking the bus also allowed him to sleep while he put miles between himself and the last location the cops had on him, and he took full advantage of that.

CHAPTER TWENTY-FOUR

The St. Louis courtroom was filling up rapidly, Jackie saw as she turned to look behind her. Many of those in the courtroom were press.

She was seated beside Wayne Simpson, her assistant for several years, who had brought his heavy briefcase from which he could always produce exactly what she needed, although she didn't expect to be required to do anything at this hearing.

Truth be told, she wouldn't have had to be at this hearing at all, but it was so important, she couldn't stay away.

On the other side of her was Special Agent Darren Wheeler of the FBI, whom she had spoken to on the phone several times, but only met face-to-face today.

They were directly behind the plaintiff's table where four lawyers were seated: Marcus Williams, Axiom's Legal VP, Daniel Moreau and two other lawyers of Sinclair-Roberts-Dubois from Washington, D.C. She was acutely aware of the hourly rate Axiom was paying them.

"All rise!"

Those assembled in the courtroom obeyed the bailiff and stood to their feet with a loud rustling of papers and clothing.

"Court is now in session, the honorable Judge James Jackson presiding."

The African-American judge, in his 50s, cloaked in a black robe, entered and motioned for them to be seated. Again, they obeyed with another, less-pronounced rustling.

"This hearing," Justice Jackson began, "is to decide the disposition of the injunction to halt the repeal of the Petroleum Independence Act, which injunction my late colleague, Judge Everett Walker, handed down.

"The petition before the court asks for a direct appeal to the Supreme Court, bypassing the Eighth Circuit. However, I'll point out that it is the prerogative of the Eastern District of Missouri to adjudicate the injunction, reassigning the trial for a permanent decision on the matter. Mr., uh, Moreau, you represent the plaintiff, Axiom Oil Incorporated?"

"I and my associates, yes, your honor," Moreau said, moving quickly to the lectern in the center of the room.

"I look forward to hearing your reasoning why I should forego the established procedure of having the trial here in St. Louis where the injunction was handed down. Do you have something against Missouri's Federal courts, Mr. Moreau?"

"Not at all, your honor. We have the utmost respect for the Federal judiciary and its important work at every level. Our petition relates to an extraordinary set of circumstances."

"Such as?"

"Such as concern for the people being adversely affected by the Petroleum Independence Act. The general public is directly affected by the artificially increased price of motor fuel mandated by the tax. The cost to consumers of all goods generally has been increased due to increased fuel costs for trucking those goods to market. This has resulted in hardship for virtually everyone in the country. The American people spoke concerning the fuel tax in the election just past, but the injunction has prevented the relief they sought at the ballot box. The elected representatives of the people enacted legislation to give the American people relief, but the injunction has frustrated this effort.

"Also, one of Axiom's competitors, Petrocom, has already failed, causing a cascade of other failures and thousands of people being put out of work."

"And you think Axiom could be next?"

"Your honor, Axiom's Vice President for Legal Concerns, Marcus Williams, can address specifics of Axiom's position."

Marcus stood and shuffled to the lectern, pulling the microphone down a little.

"Thank you for this opportunity, your honor. I am Marcus Williams. As Axiom's legal vice president. I'd first like to say I was saddened to hear of the death of Judge Walker. I had the opportunity to be in his court room to testify about this matter.

"Your honor, I have watched as our great company has been forced to lay off several thousand of our workers, most of whom are people with families to feed.

"Our stockholders have also seen the value of their investments evaporate. Many of them are small investors, some retirees on fixed incomes who depend on the value and stability of Axiom as a company for their own survival.

"Because of these facts, we have submitted this petition because a final resolution to the question of repeal of the Petroleum Independence Act is urgent. With all due respect, your honor, if you rule against our petition and have the trial here in St. Louis and the injunction against repeal is ultimately upheld, we will then have no choice but to appeal the ruling to the Supreme Court anyway, greatly extending the time required for ultimate resolution. Many innocent people will suffer in the meantime, so we would prefer to move right away to what might be the final disposition anyway."

The judge looked over the reading glasses perched precariously on the end of his nose, apparently measuring the sincerity and fortitude of the man before him. Then he spoke.

"While the anecdotal hardships of Axiom's customers and stockholders may be a concern, they do not bear directly on the decision I have to make." The judge looked down at the petition before him. "And I'm not sure Axiom has standing to appeal the injunction handed down by the Eastern District in any case, since the company was not named in the injunction."

"That is true, your honor, but Axiom was also not named specifically in the Petroleum Independence Act," Marcus responded, since this was a point the legal team had anticipated and rehearsed. "But the Act was written purposely to directly and adversely affect our employees, stockholders and customers and those of our competitors. But more importantly, a terroristic attack on one of Axiom's installations was the impetus for the Act in the first place, so we lay claim to special interest in the outcome."

"Umm hmm."

"And Judge Walker did allow me to testify at the hearing on the injunction on behalf of Axiom Oil and, had the trial occurred, I was to have testified there as well."

"All right, I take your point. I see you have some other items to present," Justice Jackson said. "Let's hear them."

"I'll return the floor to Mr. Moreau."

Daniel Moreau once again stepped to the lectern as Marcus sat down.

"Your honor, I don't have to tell you of the events which have called Judge Walker's injunction into question: law

240

enforcement's suspicion of funds apparently provided from out of state, possibly outside the jurisdiction of the Eastern District Court, to bring the petition, and how the petitioner, George Donaldson of O'Fallon, Missouri, has since been found murdered, apparently to obstruct justice and prevent the discovery of the source of the funding."

"None of that has yet been fully investigated and adjudicated. You are taking a big leap to say the funding was provided through some kind of conspiracy, if that is what you are implying."

"That is true, your honor, but the investigation is proceeding; arrests will hopefully be made and criminal conspiracy charges surely filed, along with charges of murder against those involved in funding the original oil platform bombing. We have with us today a representative of the St. Louis field office of the Federal Bureau of Investigation who will shortly give us more information about the ongoing investigation into the events that have brought us here. I'm confident that law enforcement's theory of conspiracy behind the injunction will also be borne out when the conspirators are identified and tried."

"Are you connecting the oil platform bombing last year to the murder of the petitioner?"

"Yes, your honor, that is the theory of law enforcement at present."

"That seems like a stretch to me."

"We have more to present on that, your honor. I would also like to join Mr. Williams in pointing out again that the bombing of Axiom's drilling platform in the Gulf of Mexico was used as a pretext to pass the Petroleum Independence Act in the first place. Since law enforcement has charged and convicted some of the people directly involved with the conspiracy, including indicting the former United States Senator who sponsored the Act, the original law is called into question, and the injunction to keep the law in place is under similar suspicion, perhaps with some of the same players. That, I believe, gives Axiom Oil Incorporated a more-than-ordinary interest in the disposition of the injunction.

"To underline this point, I'd like to have Special Agent Darren Wheeler, the representative from the Federal Bureau of Investigation, make a statement, if it please the court. You have a summation of his statement in Exhibit B."

"Proceed."

Moreau nodded to Special Agent Wheeler, who turned and nodded to Jackie, then stood and walked to the lectern.

"Thank you for this opportunity," Wheeler began.

"State your name and position for the record please," the judge said.

"Yes, your honor. I'm Special Agent Darren Wheeler. I am Special Agent in charge of the St. Louis field office of the Federal Bureau of Investigation."

"Have you been in my court before, Agent Wheeler?"

"I don't believe so, your honor, but I have had occasion to be present for several trials before some of your colleagues in this building in past years."

"All right, please continue."

"My involvement in these events began with the murder of Judge Walker, because it happened in my jurisdiction, but I have since been brought up to speed on the other related events in this case by my colleagues in the nation's capital. Since the original attack on Axiom Oil Incorporated's Gulf of Mexico drilling platform last year, which was the reason cited for the Petroleum Independence Act in Congress, my fellow agents at the Washington, D.C., and New Orleans field offices of the FBI have been investigating the conspiracy behind the bombing. Convictions have been obtained for those who directly perpetrated the attack and others thought to be involved are in custody. We know that money was provided to the bombers by a third party and we have the courier in custody.

"In view of the recent suspicious murder of the plaintiff in the petition for the injunction to keep the Petroleum Independence Act in place, we believe that the persons behind the conspiracy are still active in the effort to maintain the Act. We believe the key player we have in custody will eventually give us the names of who is behind all of this."

"Are you telling me that whoever the shadowy characters are behind the alleged conspiracy are so desperate to keep the gas tax in place they are willing to kill?"

"More likely the murder was an attempt to cover up the conspiracy."

"You are saying the death of the judge and the plaintiff in this case is part of the original conspiracy?"

"The murder of the plaintiff, yes, but not the murder of the judge. We know who perpetrated that crime and we believe he had personal reasons for the act, unrelated to the conspiracy."

"This is all pretty thin, until you have the evidence and can make an arrest in these cases," the judge remarked dryly.

"Yes, I know, your honor. Nothing would make me happier than to be able to tell you we had the parties of the conspiracy in custody."

"I'm sure there's an 'allegedly' in there somewhere, Special Agent Wheeler."

"Yes, your honor. Those *allegedly* behind the conspiracy, who provided the funding for that attack, we believe, also provided the funds used to submit the petition here in the Eastern District to issue the injunction – allegedly."

Jackie watched as the FBI agent squirmed a little and she was glad that she didn't have to do anything but observe.

"I'm giving you a great deal of latitude, Special Agent Wheeler, because you are a man of some responsibility in our Nation's law enforcement arm and because you are local to our jurisdiction. Tell me again why you are linking these two things: the financing of the attack on the oil platform and the injunction?" The judge looked down his nose at Wheeler.

244

"We at the FBI are quite certain that we have yet to apprehend the persons ultimately behind the original conspiracy. Now that the petitioner in this case has been murdered, it stands to reason that the same person, or persons, is acting because the first crime enabled passage of the original Act and the injunction kept it in place."

"Are you saying that the man, the Axiom employee, who killed Judge Walker, is not a suspect in the murder of – what's his name? – Mr. Donaldson? I would think he would also be a potential suspect, since it was he who petitioned for the injunction."

"We have not ruled Mr. Jones out entirely, because he's a logical suspect, but the methods used in the two crimes are very different and we found no evidence that Jones had been at the scene of Mr. Donaldson's murder. Plus, we know Jones was several hundred miles from there, having left Missouri a couple of days before Donaldson was murdered."

"Well, Mr. Wheeler, this is all highly interesting, but I'm not sure how it bears on the decision of whether or not to move forward with a trial concerning the injunction here in the Eastern District. It seems we are getting far afield."

"Your honor, it may not be my place to draw this conclusion," Wheeler said tentatively, "but, if you will indulge me, it seems to me that the facts of our investigation call into question the motivation for passage of the Petroleum Independence Act in the first place, and the fact that the petition for the injunction is similarly tainted by the murder of the petitioner calls its legitimacy into question as well."

"Umm hmm. All right, noted. Is that all?"

Wheeler stole a quick look at Moreau who nodded slightly.

"Yes, your honor. Thank you," Wheeler said as he returned to his seat.

"What else is there, counsellor?"

"Finally, your honor," Moreau continued when he arrived back at the lectern, "If Judge Walker was still alive, he could have adjudicated his injunction in a timely manner, but because of his untimely death, that task would be added to the already busy schedule of one of his colleagues."

"Yes, whereas the United States Supreme Court doesn't have anything to do, does it?"

The judge's remark was met with a ripple of muffled laughter in the crowded courtroom.

"Of course, your point is well taken, your honor. Rest assured that our desire to go directly to the high court does not mean we wish to increase the docket load there, nor does it reflect at all on the sense of fairness and jurisprudence here in Federal Court in St. Louis."

"I should hope not! It occurs to me that Judge Walker would still be here and able to follow through with the trial if an Axiom employee hadn't allegedly killed him!"

Moreau didn't answer immediately. It was so quiet it seemed no one in the courtroom was breathing.

"I in no way excuse the actions of the Indiana man who is alleged to have killed your colleague, Judge Walker," Moreau said finally. "He acted rashly when he was laid off from his job and he wrongly blamed the judge. He wasn't thinking straight. Law enforcement is working to bring him to justice, as well.

"But, with all due respect to this court, your honor," Moreau continued, "The need remains for an expeditious resolution of this matter, for the sake of literally millions of Americans who are being harmed."

Jackie watched the judge's face closely to see if she could read his mood and how the arguments were hitting him, but she couldn't tell.

"All right, if there's nothing else?"

"No, your honor."

"Court will reconvene at 10:00 o'clock tomorrow. I'll announce my decision then," the judge said, striking his gavel.

CHAPTER TWENTY-FIVE

"How's the salad?"

"Not sure," answered Marcus Williams between bites. "I'm not really tasting anything right now."

The question had come from Jackie as they sat with the rest of the Axiom management and the legal group from Washington, D.C., in a hotel restaurant in a massive booth wrapped around an oblong table covered in a white table cloth.

Axiom was footing the bill for the meal, as well as the hotel and travel. It was early evening after the hearing.

"I think it went well," Daniel Moreau said with his trademark authoritative voice, reading the group's minds.

"It was hard for me to read the judge," Jackie said.

"Judges purposely mask what they're thinking, unless your arguments are really stupid," Marcus said, bringing a burst of laughter which quickly fell back into contemplative silence.

"The important thing," Moreau gestured with his fork after a few seconds of silent chewing, "is that our presentation was sound and broad-ranging. Agent Wheeler gave us some key arguments in tying in the recent murder of the plaintiff in the injunction. While it's not a slam dunk until the murderer is found and convicted, it showed that the petition for the injunction was probably a sham to begin with."

"That doesn't mean the judge is required to rule in our favor," it was Marcus again, "but it can't hurt."

"I just have a feeling I'm not going to sleep too well tonight," Jackie said grimly.

* * *

The next morning, Jackie and the others were again seated exactly where they had been twenty-four hours earlier, except for Special Agent Wheeler, who was back at work across town. Again, they rose when the bailiff told them to and again sat when the judge motioned to them.

Judge Jackson slowly took his reading glasses out of a black case and placed them low on his nose. Then he began reading something silently, taking his time as if no one else was there.

Jackie suddenly was conscious that her neck was very tense. Without moving perceptibly, she tried to will her muscles to relax. It was no use. She silently lifted her right hand and lightly massaged her neck as unobtrusively as possible.

Finally, the judge spoke.

"I have examined the factors in this petition. It is not uncomplicated. There are many players, many with a stake in the outcome and many people affected."

Jackie stole a glance at Wayne that said, *Is that a positive sign?* He looked back as if to say, *It's too early to tell.*

"This whole situation is a morass of conflicting interests," the judge continued. "There are the Environmentalists and their concerns and corporate interests, with their employees and customers affected. The Federal Government is a player in this; all three branches, the legislative, administrative and judicial branches have played their parts. Ultimately, pretty much everyone has a stake and an opinion about this matter.

"That makes my decision very difficult, but nothing makes it more difficult than the fact that my good friend and colleague, Justice Everett Walker, was to have sat in judgement on this case. The plaintiffs before me, Axiom Oil Incorporated and its representatives, could, some might think, be indirectly responsible for the death of Judge Walker."

Jackie saw that none of the four lawyers sitting silently at the plaintiff's table betrayed anything by their body language.

"Others would say," the judge continued, "the events which led to the plant closing and the murder of my colleague began long before; events which cast Axiom Oil as the victim."

The judge shifted and adjusted his robe before continuing.

"This decision required me to do a fair amount of research and it appears to me that Axiom cannot be accused of causing the death of Judge Walker, directly or indirectly. The plant closing may have pushed one employee over the edge, but Axiom could not have foreseen that. The perpetrator has yet to be apprehended. That matter will be fully explored then."

Jackie allowed a quiet sigh to escape her lips.

"So, Judge Walker's fate does not have any bearing on this petition as I see it, although it's never far from my mind.

"Unfortunately for Judge Walker, it appears that the basis for the injunction may have been fraudulent to begin with. I refuse to believe that Judge Walker was part of any conspiracy." The judge looked over his reading glasses at the lawyers. Almost imperceptibly, Moreau shook his head.

"Law enforcement believes that the money used to petition for the injunction was allegedly provided by the same entity that conspired to attack the oil platform that started all this.

"If that turns out to be true, it calls into question the basis for the original bill," he looked down at his notes, "The Petroleum Independence Act. Of course, we don't know yet if it will be found to be true, do we?

"In addition, the result of the election last November appears to have indicated the opinion of the American people regarding the law and the fuel tax. However, the outcome of elections is not part of what I must consider here. The Federal judiciary must make its decisions based on the law, not the ebb and flow of electoral politics.

"And I remain ambivalent as to how Axiom Oil Incorporated has standing to challenge the injunction by my late colleague, when the Federal government was its actual target."

Jackie was completely unsure where the judge was going.

"The law does not give me a clear direction in this case; I would be within my rights to assign the trial for the injunction here in the Eastern District as originally intended, or I could grant the present petition to appeal to the Supreme Court.

"So, what do I do?"

The judge looked out at the courtroom. Everyone there knew it was a rhetorical question and no one made a sound.

"In the absence of a clear direction by law and precedent, I must be careful not to allow my personal attitudes and opinions to hold sway. I was, however, drawn to the argument about the affect the original bill and its attendant fuel tax is having on the people of this country. I, of course, understand the pain that has been caused by the arbitrary nature of the tax. The authors of the bill apparently hoped to punish the oil companies for environmental transgressions, but they have, in the end, punished the American people. Such is the nature of 'unintended consequences'."

"For this reason, and primarily this reason, I am going to grant this petition, and allow the plaintiff to appeal the injunction directly to the Supreme Court, where a resolution can be ultimately and expeditiously found for the whole matter."

Thank God! Jackie lowered her head and practically fainted for a second. Then she felt herself starting to cry.

CHAPTER TWENTY-SIX

I will never get used to this, Marvin Borelli thought as he filed out into the prison "yard" with scores of other inmates. He still couldn't believe that his $500-per-hour attorney hadn't been able to get him released from FBI custody.

And now I am HERE? In a Federal prison somewhere in "Podunk", Virginia?

It seemed to him they had locked him up and thrown away the key. He knew he would have his day in court someday, but he didn't relish it. He was guilty after all.

He was just thinking that he probably needed to cultivate some friendships among his fellow inmates; they might come in handy in the future, but he immediately recoiled from the idea of a future in HERE.

Several of the men were shooting baskets in a pick-up game, as always happened when they were given an hour for exercise. Borelli turned to walk toward some bleachers to sit down and watch, when a tall, barrel-chested man approached him and spoke with a Russian accent.

"Hey, Borelli!"

"Yeah, what can I do for you?"

"I got a message for you. It's Friday the Thirteenth."

Borelli stopped cold and watched as the large man reached into a pocket and brought out something shiny. He barely had time to process the "Friday the Thirteenth" reference when the man pulled back and tried to stab Borelli in the neck.

Alarmed and acting instinctively, Borelli raised his left hand in time and the shiv plunged deep into his palm. He screamed in pain and grabbed his left hand with his right. The Russian pulled back to stab him again and Borelli fell backward, pumping his legs to scoot away from the thug as fast as he could. The Russian pursued him, but tripped over the foot of another inmate who was seated nearby. Indignant, the seated inmate stood and grabbed the Russian's collar. The Russian was momentarily distracted long enough to push the interfering inmate away and then continued pursuing Borelli, who was by this time several feet away, though still on the ground.

The inmate the Russian had tripped over pursued the Russian and grabbed his collar once more, slowing him down again. The Russian, angry at the interference, turned to attack the other inmate and they struggled hand-to-hand. Other inmates noticed the fight and gathered around, shouting encouragement to one or the other.

Finally, prison guards arrived and tasered the two fighting inmates. Another guard came to Borelli's side, took a look at his hand, which was bleeding profusely, and got him on his feet.

"You're going to the infirmary!"

* * *

The prison yard and two cellblocks were locked down, but Borelli could only see the four walls of an infirmary exam room. He was alone, lying on an examination table, but had faith to believe that a doctor would be with him shortly.

He had pled with the guard who had brought him to the infirmary to let him call his lawyer, but he was ignored.

Shortly a man in a white coat did come into the small room.

"Doctor, I..."

"I'm not a doctor; not yet anyway."

"I just need to call my lawyer. I know why I was attacked."

"Let me see that," the not-yet-doctor said, taking hold of his injured hand.

"I know who wants me dead. Please let me call my lawyer."

"This is going to hurt," the medic said, as if it was no concern of his.

Borelli gritted his teeth to keep from crying out as the man drenched his wound in one fiery liquid after another. Borelli recognized the alcohol and saw the Peroxide fizzing but couldn't identify the ugly, brown liquid that came next.

"Lie back!" the man commanded. "You're going to need stitches."

"I just need to talk to the FBI," Borelli pleaded.

"You're not going to talk to anyone anytime soon."

* * *

"So why the sudden change of heart?" Special Agent Samuel Jorgensen asked Marvin Borelli, who was sitting across from him in the visitation room of the prison the next day. "Last time I saw you, you swore you'd never turn on anybody."

"You've gotta get me out of here. My life is in danger," Borelli said, lifting his bandaged hand. "I'm ready to tell you everything I know. I know who wants me dead."

"Okay, slow down," Jorensen said looking down at Borelli's bandage. "What happened there?"

"That's what I'm trying to tell you. I know who provided the money for the bombing of the oil platform and they're trying to kill me."

"Okay," Jorgensen took a well-worn pocket-sized notebook from his suit pocket. "How do you know somebody's trying to kill you?"

"Because the thug who attacked me said, 'It's Friday the Thirteenth'."

"Is that supposed to mean something?"

"Jason is the name of the killer in the Friday the Thirteenth movies and that's the name of the man who's trying to kill me, who gave me the money to funnel to the Knights of Mother Earth: Jason Wood, of Champions of Mother Earth."

"The 'green' outfit?" The FBI had looked at Champions because they knew it was one of Borelli's clients, but they hadn't found any reason to suspect the organization.

"Yes, in Seattle."

"And you concluded this because he said, 'Friday the Thirteenth'? Couldn't he just have meant it wasn't your lucky day?"

"He's not the first person who has said those words to me. There was also a lawyer for Champions of Mother Earth who visited me."

"And he said it, too?"

"Exactly. It was a warning. You've got to get me out of here!"

"What makes you think you'll be safer out of prison?"

"You need to put me in protective custody!"

"So now you WANT to be in custody?"

"I need to be protected, yes."

"This Jason, 'Wood' was it? He runs a touchy-feely, non-profit organization? You're seriously trying to tell me he's capable of putting hits on people?"

Borelli paused a moment before speaking next.

"Look, there are people in the Movement who are True Believers, and they will do anything to see the Cause succeed."

"Aren't you one of them?"

Borelli hesitated again. "I was."

Jorgensen looked into Borelli's eyes, apparently trying to judge his sincerity.

"OK, so it was Wood at the 'Champions' group that provided the funding. How did they get it to you?"

"Do we really need to go through all that now? I need to get out of here!"

"Nobody's going to hurt you while you're here with me. I need to understand your whole story before I can know if it's credible."

Borelli's head lowered in disappointment, then he raised his eyes to Jorgensen's and began at the beginning.

CHAPTER TWENTY-SEVEN

Agent Peter Gersich pushed his glasses back to the top of his nose for the third time since sitting down in front of Special Agent Jorgensen's desk. After Borelli cracked, Gersich had known where to look, so he was able to uncover a wealth of information on "Champions of Mother Earth."

"I think we've got him. Jason Wood, that is."

"What've you got?" Jorgensen asked.

"Shell Corporations. Several levels."

"I didn't know non-profits could have shell corporations," Jorgensen said.

"Oh, these corporations don't have anything to do with Champions of Mother Earth," Gersich replied. As a forensic accountant for the FBI, his job was to ferret out criminal financial dealings that people worked hard to keep hidden.

"No, these corporations aren't even directly owned by Wood himself. Several distant relatives are the principals, although I doubt any of them know it. I had to research his extended family and locate all their holdings to piece it together.

"For instance," the thin, young bean counter continued, handing Jorgensen a flowchart, "Consolidated is the holding company for all the others and it's 'owned,' so to speak, by Wood's second cousin's husband. It owns Amcor, LLC, for which the principal is apparently Wood's sister's dog, as near as we can tell from her Facebook page."

"Somehow, I doubt the dog contributes much to the corporate meetings," Jorgensen quipped, but Gersich only realized he should have laughed after he had continued.

"The other two, well what does it matter? It's all as bogus as a three-dollar bill. The last one, Adams-Greenwich, LLC, is where the action is."

"That's where the funding for the bombing and the petition for the injunction came from?"

"Actually, he seemed to never take money from the same place twice. Some came from 'Champions,' other would come from one of the for-profit shell corporations. Sometimes money was moved several times before it got to its destination. Adams-Greenwich, LLC, however, was where he did his stock manipulation."

"Oh. How did that work?"

"Well, as near as I can tell from trading records, Adams-Greenwich owned a boatload of Petrocom and Axiom stock, several thousand shares each, and suddenly decided to sell it. Within days, the stock price tanked and there was a panic among shareholders and Petrocom collapsed."

"Where did he get the money to buy that much stock?"

"I'll have to dig some more to know that for sure. It's quite possible that there could be an embezzlement charge in his future. I'll know more, later. For now, I can give you enough to bring him in."

"So, the Axiom folks were right? He tried to do the same with Axiom's stock price?"

"Yes, he did, but I guess Axiom was just enough stronger that it didn't go all the way down."

"What about the injunction? Where did that money come from?"

"It looks like some came from Champions and some from one of the LLCs. He worked hard to cover his tracks, always pulling one amount out and transferring a different amount. I've still got to run down the exact payments to the law firm in Bellingham, Washington, that gave the money to the Aquarian Community. Then I'll have it all sewn up."

"You've got this all documented so I can charge him?"

"Yes," Gersich answered, handing him the manila folder. "It's all here, complete with the charges and the statutes you can list."

"Charges concerning both the funding of the bombing, the petition for the injunction and the stock manipulation?"

"Yes, and don't forget the Donaldson murder in Missouri. Some money changed hands for that as well."

"And do we know who pulled the trigger?"

"It's in the file."

"Right. Good work," Jorgensen said, taking the folder and opening it. "I guess I'm going to Seattle. Want to come?"

Gersich's smile froze and he couldn't say anything.

* * *

"Hello Doris."

"Mr. Garrity! What are you. . .? I mean, you can't go in there. She doesn't want to see you!"

Patrick charged ahead and went through the large double doors. He was determined that Jackie would hear what he needed to tell her. Once inside, he stopped cold when he saw her at her desk, concentrating on some report. Doris came through the door and sped past him.

"Ms. James, I tried to stop him!"

Jackie looked up and instantly saw what Doris meant.

"I – I'm sorry," Patrick stuttered. "I have something important to tell you. About everything that's happening. You need to know..." Patrick trailed off, not finding the persuasive words he had rehearsed on the flight he had impulsively taken from D.C.

"Doris, please stay," Jackie said finally. "I want a witness." Then to Patrick, "Sit. Have your say."

Patrick slowly sat in one of the leather, wing-back chairs in front of Jackie's desk as Doris sat in the other.

"There's so much I need to say – so much I should say to you," he began, "but I came because I need to tell you: I think I figured out who is behind everything that's happened."

"Everything?"

"I mean, I think I know who bankrolled the attack on the oil platform and greased the palms of the senators and congressmen to get the Petroleum Independence Act passed."

Jackie considered what Patrick said, her suspicions only slightly lessened by wanting to know what he was going to say.

"And the injunction too," Patrick continued. "It's all tied together; it's all part of the same conspiracy."

"So how did you come to this conclusion?" Jackie said skeptically.

"One time you told me you wished you knew who was doing this to you. The other day, I thought, I wonder if I could find out? So, I put my investigative reporter hat on and found out who filed the petition for the injunction."

"George Donaldson in Missouri. Now dead."

"Right, murdered. He was head of a defunct environmental group called the Aquarian Community, but he didn't have the money or the smarts to petition for the injunction.

"So, I called him, and he was high as a kite. Thanks to that fact, I learned some important information. Like I said, he didn't have the money to petition; he told me that a law firm in Bellingham, Washington, gave him $100,000, half of which he could keep, to get the injunction."

"Washington state?"

"Yeah, that was news to me," Patrick said feeling, like he was finally able to tell a coherent story. So, I checked to see what law firms in Bellingham have environmental groups as clients and I found a big one in Seattle, Champions of Mother Earth."

"So, what makes you think they're behind it?"

"Because I already knew that name from somewhere. I had a brochure from the lobbyist they arrested who gave the money to the group in Houston that bombed the oil platform, and guess who was the first client on the list on his brochure?"

"Champions of Mother Earth?"

"Exactly."

Jackie considered this news before continuing.

"That doesn't really prove anything."

"But it adds up," Patrick insisted. "the lobbyist, Borelli, had to get the money for the bombing from one of his clients, and Donaldson got the money for the injunction from a law firm that also happens to have 'Champions' as a client. See, here is

265

Jason Wood," Patrick said, handing a printout of a photo from the Champions website.

"So why do you want to help me now?" Jackie almost shouted, barely looking at the photo. "After betraying me the way you did?"

"I know. I'm sorry. My desire for a scoop got the better of me."

"But you didn't even get the scoop, you passed it off to another paper!"

"I know, I know!"

"Ms. James," Doris spoke calmly and seriously. "I know there are issues the two of you need to hash out, but I think you need to seriously consider what Mr. Garrity is telling you. And you," she said turning to Patrick, "you need to give this information to the FBI. This is important."

"You trust him?" Jackie asked Doris, frowning.

"He hasn't asked for anything but for you to listen, and what he says makes an awful lot of sense."

"I came because I thought you needed this information," Patrick pleaded. "It might help bring it all to an end. What you think of me shouldn't matter."

"Okay, then let's call your source at the FBI," Jackie said. "Special Agent Jorgensen. That's one of the agents who's been keeping me up to speed about things. You need to tell him what you've told me."

"Okay."

Jackie dialed the number and put the phone on speaker. They had to wait a while for the call to be routed. When Jorgensen answered, Jackie spoke.

"Special Agent Jorgensen, this is Jackie James at Axiom Oil. I have Patrick Garrity with me and he has some important information he needs to share with you."

"Okay. Patrick?"

"Hi, Sam."

And Patrick proceeded to relate to Jorgensen everything he had shared with Jackie.

"Well, that's some good investigating, Garrity," Jorgensen said when he had finished. "It so happens that I've just heard the same thing from another source; an eyewitness and coconspirator, as it happens, so thanks for confirming it."

"Borelli finally talked?" Jackie asked.

"Yes, after Wood attempted to put a hit on him."

"Oh my God!" Patrick exclaimed.

"I guess we can tell Judge Jackson that what the FBI suspected is true," Jackie said. Patrick had no idea what she was talking about.

* * *

The next morning Patrick ventured once again to the black-and-gold tower with the Axiom logo on the side. When he entered the CEO's suite on the twentieth floor, Doris looked up with wide eyes but didn't stand.

"Doris, I want to talk to her. I know she won't want to. . ."

"She's gone."

"What? Gone where?"

"To Seattle. With Bill."

Patrick could see that Doris was upset. "What do you mean, she's gone to Seattle? And who's Bill?"

"Bill is her bodyguard. I'm really worried about what she might do."

"Since when does she have a bodyguard? What are you afraid she's going to do?"

"I'm afraid she's going to confront that Mr. Wood person," said Doris, putting her hand to her mouth.

Patrick's mind raced. Doris knew Jackie as well as anyone. If she was afraid she would do something that foolish, well.... *It does sound like something she would do. She is fearless.*

He took out his cell phone, found a number in his contacts and pushed the "Send" button.

"Special Agent Jorgensen's office," the female voice answered.

"I need to speak to Sam! This is Patrick Garrity of the *Washington Herald*."

"Special Agent Jorgensen is out of town. May I take a message?"

"Where is he? It's a matter of life and death!"

"He left for the airport a little over an hour ago, headed to Seattle."

Patrick wondered at the coincidence. "I need to reach him before he leaves. Do you have his cell number?"

"I'm not allowed to give that to you, but I can ask him to call you."

"Yes, please I need to reach him urgently!"

"All right. I have your number in my recent call list. I will call him and ask him to call you."

"Thank you."

Patrick sat down on a couch in the sitting area in front of Doris' desk.

"He's going to call?"

"Yes, if he's not already on the plane to Seattle, too. Did you try to stop her?"

"Of course, but she just called in to tell me she was taking the jet. She didn't come into the office at all."

Patrick's cell rang and he answered immediately.

"Patrick Garrity.... I see. Thank you. Are you sure someone can't give you permission to give me his cell number? . . . Yes, I understand. Thank you."

"What did they say," Doris asked when he had hung up.

"He's already in the air. She couldn't reach him."

"What are you going to do?"

"I don't know. I've got to go. I'll let you know what I find out."

Patrick nearly ran out the door and headed to the elevator.

In the time it took to descend twenty floors, he decided what he had to do. A half hour later he was at Houston Hobby airport buying the second impulsive airline ticket he had purchased in as many days.

* * *

The flight to Seattle was comfortable and fast as usual. There was no security to go through when one flew in Axiom's Learjet. The plane could hold eight passengers, but Jackie was only taking her bodyguard. Bill seemed awkward in the big, plush seat. *He is not used to this kind of travel*, Jackie thought, bemused.

They landed at the General Aviation terminal at the Seattle airport and took a shuttle to the rental car center. It was late afternoon by the time they had their car and were on the road.

"So how are you going to play this?" asked Bill from the driver's seat.

"I think the direct approach. We'll just walk in and ask to see the man himself."

"Okay." Bill didn't sound convinced, but he didn't say more.

They arrived at the Champions of Mother Earth building in downtown Seattle, parked in the lower parking level and took the elevator to the lobby.

Jackie strode ahead of Bill and approached the receptionist.

"Hi, can I help you?" the receptionist asked.

"Yes, I need to see Jason Wood," Jackie replied.

"Your name?"

"Jacqueline James."

After looking at her computer screen briefly through eyes that had way too much mascara, in Jackie's opinion, the receptionist asked, "Do you have an appointment?"

"No, but I think he'll see me if you tell him my name."

"It's very late in the day, I'm not even sure he's still here. He doesn't see people without an appointment. Would you like me to check his schedule tomorrow to see if he has a slot open?"

"Uh. Yeah, Okay," Jackie said, not sure what else to say.

"I don't see much availability tomorrow. Are you local?"

"No, we're only in town for a couple of days."

"Well, I can see a possible appointment tomorrow at two, but I would need to check with his administrative assistant to make sure I can schedule it. Do you have a contact number so I can reach you?"

Jackie reluctantly gave the receptionist her cell number.

"Come on, Bill."

They went to the elevator and descended to the parking level. Jackie looked at a row of cars on their way to their rental.

"Hmm."

"Did you say something, Ms. James?"

"Just had an idea."

CHAPTER TWENTY-EIGHT

A United Airlines flight touched down in Seattle late that same day. Samuel Jorgensen emerged from the jetway and was met by a young man in a navy suit and tie, holding a sign with Jorgensen's name on it.

After terse introductions, the young agent led Jorgensen to a dark SUV in the parking deck and they sped off toward the Seattle field office of the FBI.

"The Special Agent in charge has briefed you on the arrest?" Jorgensen asked.

"Yes, sir, absolutely. Everything's arranged for tomorrow morning. Special Agent Davis is waiting for you in his office."

"Good."

Jorgensen then checked his phone for messages and saw that his administrative assistant had called, leaving a message for him to call Patrick Garrity. It was urgent, she said. He scribbled the number from her message into the notebook he always carried and dialed it on his cell. There was no answer, so he left a message. He hesitated but he did give his cell number in the message.

* * *

Jackie insisted they not leave the parking level immediately. It was obvious that Bill didn't know what she was up to, but he wouldn't have long to wait. They were sitting in the car on the parking level of the Champions of Mother Earth headquarters and Jackie was looking in the direction of the elevators.

Sure enough, right at five o'clock, Jason Wood exited the elevator and strode toward his car. Jackie recognized him from the glossy photo on the Champions website.

"I knew that would be his," Jackie said loudly.

A red Porsche Carrera convertible roared to life and quickly moved out of the parking level of the Champions building.

"That's him. I'm sure of it. Follow him." Jackie said.

"I don't know if that's a good idea, Ms. James," Bill protested as he started the car.

"Just follow that car. I want to see where he goes."

Bill reluctantly started the car, put it in gear and eased out of the parking space. Once out on the street, he followed Wood's car at about four car-lengths back.

It hadn't gone far when the Porsche stopped in front of a town house in what appeared to be an upscale, gentrified area of town. Bill pulled off into an empty parallel parking space across the street. A light rain was beginning to fall as Wood hurried inside after he raised the motorized convertible top.

"So, is this where he lives?" Jackie wondered aloud, twisting around to watch what was happening behind them.

Bill didn't say anything as he watched the rear-view mirror, but squirmed in the driver's seat, which was pushed back as far as it could go.

Suddenly Jackie's iPhone® rang. She hastily checked it and saw that it was Patrick. She knew he was probably put out with her for leaving him in Houston to come to Seattle, but she couldn't think about that right now. She silenced the phone, so it wouldn't bother them.

Bill watched her dealing with the phone then looked away.

They didn't have to wait long before Wood came out again. By this time, the dark cloud overhead and rapidly sinking sun made the evening extremely dark. The only light came from car headlights and street lights that were obviously newly installed but did their best to imitate nineteenth century street lamps.

Wood was followed out the front door by a young woman who looked half his age with a stunning figure under an expensive designer dress, opening an umbrella. They got in the sports car and left, driving past Bill and Jackie.

"Okay, let's see where they go now."

"Shouldn't you just call the FBI, Ms. James? I mean, I'm not sure what we're doing is legal."

"This guy has been hurting my people and I want to look him in the eye!"

Bill pulled the rental car back into the lane and followed the sports car. The Porsche only went about three blocks before stopping again, this time in front of an upscale restaurant with a large canopy over a circular drive which was illuminated by soft path lights.

Jackie and Bill pulled up, parked across the street in their rental and watched as Jason Wood handed his car keys to a valet, walked around the back of the car and opened the door for the woman. They went inside while the valet drove to the parking lot beside the building.

"We'll give them time to get seated and then we'll go in and have a talk."

"Ms. James, I don't think that's a good idea. Maybe you should just take the appointment and go back to his office tomorrow," Bill pleaded.

"No, we're here. I'd prefer not to talk to him on his own turf anyway. I want him to be off balance. This is perfect."

They waited in silence for about fifteen minutes and Jackie said, "OK, lets go in. They probably have a table now, assuming he made a reservation."

Jackie jumped out of the car putting the strap of her bag on her shoulder. She was halfway across the street when she looked back to see Bill slowly exiting the car. She started walking again as he followed her across the street. Together they went in and were met by the maître d'.

"The rest of our party is already seated," Jackie said as she breezed past the front desk with Bill following.

Jackie did a quick survey of the room, dimly lit mostly by warm light from wall sconces and a huge, round chandelier. At first, she didn't see Wood, but then she saw the young woman at a table on the other side of a pillar. She made a b-line for it, looking behind her to ensure Bill hustled to catch up.

The table had four chairs and the two empty ones were at right angles. As she rapidly approached, the woman suddenly looked up and her heavily mascaraed eyes widened as she saw Jackie looking at her and coming in her direction.

Jackie grabbed the nearest chair and sat down, turning to face Wood. Bill remained standing, looking around furtively.

Jason Wood was now wide-eyed and sputtering, "Wha-what's this? Who -- ?" Then the light of recognition dawned in his eyes.

"I don't think I need to introduce myself," Jackie began, her voice low and calm, but menacing. "I represent several thousand people you've been trying to destroy!"

"I know who you are! What are you doing here?"

"Yes, I know you know who I am, but you didn't expect to see me, did you? I figured it was time I brought you out in the open, rather than letting you skulk around like the murderous thief you are."

"What are you talking about? Are you mad?"

"Honey, who is this woman?"

"Now that you mention it," Jackie continued, ignoring her, "I AM mad and I think it's time we got some things straight. You better leave my company alone. The FBI knows everything you've been doing."

"Are you really threatening me?"

"You catch on fast for someone as stupid as you are! I know you were behind the bombing of my oil platform and my service station in Atlanta and I know you're still trying to destroy my company, but the bodies are piling up and the Feds are coming for you."

Wood blinked and his eyes moved quickly from side to side, then he recovered and leaned toward Jackie. She glanced at Bill, whose eyes widened and his hand went inside his coat.

"You better be careful who you threaten young lady," Wood said and he raised his smartphone which showed an app Jackie didn't recognize.

"What's that?" Jackie asked.

"That's what I just used to call my security detail. They're as big as your goon but there's three of them."

Jackie quickly reached inside her shoulder bag, pulled out her chrome, .38-caliber revolver and laid it on the table without taking her hand off it. The woman screamed. Wood almost fell out of his chair backing up. A few people at nearby tables looked in their direction.

"Ms. James, please!" Bill whispered.

"I know who you are and I'm talking to the FBI," Jackie said in a loud whisper as she continued to hold the gun but not pointing it at anyone. "I've gotten to know them pretty well the past few months. If anything happens to me they'll know where to look."

Jackie turned to Bill. "Let's go!"

She stood and put the gun back in her bag, then started toward the front door.

* * *

Bill started to follow, but then he saw in a gilt-edged mirror on the dining room wall three burly men dressed in black suits entering the foyer of the restaurant.

"Ms. James! This way! Now!" Bill shouted and he grabbed her arm roughly and hustled her the other way toward the kitchen. "Now you're doing what I tell you!"

As they passed through the kitchen door, Bill paused long enough to look back and see the three men talking to Wood, who then gestured toward the kitchen.

"Coming through! Out of the way!" Bill's booming voice scattered the chefs and wait staff at work in the large commercial kitchen as he moved Jackie along forcefully.

Soon they were at the back of the restaurant. On impulse, Bill grabbed a mop from a bucket parked by the double doors and then pushed Jackie through into the alley. He looked back again and could hear commotion behind them but couldn't see anything because of racks of pots hanging from the ceiling.

He followed Jackie out the doors and quickly slid the mop through the metal handles. *It won't slow them down for long, but maybe it will be enough*, he thought.

"That was NOT COOL, Ms. James!" Bill exclaimed as he turned from the door. "How am I supposed to protect you when you do things like that? Wood's gorillas are right behind us."

"I can handle myself!" she said, taking the revolver out of her bag again.

"I don't doubt you can handle a .38, but do you know who you're dealing with here? You told me yourself that this guy orders people killed. The 'security' he called are not night watchmen. They're more likely borderline criminals he's got on a leash. Now let's go!"

They were in a narrow alley and had to thread their way carefully because it was littered with junk and crowded with garbage dumpsters. The rain had made puddles and there wasn't much light.

"Now, we've got to get back to the car but we don't want to run into his security," Bill said in a commanding whisper as they rounded the back corner of the building. "So, you stay behind me and keep an eye out for anyone coming toward us."

Bill started around the corner of the building and took a semi-automatic pistol from under his coat, holding it low against his side with his finger outside the trigger guard.

"You've had that the whole time?" Jackie whispered.

"Shh!"

"That's another benefit of flying your own private jet."

Bill saw nothing funny about Jackie's remark. Soon they were at the front corner of the building and they could see the rental car across the street.

Just then Bill heard a cracking sound and the noise of a door opening at the back of the building.

"I think they're coming!" Jackie whispered.

"No doubt," Bill answered. "We gotta run across the street and get in the car. Now!"

As they started across the street at a trot, Bill looked across toward the awning over the entry to the restaurant and stopped dead still in the middle of the street.

"What's going on?" Jackie whispered.

"Get in the car, Ms. James," Bill said throwing her the keys.

He heard the keys fall to the pavement but continued looking at the restaurant where two of Wood's security men were coming out the front door and he knew the other was coming around from the back of the restaurant.

"Get the keys and get in the car, now!" Bill said.

Still standing in the middle of the street, Bill raised his pistol and the two men coming from the front door of the restaurant saw him and dove behind a low brick planter at the entrance.

That was exactly what Bill was counting on. He immediately turned and hopped into the driver's side of the car.

"Keys!" he demanded.

"Already in the ignition."

Bill started the engine of the late-model compact sedan, slammed it into gear and stomped the gas pedal to the floor. The car leapt away from the curb and careened down the four-lane boulevard, water spraying from under the tires on the wet street. Startled drivers in other cars swerved out of the way.

"They're getting in a black SUV," Jackie said, looking back. "They're following us!"

Bill said nothing, but was thinking as fast as he was driving.

* * *

"Look back! Tell me how many cars between us," Bill demanded.

Jackie readily obeyed, thinking she knew what Bill was going to try to do.

"Across the two lanes, looks like about five," she said, counting headlights through the rain-soaked back glass.

The street was four-lanes wide. Jackie knew that would make it easier for the SUV to move closer to them than if they were on a two-lane road. Sure enough, the SUV was swerving, changing lanes dangerously to get closer.

"Oops, make that four," Jackie said.

"Can we turn off without them knowing?"

"I doubt it. The road's too straight."

"Better get that .38 ready!" Bill shouted and changed lanes himself, apparently to get positioned for a sudden right turn.

Jackie was suddenly paralyzed by fear. Would she have to actually fire her revolver from a moving car?

"I don't know if I can!"

"Don't wimp out now! You may have no choice!"

Jackie took the chrome revolver from her bag and looked down at it. It was reflecting the ever-changing light from street lamps as they sped under them. She willed herself into action, tamping down her fear.

"Okay, get us in the left lane so they'll come up on the right," Jackie said, her mouth suddenly dry.

"How many cars now?" Bill asked, changing lanes again.

"Three."

"They'll be on us soon. That SUV has a lot more power than this compact."

Jackie gulped and turned to face the window as Bill changed lanes again. She pushed the button to lower the window and ignored the rain coming in. Releasing her seatbelt, she turned around in her seat and got up on one knee facing back. There were just two cars between them now, one in each lane.

Then the car in the right lane turned off on a side street and there was nothing between them and the SUV, which now changed lanes again so it could come up on their right, just as Jackie had planned, but she felt like she might faint as she slowly raised the revolver.

"What should I do?" she asked Bill.

"Shoot the front tire, if you can."

Just then, she saw the back window of the SUV roll down and a black-suited arm come out holding something shiny. It was a gun!

What happened next took Jackie's breath away.

She heard a CRASH and the SUV abruptly swerved to the left, barely missing the back of Jackie's rental car and then the rear was airborne! It was like the right front wheel buckled under and the back of the vehicle flew up in the air and went over the front as it tumbled end for end on the wet pavement. For a moment Jackie feared the truck would come down on top of them.

The SUV came down on its roof with a terrific crash and the sound of glass shattering, then a loud scraping noise as it slid along the street, finally rocking to a stop. Other cars squealed to sliding stops, trying to avoid hitting the wreck.

"What happened?" Bill shouted, letting up on the gas slightly and looking in the rearview mirror. "Did you shoot their tire?"

"No, they just all of a sudden flipped over! They might have been hit by another car," Jackie said still looking back at the wreck. "Wait! What's this? A car coming up fast past the SUV and it appears to be damaged."

Jackie's grip on the revolver tightened again as she saw the car speed past the wreck, changing lanes and move to come even with them on the right.

She had begun to raise the barrel of her gun and put it out the window when a street light illuminated the driver's face.

"Patrick?"

CHAPTER TWENTY-NINE

Bill pulled into a well-lit service station and Patrick's car limped in behind.

Jackie was first out of the car.

"What are you doing here?" she asked Patrick, bewildered.

"Destroying a rental car, apparently," Patrick answered as he got out. "Are you okay?"

Jackie didn't answer immediately but just sputtered, trying to understand.

"Hi, I'm Bill, and I guess you're the 'Patrick' I've heard about," Bill said, stretching out his hand.

"Yeah, well, I hadn't heard about you until this morning," Patrick answered taking the proffered handshake.

"Do we have you to thank for what happened back there?"

"Yeah, I think I may have just committed a hit-and-run."

"Was that a PIT maneuver?" Bill asked.

"Yes, that was my first. Years ago, I reported on police practicing moves like that but I never did one myself," Patrick looked at the front of his rental car, which had the bumper nearly torn off and one fender badly damaged. "I don't think I'll be getting my deposit back."

"I don't understand. What did you do?" Jackie asked.

"A PIT maneuver. I pulled up next to them with my front fender next to their rear fender, gave the steering wheel a hard jerk to the right," Patrick showed with his hands what he had done with the wheel, "to bang into them and that caused them to go into a spin. I didn't expect them to flip over, but I guess the wet pavement helped that along."

"How did you find us?" Jackie asked, still really confused about everything that had happened.

"Well, you remember when I helped you set up your iPhone®?"

"Yes, of course."

"Well, don't be mad. I installed an app that let me know where your phone was."

"You were spying on me?"

"No! I turned the app off right after we got it all set up, but, thank God, I didn't delete it. When you didn't answer your phone, I was afraid you would have done something foolish and would be in danger so I turned it on to see where you were. I had just driven up to the restaurant, when I saw the SUV take off after you."

"Wow," Bill said. "That was a good intuition you had about our situation right then."

"I didn't know what was going on, but I knew it looked like you were being chased so I got as close as I could to see who was after you. That's when I saw the gun and decided I had to try to ram them."

"Well, I'd say you likely saved our bacon," Bill said extending his hand, which Patrick shook again. "Thank you."

"Yes, thank you so much, but why did you come?" Jackie asked Patrick.

"When I found out you had gone to Seattle I was afraid you would confront Wood and be in danger. And I was right to be concerned, wasn't I?"

Jackie looked over at Bill, who scowled.

"Well, we did have occasion to meet the upstanding Mr. Wood," Jackie said.

"How did that go?"

"I guess it could have gone better," Jackie answered, glancing over at Bill again, whose look said, *not cool.*

"How did you know I was in Seattle?"

"Doris told me. She's worried about you too."

"Good old Doris," Jackie said.

* * *

Soon Jackie and Bill were back in the car with Patrick following in his damaged rental. They had decided to find an out-of-the way motel to stay the night, rather than the upscale lodging Jackie had reserved.

"What were you thinking, pulling a gun on him?" Bill demanded as he parked the car.

"Hey, I grew up in the rodeo, where we literally take the bull by the horns!" Jackie defended herself.

"Not cool," Bill muttered.

Jackie knew he was right, but it felt good to actually take action.

* * *

"Let's go," Special Agent Samuel Jorgensen ordered the young agent behind the wheel of the black Suburban. The long SUV eased away from the parking garage and onto the street in the early morning, leading the way as a caravan of four black vehicles left Seattle's FBI field office, where Jorgensen had arrived from D.C. just yesterday. Two of the three other cars were long sedans and the fourth was another specially equipped Suburban. Their passengers were agents who were armed with much more than the semi-automatic pistol Jorgensen carried, though he wondered if they would need weapons.

He checked the safety on his Glock 17. The fact that this suspect was a corporate type, and a tree-hugging non-profit corporate type to boot, meant he himself was likely harmless, in spite of his crimes. But cornered animals can be ferocious. So, Jorgensen made sure his standard-issue sidearm was ready.

The arrest of Jason Wood would bring to a close an investigation that started months ago, Jorgensen thought, rehearsing what they had learned. Wood had apparently been the mastermind behind the bombing of the oil platform and other acts of environmental terrorism, the gas tax bill with the damage it had done to the whole country's economy, the injunction against the bill to repeal the gas tax and, most recently, the manipulation of the financial markets that brought down one company and almost sunk another.

And the worst part was that people were dead either directly or indirectly because of Wood's actions. Wood was obviously smart and ambitious, but misguided. Others involved in his plot had been rounded up months ago, and now they would get the ringleader. It would be good to put him behind bars and end his criminal career.

"This guy Wood," said Special Agent Brett Davis to Jorgensen from the front seat. "He's a big deal around here, you know?" As section chief of the Seattle field office, he appeared anxious to connect with the guy from Washington.

"Yeah, I figured," Jorgensen replied.

"He's given money to the police and the Mayor's charity drives."

"Yeah, he's a prince."

"Hard to believe he was into all this."

"Well, you can believe it."

"I'm not doubting it," Davis hastened to say. "Just hard to believe, that's all."

Jorgensen didn't say any more. He knew prolonging the conversation would just be distracting to the other men in the car, who hadn't spoken but were looking intently through the windshield, apparently mentally preparing for their task. Davis was directing his men for the arrest and Jorgensen was just there to see his investigation to its conclusion.

They arrived at the high-rise headquarters building of Champions of Mother Earth, and Davis began positioning his men as they exited the cars while Jorgensen walked toward the large gold-framed front door.

"Taylor and MacDonald, get around to the back of the building," Davis ordered. "Make sure no one gets out that way. You guys, Jackson and Thompson, eyes on the front door. Everybody else, inside with us."

Davis stationed two more agents in the lobby near the elevators. They were taking no chances on their target slipping out. Jorgensen, Davis and four remaining agents got into an elevator for the ride to the penthouse.

"Pretty sweet digs for a non-profit," Davis remarked, as the elevator slowly ascended.

"Yeah," Jorgensen replied. "Yeah, he has his fingers in a lot of pies."

When they arrived at the top floor, they exited the elevator and turned toward the huge polished wood doors with large letters on the wall and a green and gold logo that said, "Champions of Mother Earth."

Jorgensen was right on Davis' heels going through the large doors. A pretty receptionist looked up but her automatic smile froze then faded as she saw the six men in their dark suits, some with weapons out.

Davis took out his badge and showed it to the receptionist. "I'm Special Agent Brett Davis of the Seattle field office of the FBI. I and my colleagues need to see Jason Wood immediately."

"Uh, I'm afraid you can't," stuttered the receptionist.

"You tell him to get out here, now!" Davis demanded.

"No, I mean..." began the receptionist, her voice cracking a little.

"You can't tell me no, little girl," Davis shouted as other people in the office took notice.

"He's not here!" the receptionist finally blurted out.

"Where is he?"

"He and his wife left on vacation today."

"Vacation? Where?"

"Somewhere in Europe I think. Ann..., Ann...?"

"Andorra?" Jorgensen asked loudly.

"Yes, I think so."

"The one country in Western Europe that doesn't have an extradition treaty with the U.S.!" Jorgensen said to Davis. "When did he leave?" he demanded from the trembling receptionist.

"Just an hour ago or less," said the receptionist meekly.

The six men turned without needing orders and fairly ran out the large double doors and back to the elevator.

"Thompson, you and the others on the ground floor," Davis shouted into his comm. "Wood is at the airport headed out of the country. Leave now. He's boarding a flight to Andorra. We'll call to get the flight grounded then we'll be right behind you."

The other three vehicles were long gone when the six agents exited the elevator in the lobby and ran to their parked SUV. On the way to the airport, Davis had another agent begin calling airlines to see who had flights to Andorra.

"How long to get to the airport?" asked Jorgensen. He didn't know Seattle at all.

"A half hour on a good day," Davis answered.

Let's hope this is a good day, Jorgensen thought.

* * *

The doors were closed on the Airbus bound for Newark, but it was still at the gate when Jorgensen, Davis and the other agents got there. Thompson and the others who had arrived first were standing at the end of the jetway with a small, nervous man in a United Airlines uniform.

Seeing Jorgensen and Davis coming down the jet way at a trot, Thompson said to the United gate attendant, "Open it up."

The man's voice cracked a little as he spoke into a walkie-talkie, "Open the door now, please. The FBI is here."

Thompson turned to Jorgensen and Davis. "They're in row 3, A and B."

"First class to the last," Jorgensen said.

The massive airplane door pivoted open and the agents poured through, past the flight attendant who opened it and a curious pilot standing outside the cockpit.

It was a very short walk to row 3, so soon Jorgensen and Davis, with pistols drawn and held low, were standing facing Jason Wood and his 20-something wife. Both faces were gray with fear.

"Jason Wood, you are under arrest for funding the terrorist attack on the Gulf Pride oil platform, for the murder of George Donaldson and for assorted other crimes," Jorgensen said loudly.

The other passengers in first class were obviously terrified, not knowing if Wood would resist arrest and bullets would fly. But Wood, sitting in the aisle seat, raised his hands and slowly rose and stood in the aisle. Davis roughly spun him around and jerked his hands behind him, tying them with nylon slip ties he pulled from his suit coat pocket.

The agents stood aside while Davis led Jason Wood to the door of the airplane and up the jet way, the other agents following. Wood's wife, half sitting, half standing in the window seat, watched in fear as her husband was led away, bound.

"Mrs. Wood," Jorgensen said.

She turned to him, her fearful face suddenly changing to defiant. "You'll never get away with this!"

"Come with me," Jorgensen said, his pistol still held downward. "You may not have been involved in your husband's criminal activity, but come with us until we sort it out."

Mrs. Wood's face finally changed again when she looked down at Jorgensen's gun and the full impact of what was happening dawned on her.

"Can I get my carry-on?"

"We'll carry it for you," Jorgensen said, as if he was being a gentleman, but really ensuring she had nothing in it she could use against him. "Thompson, could you carry the lady's bag?"

Thompson came forward and took the bag she pointed out from the overhead bin and headed out of the airplane. Jorgensen motioned for Mrs. Wood to go ahead of him. She did so, obediently, but held her head high, trying to maintain a minimum level of dignity.

* * *

Jackie, Bill and Patrick watched from Jackie's rented car as Special Agent Jorgensen and the other agents loaded Mr. and Mrs. Jason Wood into a Black SUV preparing to drive away.

"So, the FBI called you?" Bill asked Jackie, obviously in awe.

"Yes, we've become quite chummy," Jackie answered, laughing. Jorgensen had called her to let her know they had arrested Wood and she had surprised him by telling him she was in Seattle. "Actually, I've only talked to a few of them and they were mostly pumping me for information that would help in their investigations."

"Too bad we can't sit down with Jorgensen," Patrick said from the back seat, thinking about the work he was missing and maybe an interview would justify his being AWOL. "But I suspect he'll be pretty busy. Anyway, I've got a rent-a-wreck to return and face the music."

"Patrick, I'll pay whatever you have to pay," Jackie said. "You probably saved our lives last night."

"Wow. That would be much appreciated. The bill will probably be large though."

Just then Jorgensen apparently noticed the trio in the car and walked over. Jackie rolled her window down.

"What have we here?" Jorgensen said, looking first at Jackie then Patrick in the back seat. "I must say I'm surprised to see you both here."

"Yes, well, that's my doing," Jackie admitted. "I wanted to give Jason Wood a piece of my mind."

"That doesn't sound like a great idea to me, Ms. James."

"Yeah, you're right, as it turns out."

"Sam," Patrick said, opening the back door of the car and standing to look Jorgensen in the eye. "I might need your help with something."

"Oh, and what would that be?"

"Well, Wood sent his security goons after Jackie and Bill, here, last night and I had to stop them."

"Stop them how?"

"While they were chasing them in their car, I kinda upended their vehicle using a PIT maneuver. In the process, I caused a messy accident and trashed my rental car, so I need some smoothing over with the local cops."

"This happened last night? Was anyone hurt?"

"Only the bad guys, I think. I kinda left the scene, due to the gun the security guy was pointing at their car."

Jorgensen looked at Patrick, then at Jackie, then back at Patrick.

"You do know how to make a mess, Garrity."

"If he hadn't done it, we might not have lived to tell it," Jackie said.

"Okay, you'd better be on the up-and-up. Since yesterday you called with information that confirmed what we had, we were able to make an air-tight arrest, so I guess I owe you one. I'll talk to the police, but you'll need to come with me so we can sit down and explain the whole business."

"Yes, of course."

296

"I guess you'd better all come, since you were all involved."

"Yes, sir. Thank you so much," Jackie answered.

"Stay here so I can make arrangements and find the precinct doing the investigation. I'll be right back."

Jorgensen walked back to the SUV and talked to the other agents for a few minutes. One of them made a phone call and Jorgensen wrote down some information.

"Do you think Jorgensen will take Wood to D.C.?" Jackie asked while they waited for him to return.

"Probably. That's his jurisdiction," Patrick said. "But this was a nationwide case, so that's where they'll want to prosecute."

"I'm just glad it's all over," Jackie said. "Well, the danger anyway. We've still got to go to court."

"You haven't told me what you said to Wood," Patrick said.

Jackie looked at Bill.

"You were right to be concerned," Bill said from the driver's seat, turning his thick neck to sort of be able to see Patrick in the back seat.

"What happened?"

"Let's just say she is fearless, even when she should be afraid."

"What did you do?" Patrick persisted, directing this question to Jackie.

Jackie said, "Maybe I'll tell you all about it sometime."

Jorgensen concluded his conversation with the other agents and walked back to Jackie's rental car.

"Okay, I know which precinct is investigating the accident. The other agents will take our lovely couple to lock-up and I'm with you. I don't have a car, so you'll have to take me there with you. I've got the address."

He didn't give them a chance to invite him, but opened the back door and slid in beside Patrick.

"I'd better not regret this," Jorgensen said as Bill pulled the car away from the curb and headed for the airport exit.

CHAPTER THIRTY

Jackie was not eager to have him, but it made no sense for Patrick to fly commercial back to Houston, so she invited him to fly with them on the Lear. He had bought a one-way ticket to Seattle, not knowing when he would be coming back, but he had bought a round-trip ticket to Houston from D.C.

The time at the car rental agency and the police precinct had taken most of the day. Thanks to Jorgensen vouching for him, Patrick would not be charged. The police did find several weapons at the scene of the accident, so the story the trio told was plausible, even though the policemen were surprised to find out that the well-known citizen and philanthropist Jason Wood was being arrested for murder and other crimes and employed armed thugs to do his bidding.

Jackie and Bill somehow forgot to mention the weapons they themselves were carrying.

Once they were underway in the jet, Bill sat in a seat in the rear of the plane and was soon sleeping. Jackie was sitting in the front row, lost in thought and Patrick appeared at her side.

"Must be nice," Patrick said with a sheepish grin.

"What?"

"Must be nice to have your own private jet to go anywhere, whenever you need to."

"Actually, it IS nice," Jackie answered. "I make no apologies for it. It actually saves us money when we need to take a bunch of people somewhere."

"That's a little hard to believe," Patrick said, still awkwardly standing in the aisle.

"Go ahead, sit down," Jackie said, finally.

"Thanks," Patrick said, sitting in the single seat across the aisle from her.

"Well, it does save us money, especially since it's shared."

"Oh?"

"Yes, it's a four-way, time-share lease. That way, we don't pay for time we don't use, we don't have to hire the pilots and we don't have to maintain it. We do have to reserve it, but we can usually get it on short notice."

"That's cool," Patrick said nonchalantly.

* * *

They sat in awkward silence for a minute or two. Patrick wanted to take the opportunity to finally apologize for leaking the news about the merger, but he was having difficulty finding his voice. Then Jackie spoke.

"Why did you come?"

"To Seattle? Or Houston?"

"To Seattle."

"Because I was worried about you."

"Worried for my safety or worried I would do something stupid?"

"Both, I guess," Patrick answered cautiously. "I didn't know what was happening and I felt responsible because I told you about Wood. You've never told me what happened when you – went to talk to him."

Patrick could see anger flare in Jackie's eyes for a second when he said he had been afraid she might do something stupid, but then she spoke, avoiding looking Patrick in the eye.

"Well, you heard Bill say you were right to be worried," she began. "I came to Seattle not knowing what I was going to do or say; just that I wanted to give him a piece of my mind."

Patrick knew better than to say anything, but just let her talk. She hesitated and looked down as if trying to decide how to continue.

"When we got there, we went straight to the Champions of Mother Earth building and I demanded to see Wood. The receptionist pretty much told us he wasn't available and said we should come back tomorrow; that is, today."

Patrick nodded, encouraging her to continue, but still not wanting to interrupt.

"But, of course, I wouldn't take 'no' for an answer, so we waited until he came out and got into his car, then we followed him, saw him pick up his wife and followed them to a restaurant."

You followed him? Patrick thought, alarmed. With difficulty, he still said nothing.

"We waited a bit for them to get seated, then we went in and crashed his dinner."

"What did you say?" Patrick said, instead of saying what he was thinking: *Are you crazy?*

"I told him I knew who he was and what he'd been doing and he'd better stop attacking my company and my people."

"Did he admit it?"

"No, but he didn't deny anything either."

"How did he react?"

"He was confused and mumbling at first, but then he got defiant. Of course, that was after I showed him this."

Jackie reached into her shoulder bag and withdrew her chrome-plated revolver.

"Oh, my God!"

"That's what he said," Jackie said. The corners of her mouth tightened and, for a moment, he saw a bit of the playful impishness he had grown to love in her, but he couldn't focus on that.

"You pulled a gun on him in a public place?"

"I didn't point it at him; I just laid it on the table and he responded by using an app to call his security detail."

"And I guess that's when I got there?"

"Apparently, so you know the rest."

"You WERE in danger," Patrick said, while thinking, *and you did do something stupid*. "Thank God you're all right."

"What do you care?" Jackie snarled then turned to face him. "I'm sorry. I appreciate what you did. You saved us."

Patrick knew it was now or never.

"I've never had a chance to apologize," Patrick said, not being specific. They both knew why she was angry.

"I'm not sure an apology will cut it," Jackie said.

"Yes, I know I can't undo the damage. . ."

"Petrocom failed after your leak! No, that can't be undone."

Patrick didn't think his leaking the merger talks was the only cause of Petrocom's bankruptcy, but he knew better than to argue that point with her. Somehow, he had to get her to forgive him.

"I know it was wrong. Please forgive me," he pleaded, reaching across the aisle, but not quite touching her.

Jackie turned to look at him intently as if trying to judge his sincerity. Patrick quickly continued, with a speech he had gone over in his head many times.

"I've been going to meetings again and one thing I have to do is ask forgiveness of those I've wronged. You're certainly not the only one, but you're the one I want forgiveness from the most."

"Meetings?"

"Yes, I've had to get back in touch with my 'Higher Power' and..."

"Twelve Step meetings?"

"Yes." Patrick thought Jackie's face softened a bit at that. "I have struggled a bit since.... Quite a bit, actually."

"Are you out of the woods?"

"You're never out of the woods with alcoholism," Patrick said, knowing he was stating the obvious. "But I've been sober again for a couple of weeks now."

* * *

Jackie stared straight ahead for a while, then her gaze dropped to her hands folded in her lap. She was struggling too. Patrick had asked her to forgive him, but she didn't know if she could. She briefly wondered if it was stubbornness and pride that prevented her or if she was justified in holding him at arms' length.

She continued arguing with herself, the side that didn't want to forgive using Patrick's alcoholism as a reason to push him away. Did she really want that problem to be part of her life?

But while they were together in the plane she couldn't push him away very far. Her Christian side was arguing for forgiveness and reminding her that she had done some foolish and impulsive things, too. And didn't the fact that he came to Seattle mean he cared about her?

Back and forth she battled with herself while saying nothing. She could feel Patrick glancing over at her furtively, but staying quiet. The silence between them was becoming unbearable.

If she forgave him, what would that mean? Would they pick up where they left off; building a relationship that might or might not lead to something permanent? They were from different worlds, as his indiscretion showed. *Could they keep their professional lives from interfering with one another?*

* * *

Patrick shifted his weight on the plush seat and tugged at his collar which was already unbuttoned. He was beginning to think she would never forgive him. As she sat there looking down, he wished he knew what she was thinking; what he could say to make it better.

Then the old fears came back: how they were so different; she was rich, he lived relatively hand-to-mouth. It was true that she had more of a middle-class, practical approach to life and didn't put on airs, but there was still that economic space between them.

He had influence through his writing and reporting, but she and her industry directly affected the lives of everyone in the country every day.

His chosen profession expected him to be skeptical – indeed cynical - about business people, whereas she was totally convinced of the benefits of capitalism to people at all levels of the economic ladder.

Finally, he decided to break the uncomfortable silence.

"Look, I know what I did was wrong. I have wished over and over I could go back and do it differently, but that's impossible. I've asked you to forgive me and I'll keep asking, but if you can't, I understand."

She turned to look at him with flushed cheeks and wet eyes.

"How could you?!" she said in a loud whisper. "I'm upset about more than just the betrayal, which was bad enough, but it highlighted the differences between us. I could accept your apology, but I don't know if it would be a good idea to continue a relationship."

Patrick didn't say anything, knowing the question was not for him to answer. He swallowed hard, thinking he could sense where she was going.

"When I was engaged before," she continued quietly, beginning to cry, "my fiancée left before the wedding because he said we were too different. But in that case, the main difference was just that his parents' business was smaller than mine. We had other things in common. But with you and me, there are so many ways we are different."

"I know you are in a totally different league economically," Patrick admitted.

"I don't care about that," Jackie snapped. "You know that I've worked shoulder to shoulder with many of the laborers in my company before becoming CEO: men and women working by the hour, doing jobs that are dirty and dangerous. Most people would say you and your profession are an order of magnitude above them, but that's not how I value people. I should think you would know me better than that by now."

Patrick had to look away slightly, now that she was unloading. He had wanted her to talk, but he was overwhelmed.

"No," she went on, "what concerns me is our different backgrounds regarding family and faith. I know your divorce was because of alcohol and that concerns me. I'm not saying divorce is a deal killer, but even you said you're never out of the woods with alcoholism."

Patrick wanted to jump to his own defense as he heard his recent words thrown back at him, but he knew better.

"And you don't know about my upbringing in church," Jackie continued. "To say my people are strait-laced is being kind. I might want to loosen up, but my father's influence is still very strong."

"You don't know strait-laced until you've been taught by nuns in Catholic school," Patrick said finally, trying desperately to lighten the mood.

"Yes, that's another thing," Jackie continued, ignoring the joke. "My grandfather would turn over in his grave if I married a Catholic, and a lapsed Catholic at that!"

"Married?"

"What did I say?" Jackie's face went red as she and Patrick looked at each other across the aisle. "I meant if I was together with a Catholic."

"I understand," Patrick answered, continuing to look deep into her moist eyes.

"Oh, my stars!" Jackie put her hands over her face, obviously embarrassed.

To his surprise, he felt emboldened by her slip of the tongue. "You're wondering if there's a future in a relationship with me. I hope the answer is 'yes'. Yes, I'm a lapsed Catholic and you're a Baptist who feels the need to loosen up. But I'm pushed toward a relationship with God whether I like it or not because of my alcoholism and if I'm not a good Catholic that just means there may be less to conflict with you as a good Baptist.

"By the way, Baptists don't handle snakes, do they?"

She finally laughed and the tension broke, then she looked at him earnestly.

"You just need to know that my faith is important to me."

"And mine is important to me" he replied. "They may look different, but we both know we need it."

She didn't look away, but appeared to be studying his face for signs of sincerity.

"If I say I forgive you," she began slowly. "Can we talk about other things for the rest of the flight and worry about the future another time?"

Patrick felt a wave of relief wash over him so he found it difficult to finally say, "Sure. Thank-you."

CHAPTER THIRTY-ONE

Texas is such a big state, Jonesy thought. He had spent a week in San Antonio, once again finding a homeless shelter where he could get a meal once a day and a reasonably nice bed, but now he knew he had to move on. If he stayed in one place too long, someone might recognize him. So, he checked his dwindling supply of cash and began walking to the bus station where he had come in from Texarkana.

The shelter didn't allow its residents to stay there all day, so his days had been spent walking, avoiding police, learning the town and finding places he could go to get out of the sun or the rare rain shower. He now knew his way around pretty well, so returning to the bus station was easy.

He had resisted efforts by those at the shelter to help him. They had suggestions for finding a no-skills-required job and cheap places to stay. But applying for jobs meant showing a drivers' license and supplying a Social Security number, two things he couldn't risk doing.

The more he thought about it, the more he realized that getting into Mexico would not be an option. He didn't have his passport and Mexico was much stricter about illegal border crossing than the United States seemed to be. He realized he might have to float from shelter to homeless shelter forever.

Or he could just turn himself in. That would end the running. He wasn't sure how many law enforcement agencies were seeking him, but he knew the murder of a Federal judge would not be ignored. He had been surprised that he had survived the explosion, but was even more surprised that he hadn't been caught. The close call in Texarkana was as close as law enforcement had gotten, as far as he knew.

Once he got to the bus station, he went inside to the rest room and tried to make himself presentable. Walking for miles in the heat undid everything he had done before leaving the shelter and he didn't want to attract any undue attention because of an unkempt appearance.

That done, he went to the ticket window.

"I need a ticket to Corpus Christi," he told the young, heavy-set woman at the window.

* * *

Darla Stowe was bored with the drudgery of her job at the Greyhound bus station in San Antonio, so she barely looked up at the man who had appeared at her window, but when she saw him, she did a double-take. A flyer from the Texas Rangers had been distributed to all ticket agents. She glanced down at it on the shelf under her counter. She looked carefully at it and then looked up at the man at the window, smiling.

"That'll be $37.55"

Darla watched the man closely, continuing to smile as he pushed two twenty-dollar bills through the window. She punched the fare into the computer and the ticket was printed. At the same time a cash drawer opened automatically and she retrieved the specified amount of change.

"Here you are," she said cheerily as she slid the change and the ticket to the man. "The bus will be leaving in an hour and fifteen minutes." He said nothing but just turned and walked toward the waiting area.

Darla immediately closed her window, put the "Next Window" sign in place and took the flyer from under the counter. *Yes*, she decided, *that is the man on the flyer. Wanted for murder!* She got up and went to find her supervisor.

* * *

Jonesy shifted his weight on the hard, plastic seat. Waiting area seats like these, where four or more were bolted together, seemed to be designed as instruments of torture. Getting comfortable was next to impossible. He looked forward to getting on the bus where he would have several hours of time in a more comfortable seat and could get some good sleep. He had slept well at the shelter, but what else did he have to do?

He wasn't a reader or he might have deigned to buy a newspaper, but there was also the off chance that his picture might be in it, so he'd just as soon not make one available on the bus. He checked the clock on the station wall: only a half hour before the bus would be leaving.

Just then, he noticed some movement out of the corner of his eye. A man in a uniform. *So what?* There were bus drivers and security guards and even janitors in uniform at the station. But this had been none of those. The uniformed man wore a cowboy hat and had gone through the door into the room where the ticket agents sat behind bullet-proof glass. He noticed that a couple of the windows had blinds pulled and signs directing to "Next Window." As he looked he saw one of the blinds being pulled apart just far enough for someone to look out.

Suddenly, he panicked and instinctively knew he needed to run. It took all his self control to get up and slowly walk toward the exit, carrying his duffle bag.

When he was out the front door of the station, he began to run as fast as his short legs would carry him. It was then that he saw two more uniformed men in cowboy hats get out of a car across the street, looking directly at him.

"Tobias Jones! Stop!" one of the men shouted, drawing a semi-automatic pistol from a black holster at his side as he began running across the street, the other man close behind.

In full-fledged panic now, Jonesy continued running and reaching into his pocket. With difficulty, he withdrew the pistol he had taken from the deputy in Texarkana, but before he could raise it, the uniformed man fired a single shot which struck Jonesy in the thigh.

Blinding pain knocked him down as surely as the bullet which hit his leg. He didn't realize he was falling, but only that his face slammed to the sidewalk. Though he was stunned, he was aware that the pistol was no longer in his hand.

As he rolled over on his back, the pain grew and he looked up to see the two uniformed officers standing over him with their guns pointed at his prostrate body. Jonesy could hear more feet running toward them. He was powerless to stop the darkness that was overtaking him.

* * *

"If we could just hold on a little bit longer," Jackie pled. Dennis Trask, Axiom's Chief Financial Officer, was in her office to propose a drastic strategy.

"With all due respect, Miss James, we don't know how long it will take the Supreme Court to rule, and when they do, we can't know the outcome beforehand. And it's even possible that the Supreme Court will choose not to hear the appeal at all."

Jackie didn't need to be reminded of that possibility. Marcus Williams had warned her that the Court had the prerogative to simply not hear the appeal, in which case the injunction would stand and the gas tax would continue at least until the Eighth Circuit deigned to set a trial date.

"So, tell me again why it's a good idea to sell assets?"

"With the gas tax in place we've been bleeding cash. 'Operation Backlash' gave us a reprieve and may have saved us, but there's a limit. With the market manipulation that took down Petrocom and has damaged us, we need a bold step to show we intend to remain solvent and strong, in spite of our loss in market 'cap.'"

Jackie considered what Marcus said. "So, selling off some properties will reassure stockholders and Standard and Poor's, I get that, but couldn't we just borrow more money until this is all over?"

"That would make our temporary cash situation look better, but it would almost certainly hurt our credit rating, so our interest rate would be higher and we would be paying through the nose for a long time. Increasing indebtedness would not likely help with investors and the ratings."

Jackie stood and walked from her desk to the floor-to-ceiling window overlooking Houston.

"What do you recommend we sell? And what makes you think anyone will buy, with the economy like it is?"

Dennis hesitated. Jackie sensed it wasn't because he didn't know what he wanted to say, but was afraid of her reaction.

"Go ahead. I'm a big girl. Give me your counsel!"

"Well, the western states have been underperforming."

"You mean like California?" Jackie knew the numbers without consulting Dennis' many spreadsheets. California had indeed been underperforming because of the gas tax. Pump prices in the state were already the highest in the nation before the gas tax. Now, all grades and blends were firmly against the cap of $6.00 per gallon. The high prices had resulted in a drop in demand in many areas of the state, making it difficult to predict the need, leading to shortages, hurting business further.

"California is not the only candidate, but it would be the most attractive to a buyer."

"We wouldn't have to sacrifice the entire state," Jackie mused. "It's already segmented into North and South divisions."

"That's true. The South is the plum."

"Which just means I hate to sacrifice it."

"So, what do you want to do?"

"Go back a year ago and have Jason Wood hit by a bus!" Then she recovered. "Sorry, I guess the strain is getting to me."

"I understand."

"So, I guess Southern California goes on the block."

Jackie thought about the 40-plus company-owned filling stations that would have a new logo, IF there was a company strong enough to buy them. Then there were all the people who would probably lose their jobs. Yes, some would be picked up by whoever the buyer was, but many would be out. She looked down at the framed photo of her father and mother on her desk. He had built Axiom by buying companies in trouble and turning them around. Now Axiom was the company in trouble.

* * *

"So, first of all, your case will pass the test of being a matter of Federal concern, because it's relating to two bills passed by Congress and signed by the president, as well as an injunction handed down by a Federal judge."

Daniel Moreau believed in giving the good news first. Those gathered in the twentieth-floor conference room in Houston included Jackie, Marcus Williams and a couple of other attorneys from Moreau's firm, Sinclair-Roberts-Dubois.

Jackie looked around the table as Moreau continued. She didn't say anything, but was thinking, "*This process is taking so long and costing so much money. Will Axiom even last long enough to get the case heard?*"

"The next step, the way it usually works, is to file suit in the local court," continued Moreau. "We've done that and gotten a judgement in our favor, so now it's on to Step Three. We have to prepare a "Petition for Certiorari." This will include the history of the case and all the basic facts we want the Court to be aware of, plus legal issues that are peculiar to our case."

"I guess that's because if there's no new precedent to be set, the court might not consider it?" asked Marcus.

"That's right. The Supreme Court, understandably I think, prioritizes cases that represent uncharted territory."

"Does our case do that?" Jackie asked.

"That's not clear cut. There may not be any earth-shaking precedent to come out of your case, but we can certainly point out the benefit to the public good of the Court hearing the case.

"Once we submit the Petition for Certiorari," Moreau continued, "the opposition is given a chance to respond. In this case, the opponent is the Federal government, specifically the District Court for the Eastern District of Missouri, where the injunction originated. Because the Eighth Circuit already ruled, I don't think there will be a stumbling block there. The Petition will then be evaluated by a collection of Supreme Court clerks, who will review all the documents, supply each of the nine justices with a summary and recommend for or against the Court hearing the case. Then the justices make the final decision."

"So, if the clerks don't like it, we don't get heard?" Jackie wondered aloud.

"That's possible, but the several clerks don't always agree, so the justices will make their own decision. And of course, they don't usually agree either. The majority decides."

"And the decision about hearing the case may not be the same as the decision about the case itself, right?" Marcus asked.

"That's right, you could have a unanimous vote to hear the case, because it's important, but a split vote on the case itself."

"How long will all this take?" Jackie asked.

"Unfortunately, the Court doesn't move quickly, unless it's an extreme need; for instance, when lawsuits concern the outcome of a Federal election. In a case like that, they can move within days. I think we will be able to make the case that the relief needed by the American people is urgent enough."

Jackie was only moderately reassured by that answer. "I sense that that's not all."

"No, it isn't," Moreau answered. "The bad news could be really bad. The Supreme Court's term usually ends in June. . ."

"June?! But it's June now!"

"Yes, they will extend into July if needed, but if they choose not to hear our case during this term, it could be as much as a year before we have a resolution."

Jackie looked at the floor and her eyes lost focus. *A year?!*

* * *

"Yes, Doris," Jackie said when the intercom buzzed on her desk phone.

"Daniel Moreau for you on line three."

"Thanks," she said, then pushed a button on the phone. It had been a tense two weeks since Moreau had been to Houston to lay out their strategy. "This is Jackie James. Mr. Moreau, please tell me you have good news."

"Well, the court will hear your appeal. They are giving it priority because of all that's happened, making sure that it gets included in this year's session."

"Oh, thank God! That IS good news."

"Yes, absolutely! Otherwise we'd have to wait until next year, or if they had decided not to hear it, we'd have to wait for it to play out in St. Louis, and then, if it didn't go our way, we'd have to go to the Supreme Court anyway, and it would definitely have to be next year."

"Yes, this is definitely the faster route."

"That's what we hoped for."

"Do we have a date?"

"Not yet, but it will be soon."

"I guess we're going back to Washington."

"Yes, you'll be coming to my town," Moreau said.

Jackie didn't say anything, but she was thinking that, in her mind, Washington, D.C., was still someone else's town.

CHAPTER THIRTY-TWO

She knew it was built purposely to inspire awe, but she was unprepared for how she felt entering the United States Supreme Court building. Jackie paused to look up at the soaring ceilings supported by their majestic columns. Everything was white marble and brass, it seemed. It gave the building an aura of permanence, of eternity really.

And that was appropriate, Jackie decided, because the decisions made here were indeed final. There was no recourse from the rulings handed down here. Future rulings were based on past precedent and would not be easily modified.

That awareness of finality was with her as she, along with the lawyers who would take center stage to argue their case, mounted the elliptical marble staircase to the great hall, which they traversed in silence, flanked by its nearly thirty-foot ceiling and Dorian columns, finally entering the courtroom itself.

Passing through the tall, wood-paneled door Jackie saw the huge room with plush, deep-red-and-yellow-patterned carpet. Dark wood was everywhere, from the leather padded chairs before the railing to the massive tables for the attorneys to the dais where the nine justices would soon sit in high-backed black leather chairs spaced as much as four feet apart.

The walls of the courtroom were white and on all four sides of the room were marble columns, with Ionian capitals this time, which left no doubt about the weight of the matters decided here.

The court had indeed given their case priority, scheduling it two weeks after they were decided they would hear their case. That didn't mean it would be ruled in their favor, of course.

Many people were filing into the room, but scarcely a sound was being made. Daniel Moreau silently gestured to Jackie and Marcus that they should take a seat in the two rows of seats before the railing but behind the tables reserved for the lawyers. There they would wait until their case was called.

Once seated, Jackie looked around again. The room itself inspired reverence, Jackie realized, thinking of some of the great cathedrals she had visited in Europe when she was in college. Their builders, like the builders of the Supreme Court building, understood the effect vaulted ceilings, elegant furnishings and grand columns would have on people. She decided that perhaps this was a type of cathedral, not dedicated to the worship of God, but to reverence for the law.

But God was not absent from the court. Jackie was able to look to the side above the soaring columns and see the frieze that she already knew included Moses, holding the Ten Commandments, as one of the world's great law givers and King Solomon, known for his wise judgements. These representatives of the God of the world's monotheistic religions reminded Jackie that, while this room was dedicated to reverence for the law, there was undoubtedly a great deal of praying that had happened here.

And she would be praying today, as Moreau made their case. She knew that they would have a very limited time – thirty minutes for each side - to make their oral arguments; that most of the deliberation would be done by the justices from the written briefs that Moreau and the attorney for the Eastern District of Missouri had supplied to the court.

So, Jackie wondered, *is the decision already made?* The justices had their briefs, bound in the blue covers that were required of petitioners. Everything about the briefs had to be done to the court's specifications, down to the type of paper and the size of the font used.

The justices could have already read them and decided. A chill went down her back as she thought about that. But, no, she decided, this hearing was important for the justices: to hear the argument made by a human being, not just dead paper. She hoped that the justices were keeping an open mind, because she knew that Daniel Moreau could be persuasive.

Just then, across the room, she saw a man she didn't recognize taking a seat at the table on the other side of the room. She assumed he was the attorney for the Eastern District of Missouri who would be taking the lead in presenting the Government's case.

* * *

Patrick Garrity was among those who slipped quietly into the gallery behind the railing. He could say he was there in his official capacity as a journalist, but he had not been given the assignment. The *Washington Herald* had its reporters who followed the Supreme Court, and they were here as well, although Patrick knew he could check with them back at the *Herald* offices to learn the angle they were taking.

It was good that he didn't have to report on these proceedings, Patrick realized, because he was hardly a disinterested observer. It had taken barely five seconds after entering the room before he spotted the back of Jackie's head. It was the first time he had seen her since he had hitched a ride on the Lear jet from Seattle to Houston.

They had not talked much since then. He was giving her space. She had said she would forgive him on the trip back, but their relationship was still on hold. Patrick wished there was a sure way to get it off dead center, but he knew instinctively that whatever he might do to try to talk to her or get things going again could wreck it permanently for him.

So, he was there to hear the case, but even more just to see her, if only the back of her head. She hadn't really even told him she was coming to D.C. That was hurtful and Patrick wondered if it was a bad, or even fatal, sign for their relationship.

A couple of hours went by as the court heard arguments in cases Patrick cared little about. Finally, the announcement came for Jackie's case.

* * *

"We'll hear arguments next in Case 142-840, Axiom Oil Incorporated versus the United States District for the Eastern District of Missouri and the consolidated case. Mr. Moreau," Chief Justice Raymond Powers announced the case that Jackie and the others were there for.

Moreau stepped up to the lectern sitting on the broad table before the dais.

"Mr. Chief Justice and may it please the court," he began, "Axiom Oil Incorporated simply asks that the will of the people be allowed to hold sway in the matter of the Petroleum Independence Act. The representatives of the people have passed bill 115-832 to repeal the Act and that is in line with what polls have indicated…"

"I shouldn't think that popular polls should influence what we decide to do in any case, Mr. Moreau." It was Marco Vega, the only Hispanic justice on the court. Jackie remembered from Moreau's briefing and from the notes that Wayne had supplied her that Vega was a Liberal from the Northwest and not likely to be sympathetic.

"Of course, this court is concerned with the law and with precedent rather than polls," answered Moreau, "but there are reasons to afford relief to the American people. Many are suffering because of the tax."

"But suffering also results from damage to the environment," Justice Vega insisted.

"That may turn out to be true someday," Moreau argued. "but uncovering an alleged conspiracy calls into question the original Act and the injunction which sustains it, your honor."

"Mr. Moreau," said Justice Simon Mayer of Florida, whom Jackie recalled was the swing vote on the court. "Is law enforcement confident that a conspiracy brought about the original Act as well as the injunction?"

"Your honor, the FBI is quite certain because they have the parties of the conspiracy in custody and at least one major player has turned state's evidence and is cooperating."

"That has little to do with the fact that the intent of the law was good," this was Justice Iris Hayden Goode, another Liberal from California. "Shouldn't that be our main focus?"

"With all due respect, your honor," Moreau answered, "I and my clients would argue that the effect of the Act and the injunction which upholds it have had very negative effects on the nation, slowing the economy and harming millions of people in the near term, while any effects on the environment are speculative in nature and would not come to fruition until the distant future."

"I have wondered if the original Act represented government overreach in mandating pricing and picking winners and losers in the marketplace?" asked Justice Frederick Waldrop, a rare Northeastern conservative from New Hampshire.

"My clients would agree that the market would be better served by allowing prices to take their natural course."

"But again," Justice Goode said, "Shouldn't we be focused on the good done by keeping the Act in place?"

"With respect, your honor, the conspiracy taints the Act and, likewise, the injunction," Moreau answered.

"Mr. Moreau, I'm curious as to why Axiom Oil Incorporated believes it has standing in this case, since it was not mentioned in the Act or the injunction? Could you expand on that?" Justice Mayer asked.

"That is a fair point, your honor, which I am happy to address. Axiom Oil Incorporated may not have been mentioned by name in the Act, but it was the attack on the Axiom facility which was used as a pretext for the original statute and that attack is now known to have been part of the conspiracy attempting to manipulate our nation's legislative process. Axiom has been at the center of this from the beginning."

"Thank you, Mr. Moreau."

"And if I might," Moreau continued, "The Act was calculated to harm companies like Axiom, and therefore has harmed the company's employees, stockholders and customers. If Axiom had not picked up the ball, so to speak, the injunction would have continued to harm the American people, whether they were directly related to Axiom or not."

Jackie watched as the back and forth of oral arguments continued. Moreau had explained that they would only have an hour for their case and roughly half that time would be given to the attorney representing the Eastern District of Missouri. Oral arguments before the Supreme Court were mainly to allow the justices to challenge the briefs each side had presented and see how they would answer.

"Thank you, Mr. Moreau," Chief Justice Powers said, by way of closing off Moreau's time after about 30 minutes had elapsed. "Mr. Phillips, please."

"Thank you, Mr. Chief Justice and may it please the court," David Phillips began his argument on behalf of the government. Jackie saw in her notes that he was the U.S. Attorney for the Eastern District and Moreau didn't expect him to do anything that would conflict with Judge Jackson's ruling.

"The case before us is brought on behalf of Axiom Oil Incorporated to appeal the injunction handed down by the late honorable Judge Everett Walker, a jurist of renown who, had he not been struck down by the hand of an Axiom employee, might have one day been nominated to sit on this court."

What in the world? Jackie thought. *Where is he going with this?*

"We at the Eastern District of Missouri believe Judge Walker's ruling should have been tried and finally decided in the Eastern District as would have been possible and should have been the case, given a little time."

"But time is of the essence for the American people, it would seem," argued Justice Rosalind Allred Gardiner. Jackie looked down at her notes and was reminded that Gardiner was a conservative from Tennessee, as evidenced by a soft Southern accent, though it was quite different from South Texas. "Mr. Moreau pointed out what we all are aware of: that there is considerable pain out in the country, as long as the Petroleum Independence Act is in effect."

"With respect, your honor," insisted Phillips, "the intent of the Act was to protect the American people from the negative effects of fossil fuels and the pollution which results from their use."

"But which is worse," Gardiner asked, "the immediate cost to their economic health or the long-term effects of pollution which may or may not come about?"

"I believe, your honor, that the Science is certain that the damage to our ecosystem could result in the death of the planet, in which case economic health will be passé."

"It seems to me that, that is a speculative issue in the future," Chief Justice Powers commented, "whereas the economic harm being experienced by the American people is easily demonstrated and observable now."

Jackie was surprised by the vigor of the District Court's arguments. She had thought that the decision of the Eighth Circuit allowing them to bring the appeal directly to the Supreme Court would mean that the District Court would virtually acquiesce, but that had not turned out to be the case.

Now she began to worry again. Soon the hour was nearly up and the Chief Justice spoke again.

"Thank you, Mr. Phillips. Mr. Moreau, your reply?"

"Thank you, your Honor," Moreau said as he arrived at the lectern once again. "As Justice Goode pointed out, the long-term benefits to the environment of the Petroleum Independence Act are speculative at best, but the observable pain being experienced by the American people having to deal with artificially inflated fuel prices is a demonstrable fact today. As long as the Act remains in place, people suffer."

"Especially, I suppose, those whose portfolios are affected," scoffed Justice David Fortier, the lone African-American on the court.

"The small stockholders like retired people on fixed incomes are just as surely affected, your honor, with all due respect, as wealthy investors. But most affected are those whose budgets are stretched by the high price of gasoline to the point that they can hardly afford to drive to work, all to satisfy those who believe in some future environmental catastrophe which may or may not come to be."

Before Jackie knew it, the hour was over. Moreau thanked the court for the opportunity and sat down. Now they would go home and wait until the court saw fit to render a decision. Jackie hoped it would be soon.

CHAPTER THIRTY-THREE

So, it all comes down to this, Jackie thought as she once again sat down facing the large dais where the nine justices of the Supreme Court would shortly appear to hand down their ruling on the injunction. It was rare for the Supreme Court to have a session so late in the year – July 30 – but they had apparently been convinced that the country needed closure on the issue of the gas tax and the injunction.

Behind the nine chairs were the scarlet drapes and yellow pillars out of which the judges had emerged ever since the building was built in the 1930s. It was odd to think that the Supreme Court had not had a permanent home until the Roosevelt administration; not even Teddy, but Franklin. There were people alive today who could remember when it was built,

Daniel Moreau told Axiom's management during one of their orientation sessions in preparation for going to the High Court.

Waiting with her on the wooden benches that reminded Jackie of church pews were Axiom's Vice President for Legal Affairs Marcus Williams, of course, and Moreau, who had guided them through the whole Federal judiciary process. Regardless of the outcome, his job would be done today. *I hope it was money well spent,* Jackie thought.

They sat quietly, since Daniel had told them that silence was required, especially during the session, and deviation was not tolerated by the Supreme Court police. Jackie found it odd that the Supreme Court had a police department distinct from the Capitol Police. She would have expected security guards, but police? She found Washington, D.C., to be an alien place no matter how many times she visited.

Axiom's was the only case to be read today, it was so late in the Court's schedule, so Jackie felt fairly exposed, with her little group being the only ones in the room so far. She had been to a salon where she had paid too much to make her hair and nails perfect. She had also invested in a new suit that was a warm, charcoal gray, and of course, new heels. She knew it wouldn't make any difference to the outcome, especially now, with the decision of the Court already made and written, only needing to be read, but it made her feel better to look her best.

Soon, people began coming in and finding seats. Jackie was aware that many were reporters, some of whom, Jackie assumed were following their specific case and others might be assigned to cover the court itself and were always there when there was a public session. She wondered if Patrick would be among them.

As she waited, Jackie was impatient one moment, then wanting to hold off the inevitable the next. It was so quiet she thought she could hear a clock ticking somewhere. She was trying not to obsess about the worst-case scenario: that the court would allow the injunction to stand and keep the gas tax in place permanently. If that happened, there was no recourse, no next step within the court system. What would she do?

Would she go back to Congress to try to get the price cap repealed? If there was no longer a $6.00-per-gallon cap, gasoline would be very expensive, but they could afford to sell it again because they could make a profit. Demand would just be curtailed by prices that could be above eight dollars a gallon, if that's what the market demanded. Hopefully that wouldn't be necessary and it could all end today.

After what seemed like a long time, but was probably only half an hour, the bailiff gave the call to rise and everyone watched as the justices entered the courtroom through the velvet drapes and sat down. Jackie felt a flicker of panic, but she scolded herself inwardly. *Think positive.*

There would be a majority decision and a minority dissent, but, Moreau had explained, the latter usually wasn't read aloud.

"Axiom Oil Incorporated v. the Federal Government of the United States," the Chief Justice began, his deep voice echoing off the marble columns. "Today's orders of the Court had been truly entered and certified and filed with the clerk. Justice Leighton has the opinion of the Court in Case 142-840, Axiom Oil Incorporated versus the United States District Court for the Eastern District of Missouri and the consolidated case."

Jackie swallowed hard and clasped and unclasped her hands. Justice Harper Leighton was a liberal from Michigan. If he was reading the majority opinion, that almost certainly meant that the judgement would be to uphold the injunction.

Yet, he had said nothing during oral arguments, so she had no read on him at all. She looked at the elderly man as he began reading, hunched over in his black robe, trying to imagine what the judgement would be.

"The Petroleum Independence Act was passed with intent to better the lives of all in the United States by reducing the burning of fossil fuels," the mostly bald Leighton began, peering over his reading glasses. "It has had the desired effect, in that demand for refined petroleum products such as motor fuel has been attenuated. That cannot be denied.

"However, there have been other effects, which were neither desired nor anticipated. Because many have suffered under the effect of increased fuel prices, Congress acted to repeal the bill, passing 115-832 and the president having signed it into law. This was petitioned in the Eastern District of Missouri and an injunction was issued to halt the repeal. This injunction has now been appealed in the case before us.

"In considering this question, a morass of conflicting information was presented, some legal in character, but most of it circumstantial. Of particular concern to those in the majority was the criminal activity of those ultimately responsible for the original statute."

Jackie was paying close attention and thought she could see a reason to be encouraged by these last words.

"While the Petroleum Independence Act was duly passed by Congress and signed by the president," Leighton continued, "a contradictory Act was passed and signed into law by a different president within just a few months' time.

"For those of us conversant with the law, this presents problems that must have been in Judge Everett Walker's mind as he issued the injunction to stop the second law."

Jackie licked her dry lips. Now she wasn't so sure there was reason to be encouraged.

"Two contradictory legislative efforts by the same body within nine months calls for careful deliberation and so, when Judge Walker received the petition, he issued the injunction to slow the process down, in case the Congress acted rashly in the second instance."

Jackie stole a look at Daniel Moreau, who raised his right hand slightly as if to say, *just wait.*

"The process has indeed been slowed now and we can witness the result. Counsel is correct that many have suffered and continue to suffer because the original Act imposed arbitrary and artificial price controls; not to hold prices down, as is usually the case in laws that seek to control the market, but to force prices up.

"This has been seen to have created hardships which can easily be remedied. Axiom Oil Incorporated has sought that relief in their appeal: to simply allow the repeal of the Petroleum Independence Act to go forward and to allow market forces to once again hold sway.

"Judge Walker of Eastern District of Missouri may have had good legal concerns for the precipitous nature of the quick repeal, but the other factors, including criminal activity of those behind the scenes, as well as hardship of the American people, lead us to vacate the injunction today, reversing the action of the United States District for the Eastern District of Missouri."

It was all Jackie could do to keep from jumping up and shouting a long "Yahoo," but instead she looked over at Moreau again who gave her a low-key thumbs-up and a smile.

* * *

"Do you feel you've been vindicated by today's decision?"

Jackie considered the first question from a reporter at the news conference following the Supreme Court ruling, standing at the top of the massive stairs leading out of the Supreme

Court building. She was not unprepared; she had been thinking about all these issues for over a year, examining her own motivations and trying to understand the motives of others.

"Obviously, I do think our position has been vindicated, but that is not really the important take-away. The point is that things can go back to normal for the millions of people who depend on the products and services we provide and the people who work for us can feel secure in their jobs, but also the scores of companies with whom we contract have a more certain future; they also can know that they can put food in their children's mouths and clothes on their backs."

"But both the law that established the gas tax and the law to repeal it were passed by the people's representatives," another reporter began. "Doesn't that kind of legislative churning just create chaos?"

"Yes, but as we now know, the original law was passed, allegedly, through manipulation of the legislative process, apparently through deception, bribes and coercion, not to mention violence. The original law was not what the American people wanted. The repeal was."

"There have been reports that you threatened Jason Wood, the person accused of being behind the attack on your facility in the Gulf."

"And he's accused of much more than that, including murder," Jackie began, struggling to control the crimson rising into her face. "I did nothing to threaten him, but the things he did he threatened me and everyone who works for me. That's all I'll say about that."

"Will you attend his trial?"

"I doubt I'll be asked to be there, but if there's anything the prosecution needs I'll be happy to help. His activities hurt a lot of people."

"Are you not concerned that the environment will be damaged as a result of today's ruling, with the increased use of fossil fuels?"

"I'm as concerned about the environment as anyone. I drink the water and breathe the air just like everyone else. The Federal government has seen to it that we are constantly concerned about the effect we are having on the environment. Whether it's the EPA, OSHA or the National Labor Relations Board, we are forced to be attentive to that issue. But to me, the bigger issue that was dealt with today is this: will an unelected judge be allowed to thwart the will of the people of the United States as expressed through their elected representatives? Will the bank account of one person be all that's necessary to prevent an end to the damage being done by an ill-conceived law? The High Court answered 'No' today. The will of the people to allow the market to work in the people's favor should be honored. That's what the court said."

There were a few more questions, some of which were directed at Daniel Moreau and concerned the legal arguments and precedents.

Then it was over.

Jackie was surprised by an ache in her chest as the reporters melted away. Suddenly she realized why.

CHAPTER THIRTY-FOUR

"Where have you been?" asked the waitress standing at the side of the table with a sly smile on her face.

"I had a lot going on," Patrick answered, failing miserably at presenting a smile in return.

"So, what'll it be?" Jenny asked, apparently choosing not to pursue her line of questioning further.

"My usual. Iced tea."

She looked at him, appearing to evaluate him, then nodded and turned to walk to the kitchen.

It had been a long time since Patrick had been to the Blue Ribbon Grill after work, but today he finally felt that he could return and not yield to temptation, in spite of the bright neon signs for various brews behind the bar.

He had not gone to the Supreme Court today. He knew Jackie would be there, but she hadn't tried to contact him since the flight from Seattle to Houston. Though he was still struggling with the aftermath of his lapse, he was firmly back on the wagon now and whatever happened, he knew that he needed to stay sober.

He was looking down at his phone, studying an early report from the Supreme Court ruling when Jenny returned with his tea. He was glad that the ruling had come down the way it had: a 6-3 split to lift the injunction. That would benefit everyone, *but especially Jackie*, he thought.

Then someone was standing at his table again. Thinking Jenny was already back for his food order, he looked up to see Jackie looking at him with a slight smile.

"Jackie!"

He stumbled as he got up to face her, then realized he didn't know how to greet her. At one time, they would have hugged and even kissed, but this was unexpected and he didn't know what her sudden appearance meant.

"Please," he stuttered, "sit – join me."

He stepped around her and pulled the dark wood chair away from the table for her. She accepted and was seated. He hurried back to his own seat and looked at her face. She was dressed to the nines and her makeup and hair were perfect, but the sparkle was missing from her eyes as she returned his gaze.

"It's good – I'm glad to see you." Patrick was suddenly not sure he could eat. *Can I just not blow this?*

"I wasn't sure I wanted to come," she answered, "and wasn't sure you'd be here."

Just then Jenny reappeared. "What can I get you?" she asked Jackie.

"Same," she said, gesturing to Patrick's glass.

When Jenny was gone, Patrick let Jackie talk.

* * *

"I got good some news today; great really. The Supreme Court ruled in our favor. The gas tax repeal can go forward."

"That's really great," Patrick said, but his voice was subdued.

"I didn't see you there."

"No. It wasn't my assignment and I knew you'd be busy."

After a pause, Jackie blurted out, "I didn't know if I – if I could get over how I felt after what you did. I don't know how we can be together if I can't trust you to be around my office because I might see some company secret in the newspaper the next day."

She had rehearsed what she was going to say, so she wasn't looking at Patrick, because she didn't want his blue eyes to distract her from what she needed to say.

She finally glanced up and saw he was listening intently with a pained expression on his face, but he didn't say anything, so she kept going. "So many times, media reports are just hatchet jobs. It seems to people like me that they just intentionally hurt people. They put fancy names on it like 'exposé' or 'whistle blowing,' but it's just vicious and sadistic. After that article, Petrocom failed and all those people lost their jobs."

Patrick didn't say anything, so she kept talking.

"I thought you were different. I thought you were sympathetic with the concerns of the people I'm responsible for. What about it?"

Patrick didn't immediately answer, but looked down for a moment, then spoke after clearing his throat.

"Uh, I'm truly sorry; truly I am. I've done a lot of soul searching. It's true that I have in the past done whatever it took to get the story and I didn't care who got hurt. I'm afraid you're exactly right about many in my profession. Many of my colleagues are jaded and cynical and assume everyone is crooked by default, so they figure they're doing the world a favor when they trash whoever they're reporting on."

Jenny rushed by the table, dropping off Jackie's iced tea, then Patrick continued.

"I don't know what to say that will fix the past. I can promise to never do anything like it again, and I do."

Jackie was now watching his eyes carefully for any signals she could detect. She saw only sincerity.

"I desperately want to patch things up with you," he said, finally.

"But how can I know that you won't find something else you stumble across too irresistible not to publish?"

He looked down at his glass of tea and then answered.

"Jackie, I have been in agony since that day, unable to get you to talk to me, unable to adequately apologize. I thought we might have a future. I – I think I might love you. . ."

She felt her heart leap! She was surprised by her own reaction. She wasn't sure what it meant, but he was still talking and his face was growing red.

"And if it is necessary, I would resign my position to remove the conflict of interest."

She was shocked by this unexpected statement.

"You would give up your career for me?"

"Yes, if that's what I needed to do."

Jackie wasn't sure what to say. She hadn't seen this coming.

"Have you thought this through?" she said finally.

"I have. I realized, belatedly, that it is a conflict of interest and if it's going to keep us apart, it's not worth it."

"But you've spent your life building to where you are now."

Jackie was surprised by her own words. *Why am I trying to talk him out of removing the thing that is between us?*

"Well, I figure, with my resume, any number of small-town papers would be thrilled to have me, or I could teach journalism, or whatever."

He shrugged, as if it was of no consequence, then continued.

"The thing is, I don't want anything between us. I want to remove the possibility of yielding to that temptation. I want a normal life and maybe that's not possible in the cut-throat world I operate in."

"I wasn't expecting this," she answered, looking down at her own glass. "I came here tonight because I have feelings for you too, and, even though I was badly hurt, I have missed you, also. I guess I want a normal life too." Jackie looked up and saw him looking at her earnestly. She could see that there was no need for either of them to explain what they meant by "normal." They were both consumed with their careers, but in the long run, career would not be enough. She needed someone and sitting across the table from her was someone who had just proclaimed his love for her. How long might it be before that happened again?

But just needing someone wasn't enough. She knew she needed to feel the same love for him that he said he felt for her, but she didn't know if she was there yet.

"Patrick, maybe we can start over. We can't pick up exactly where we left off, but maybe we can see each other again and see where we go from there."

"That would be great," he answered softly.

"Don't do anything rash, like quitting your job or anything, just yet," she continued, with a hint of much-needed humor. "We'll sort things out."

Just then Jenny appeared again. "Are you ready to order?"

* * *

At least I'm out of prison, Marvin Borelli sighed, trying to find a silver lining. The FBI had emphasized repeatedly how easy they were going on him because he had cooperated and his life had been threatened.

So now he was protected, officially a member of the Federal Witness Protection Program. He couldn't believe how fast it had happened. One moment he was sitting in a holding cell at the Washington, D.C., field office of the FBI and seemingly the next he had been flown across the continent to some two-bit town in Alaska. He had never heard of the town and hadn't completely memorized his new address yet.

He didn't always even remember his new name. He was still working to memorize his new identity, from the voluminous file that had been unceremoniously dumped in his hands as the Federal agents abandoned him in this wilderness. He wondered how long it would take before he would recognize and respond to his false name when someone called it.

But how likely was someone to call his name in this place that civilization barely touched? He had been to town and greeted a few people who looked as forlorn as he felt, living miles from one another on the tundra.

He felt an impulse to run: to take the first available transportation to somewhere with at least Wi-Fi and some decent cappuccino, not to mention a three-star restaurant, but he knew that, even with Jason Wood behind bars, he couldn't expect to be safe if he showed his face. Besides, he didn't have the money it would take to go somewhere no one would be likely to look, like Europe.

He looked out the window and felt a chill, even in the summer, as the darkness fell. His cabin – there was no other word for it; it couldn't be called a "home" – was small by any standard, and it was as rustic as his former Georgetown brownstone had been luxurious. The decor, such as it was, had no reference to any design school he could identify. Courtesy of the Witness Protection Program, the bedroom closet had been outfitted with off-the-rack flannel shirts and blue jeans instead of the designer, custom-cut fashions to which he was accustomed. To add insult to injury, his new wardrobe was completed by blue-collar baseball caps and cowboy boots. Admittedly, the clothes helped him fit in and fitting in was what would keep him alive.

But, the boredom! He could easily go for hours – even days – without seeing another human being. When he did see someone in the small town, he couldn't imagine what he could talk to them about; they would surely have nothing in common.

He had made a life for himself in D.C. complete with fast cars and faster women, greased with endless streams of cash from people and companies eager to get a leg up in the influence market of the nation's capital. There were parties and lunch meetings and elegant dinners and more parties that he relished because he was able to network and influence the truly powerful. Here, there was nothing remotely similar to that lifestyle available to him.

So even though he was not in prison, it felt like he was, with nothing to do in such a remote environment. At night he heard the cries of animals he assumed were wolves and moose. He felt sure there were even more frightful creatures such as snakes and mountain lions in the wilderness near his new home. The sounds made him shiver with fear as well as with the cold.

His main heat source was a wood-burning stove. He wondered whether it would be adequate when the real Arctic cold descended on the landscape. He also wondered how many trees were being consumed per hour in cabins like his in the surrounding wilderness and how much, soot, smoke and ash was rising into the air.

He would get to go back to D.C. once, he had been told, to testify against his former client, Jason Wood, who had put a price on his head. He relished the opportunity, but after he testified, he would once again be abandoned here where he would live a solitary, if safe, existence for who-knew how long.

Suddenly he heard a noise; a vehicle on the road several hundred feet in front of the house. Ordinarily he wouldn't notice or care, but now he rushed to the window to see what it was, just to have something to do. It was a truck, he judged from the sound of the engine and the height of the headlights in the darkness. As the truck went by he saw that it was a gasoline truck bearing the black and gold logo of Axiom Oil Incorporated!

CHAPTER THIRTY-FIVE

"Well, there's not as much work, anyway."

"That's a good thing, right?" Jackie had just asked her mother how she was liking her new place. They had just finished Thanksgiving dinner and had gone into the family room to relax. The help had the day off, so Jackie figured she would load the dishwasher after a while.

"Living here is nice enough," Florence James continued. "There were so many memories of your father at the old place."

The "old place" had been a sprawling 22-room estate in Tudor-style wood, stucco and stone which had been the James family home for more than 30 years. It had required a sizeable staff to keep it going. Now that she was downsizing, Florence kept a few people to help her, but after moving to a house that was a mere 3,200 square feet, the Florence James household was considerably pared down.

"How are things with you?" her mother asked. "I know it's been rocky since you took over the company."

"Yes, to put it mildly. It's better now; much better actually."

"I've seen our stock price doing better," Florence said. "With your father gone, I have to depend on that you know."

Jackie smiled. It had been so long since her mother had had to struggle that she had no idea how good she had it. But, she shouldn't have to worry. Jackie's grandfather and father had built something from the ground up that now fed and clothed thousands of people. Her mother deserved to live comfortably and securely as she grew older.

"Yes, I know, Mama. Things have really turned around, now that the tax is gone."

"That was such a stupid thing! Why did those politicians want to hurt so many people?"

"Good question."

"Anyway, I'm glad things are going well."

"Yes, Mama, they are."

Jackie leaned back in the overstuffed recliner that her father used to sit in. She was taking his place in so many ways now. She wondered how he would have dealt with the challenges she had faced over the past 18 months.

Then she realized there was no point in asking that question. It was up to her to do what needed to be done. At least the company had survived when many others had not. It was downsized a bit and the valuation of the company was down as well, but she had confidence to believe that, all things being equal, Axiom could again be strong and growing.

She was awed a bit to realize that what happened to her company had a real impact on the lives of millions of people. She still found it hard to believe that there were people who wanted to destroy something that so many people counted on and from which they benefited.

It had been almost four months since the Supreme Court had struck down the injunction. There were signs that the economy was recovering. With the tax gone and supplies increasing, the price of gasoline had settled down to market levels so that, in some places, people were paying $2.50 less than they had been while the tax was in place. Therefore, prices of consumer goods, pushed up by the tax on fuel, were settling back to reasonable, market levels as well. That meant a lot more money in people's pockets, which in turn would benefit the whole economy in the long run.

And finally, Jackie could look at a report from the Axiom Finance Committee without getting depressed. The company was operating in the black again. The repeal of the tax meant millions of dollars more was available to finance the company's extensive operations, pay their employees, and give their investors a return.

And that was what was important. Her personal wealth, though considerable even after the lowered valuation of the company's stock, was not the issue for her. After all, she could only wear one outfit at a time, drive one car at a time and be in one house at a time, just like anyone else. The important thing was that all the people who depended on her were able to pay their bills, put food on the table and a roof over their heads and put their kids through college. That's what gave her satisfaction.

"And what about your beau?"

Jackie struggled not to laugh out loud when her mother used the dated term. Yet there was no doubt what she meant as there might have been if her mother had said "friend."

"Well, we're back together after a rocky patch," she began. "We're taking it slow."

"Better not be too slow. You're not getting any younger."

Jackie smiled. Her mother had been worrying about her love life for 20 years, thinking she wouldn't be complete until she was married. She was never overbearing about it, but it was a recurring theme.

"I just don't want to make a mistake, Mama. Marriage is forever."

"I think so, but it doesn't seem everybody sees it that way these days."

"Yes, Mama," she said absent-mindedly as her thoughts travelled far away.

* * *

As the plane touched down at Washington Dulles International Airport, Jackie looked out the window of the first-class cabin. She and Patrick had been together several times since their truce at the Blue Ribbon Grill, alternating between Houston and D.C., but this was the first time that she felt anticipation, unmixed with suspicion. She was actually looking forward to seeing him. She felt as if she had put his betrayal behind her and could thoroughly enjoy his company again.

As the plane rolled toward the terminal, she could see the brown grass and bare trees of Autumn in the distance. She was sure the colors had been beautiful a month ago, but the peak was past and the trees were bare and ready for winter. The plane stopped at the gate and people stood to retrieve their carry-on luggage. The season was certainly farther along here in D.C. than in South Texas.

She was ready for a new season, after all that had happened. A new metaphorical season in which she would get past the constant fighting with forces beyond her control. Business was difficult enough without interference from powerful politicians, activists and judges. Before she knew it, Jackie was out of the plane and making her way to baggage claim.

As she entered the baggage area, she saw him, far across the huge room, through throngs of people coming and going. He was there waiting for her. Suddenly she felt an unexpected rush of emotion: joy, longing, affection.

He saw her too. As if they were of one mind they began to thread their way through the crowd toward one another.

As she moved forward, all her doubts evaporated; all her fear was gone. She knew that the pieces of her life were finally falling into place and she could see a little way into a full and happy future.

THE END

Haven't read the first BACKLASH?

A conspiracy of activists and politicians threatens the livelihoods of hundreds of thousands of people, so Jacqueline James finds herself in the midst of a national controversy. To save her company, her employees and her stockholders, she must launch a daring response called "Operation Backlash."

Go to www.backlashbook.com for ordering information.

Praise for "Backlash, vol. 1"

"I loved *Backlash*! I read it in less than three days. Only put it down when I had to. Now, you need to get started on your next book. Your fans are waiting." *L. R., Mississippi.*

"*Backlash* was enjoyable to read on a variety of levels. The characters were well developed. Jacqueline's years in the family business served her well, when she was thrown into managing a terrorist attack directed at her company, soon after taking over as CEO from her late father. Her grit and innovative ways of solving complex issues were evident. The storyline, including special interest groups, reporters, environmental radicals and Washington politics, was easy to follow. Jacqueline was eloquent and human in her approach to protecting her family's corporation against all odds, and I found myself cheering her on, as she took on Washington and her stockholders throughout the book. The storyline flowed, keeping me wondering 'what next?' Author meticulously conducted his research for his book, reminding me of a well-developed Grisham-like novel. Hope another book is in the works." *D. J., Amazon.com review.*

"An 'edge of the seat'er! We need more (real) people like Jacqueline Marie James who will take a stand against some of the idiocy foisted on us by our elected officials (of all parties) to further their own selfish goals. So pertinent to what is going on today in America. But not so political that you can't relate to the characters and get caught up in the emotion of the story. A great read--I didn't want to put it down. Loved it!!! *S. D., Amazon.com review.*

"When is the sequel coming out?" *P. C., Georgia.*

"Didn't have to skip sections for inappropriate language or sexual conduct. This proves a good story can be written without adding trashy content." *S. Y., Amazon.com review.*

"Get Ready for a Wild Ride! *Backlash* can be enjoyed on many different levels. As a page-turner, it keeps you on the edge of your seat from the initial...well, I won't spoil it for you...right up to the denouement. But Backlash has a deeper subtext, almost a platonic dialogue being conducted between the lines, that addresses many of the key political concerns of our time without ever lecturing or slipping into the abstract. As we become engaged by the highly colorful characters, we grapple with the political issues that confront them.
"What's unique is the way in which the author weaves a complex philosophical treatise into a plot that moves as quick as you can turn the pages. You can't help but be transfixed by the unexpected plot twists. It's not until the story is over that you realize that the book has taken on many of the nettlesome issues of our current political discourse. The ride is so fun that you don't realize how much ground you've covered until it's over. What a great read, can't wait for the next one from this author." *B. G., Amazon.com review.*

"Just finished *Backlash* by Gary L. Ivey. It was fabulous!!!! I was so intrigued by the plot...environmental terrorists, murder, politics, moral integrity, a female heroine, hard-core work ethics, and a splash of love made for a great read! (ah...and the evolution/creation thread!)." *L. Z., Facebook post.*

Watch for future books
by Gary Ivey

Thine Is the Kingdom

It was a time of triumph, but also a time of crisis when Israel's first monarchs established the kingdom.

With great power comes great responsibility. Follow the ascendancy of God's people during the reigns of Saul, David and Solomon through the eyes of fictional as well as real Bible characters in the *Thine Is the Kingdom* trilogy. The first book of the series will chronicle the ministry of Samuel and the reign of Saul. The second book, *Forever and Ever*, will trace the monarchy of David, Israel's iconic king. Finally, *The Power and the Glory* will trace the wisdom and power of Solomon as well as the strife which ended the united monarchy.

To be notified about publication of *Thine Is the Kingdom*, join the email list at **www.backlashbook.com** or **www.garyivey.com**.

Want more?

Check out **www.garyivey.com** for blog posts about freedom and the free market.

Follow Gary L. Ivey on Facebook at
www.facebook.com/GaryIveyAuthor/
and on Twitter **@gary_ivey**.

About the Author

Gary L. Ivey wrote the first *Backlash* while living in Georgia but has since moved to the state of Hawaii to be near children and grandchildren, where he finished writing *Backlash 2: Justice Denied.*

He is originally from Oklahoma, went to school for a time in Arkansas and has also lived and worked in Texas, Mississippi and Alabama. He met his wife in Louisiana.

His father retired after working as a middle manager for a large oil company for 31 years. He doesn't claim to be an expert, but growing up in Oklahoma, Ivey learned about the oil business by "osmosis."

He wrote *Backlash* and this sequel because he believes free-market capitalism is the best system to alleviate poverty in the world and government interference in the free economy is the enemy of prosperity.

An entrepreneur himself, together with his wife of 44 years, he has owned a web development company for 20 years. Before that, he owned a video production business and before that worked as a magazine editor and pastor.

Besides writing, Ivey likes to compose, play and listen to music in a variety of styles.